"You are one beautiful woman,"

Mike admitted grumpily. "But I am not so desperate for naked female companionship that I have to kick down bathroom doors."

The macho cop's words should have relieved Casey. But they left traces of irritation instead. He didn't have to be quite so positive about it. "Can I have your promise on that?" she demanded pertly.

"You've got my sacred vow," he snapped.

"Until hell freezes over?"

"That happens almost every winter here in Michigan. So let's say you're safe from me until your cats explain the mystery of life."

"My cats don't explain anything."

"So you're really, really safe then, aren't you?" Mike said smugly.

But, somehow, Casey wasn't too sure....

Dear Reader,

The holiday season has arrived—and we have some dazzling titles for the month of December!

This month, the always-delightful Joan Elliott Pickart brings you our THAT'S MY BABY! title. *Texas Baby* is the final book in her FAMILY MEN cross-line series with Desire, and spins the heartwarming tale of a fortysomething heroine who rediscovers the joy of motherhood when she adopts a precious baby girl. Except the dashing man of her dreams has no intention of playing daddy again....

And baby fever doesn't stop there. Don't miss *The Littlest Angel* by Sherryl Woods, an emotional reunion romance—and the first of her AND BABY MAKES THREE: THE NEXT GENERATION miniseries. Passion flares between a disgruntled cowboy and a tough lady cop in *The Cop and the Cradle* by Suzannah Davis—book two in the SWITCHED AT BIRTH miniseries.

For those of you who revel in holiday miracles, be sure to check out *Christmas Magic* by Andrea Edwards. This humorous romance features a cat-toting heroine who transforms a former Mr. Scrooge into a true believer—and captures his heart in the process.

Also this month, *The Millionaire's Baby* by Phyllis Halldorson is an absorbing amnesia story that's filled with love, turmoil and a possible second chance at happiness. Finally, long-buried feelings resurface when a heroine returns to unite her former lover with the son he'd never known in *Second Chance Dad* by Angela Benson.

All of us here at Silhouette wish you a joyous holiday season!

Sincerely,

Tara Gavin,
Senior Editor

Please address questions and book requests to:
Silhouette Reader Service
U.S.: 3010 Walden Ave., P.O. Box 1325, Buffalo, NY 14269
Canadian: P.O. Box 609, Fort Erie, Ont. L2A 5X3

ANDREA EDWARDS

CHRISTMAS MAGIC

Silhouette®

SPECIAL EDITION®

Published by Silhouette Books

America's Publisher of Contemporary Romance

In memory of Isabel Anderson and all the others who
lost their lives on ValuJet 592.
May the white cat's story touch others
as Isa touched us.

 SILHOUETTE BOOKS

ISBN 0-373-24144-5

CHRISTMAS MAGIC

Copyright © 1997 by EAN Associates

This edition published by arrangement with Harlequin Books S.A.

® and TM are trademarks of Harlequin Books S.A., used under license.
Trademarks indicated with ® are registered in the United States Patent
and Trademark Office, the Canadian Trade Marks Office and in other
countries.

Printed in U.S.A.

Books by Andrea Edwards

Silhouette Special Edition

Rose in Bloom #363
Say It With Flowers #428
Ghost of a Chance #490
Violets Are Blue #550
Places in the Heart #591
Make Room for Daddy #618
Home Court Advantage #706
Sweet Knight Times #740
Father: Unknown #770
Man of the Family #809
The Magic of Christmas #856
Just Hold On Tight! #883
†*A Ring and a Promise* #932
†*A Rose and a Wedding Vow* #944
†*A Secret and a Bridal Pledge* #956
Kisses and Kids #981
**On Mother's Day* #1029
**A Father's Gift* #1046
**One Big Happy Family* #1064
Christmas Magic #1144

Silhouette Intimate Moments

Above Suspicion #291

Silhouette Desire

Starting Over #645

†This Time, Forever
*Great Expectations

ANDREA EDWARDS

is the pseudonym of Anne and Ed Kolaczyk, a husband-and-wife writing team who have been telling their stories for more than fifteen years. Anne is a former elementary school teacher, while Ed is a refugee from corporate America. After many years in the Chicago area, they now live in a small town in northern Indiana where they are avid students of local history, family legends and ethnic myths. Recently they have both been bitten by the gardening bug, but only time will tell how serious the affliction is. Their four children are grown; the youngest attends college while the eldest is a college professor. Remaining at home with Anne and Ed are two dogs, four cats and one bird—not the same ones that first walked through their stories, but carrying on the same tradition of chaotic rule of the household nonetheless.

The Christmas Pickle

A century ago, in certain German areas of the United States, a glass-blown Christmas pickle ornament was considered a special Christmas-tree decoration. It was the last ornament to be hung on the tree on Christmas Eve. When the children were allowed to see the tree on Christmas morning, they would search for the pickle ornament, for whoever found the glass pickle would receive something special.

Chapter One

Something was wrong.

Mike Burnette turned off the ignition of his Michigan State Police cruiser and stared through the rain-snow mixture that pelted his windshield. A light was on in his kitchen, but the only one who should be in the house was Gus. And while his dog was big enough and smart enough to reach a switch, he'd never bothered with lights before.

An uneasiness settled in the pit of Mike's stomach as he glanced around the neighborhood. The only lights in the Randalls' house next door were from their Christmas tree; most likely no one was home yet. That would mean that Dubber hadn't been over to feed Gus this evening, and so the eleven-year-old couldn't have accidentally left the lights on. But then who had? Gus would have to be dead before he'd let a stranger in.

It had to be burglars. Burglars who'd done something to his dog.

Mike reached for his radio and called for backup, then

slipped out of his car. It could be five minutes before one of the Berrien Springs cars got here, more if something was going down in another part of town. He took a deep breath, letting the chilly evening air push back the grogginess that kept trying to swallow him up. He'd take a look around while he waited. Putting on his uniform cap, he crept up the steps to his back porch.

Damn, he was tired. What with that extradition trip to New York, he hadn't had a decent night's sleep for days, and the cold tablets were winning over the coffee. He glanced through the dining-room window—dark inside with only a patch of light spilling in from the kitchen. Looked okay. He crept farther along the wall. Maybe he should go back to his car and cancel his earlier call. It probably was nothing. But as he turned, he glanced into his kitchen.

His blood froze; his heart stopped.

Gus—his dog, his best friend and ninety pounds of pure fearlessness—was pinned on the blue linoleum floor by something dark. But Gus must have seen Mike at the window, for the dog's eyes, filled with pleading, looked his way.

This wasn't a time for caution and waiting. This was a time for action. His best friend was in trouble! Drawing his service weapon, Mike kicked in his back door and burst into the kitchen.

"Everybody freeze," he shouted, vaguely aware that although Gus hadn't gotten up, he was wagging his tail. There was a sound to Mike's right and he spun.

A young woman stood in the living-room doorway. "What are you doing?" she squealed, half raising her hands.

In her mid-twenties, with red hair, green eyes and a dash of freckles sprinkled across her nose, she wasn't like any burglar he'd ever seen. She wasn't wearing any shoes, just thick socks that hid her feet—something her tattered jeans and University of Michigan sweatshirt couldn't do to her shape. Mike felt the temperature in the room go up a few degrees. Luckily, he was immune to beautiful women who broke into houses.

"Just move on over by the stove there," he said, and waved her across the old kitchen with his gun.

"This is crazy," she protested, but did as he said. "I didn't do anything."

"Uh-huh."

Keeping her in sight, he moved carefully around the kitchen table to where Gus lay. And stopped in shock. Gus was pinned down by two cats! Mike just stared at them as Gus wagged his tail some more. Cats?

"Mrs. Jamison sent me," the woman said loudly.

Mike turned back to her at that. "Myrna Jamison?" He let his weapon drop slightly as the adrenaline surge left his body. What was going on? "Aunt Myrna?"

"Yes, your aunt Myrna." The woman lowered her arms enough to wrap them across her chest. "The one who owns this house and whose door you'll have to get repaired."

Actually, Myrna was his great-aunt, but Mike just shook his head, trying to clear the cobwebs. This woman had the most disconcerting eyes—wide, bright green and reflecting a certain gentleness. They were the kind that could hypnotize a guy, if he let them. But there was no way he was going to let her and her gang of cats pull anything on him.

"We should really shut the door," the woman continued. "The snow's blowing in."

"Forget about that and tell me why Myrna sent you."

"Have you always been so bossy or is that part of your police training?" She walked past him and tried to shut the door, but finally gave up and let it stay slightly ajar.

"I'm the one asking the questions here," he said a bit louder. "Now—"

A growl from the floor stopped Mike in midsentence, and he looked down. His dog, the big stupid mutt he'd rushed in to rescue, had his teeth bared and was growling at him. And the two cats—one white and the other black—lying against the dog's side were giving Mike looks that were as near to an assault as one could get without touching a person. Didn't any of them realize he was the good guy here?

"Hush, sweetie." The woman bent down and patted Gus's large fuzzy head. "Everything's fine. Your daddy's not mad. He's just tired."

Mike stared at his dog, whose demeanor had reverted to happy and stupid, and seriously considered turning around and leaving. He had to have stumbled into the wrong house.

"His name is Gus," Mike said. "And I'm not his 'daddy.'"

"Sure, you are." The woman gave Gus one last pat before straightening up. "You're Mike Burnette, aren't you? Mrs. Jamison described you perfectly." She held her hand out to him. "I'm Casey Crawford."

Mike swallowed hard and transferred his weapon to his other hand. He shook her hand as briefly as possible, but it wasn't brief enough. He felt as if he'd touched a live wire; a charge raced through him, leaving him feeling weak and weary.

What was this woman really doing here? This was just too weird for words. Myrna rarely ventured out of her house except to…

Mike frowned at Casey. "You're not her psychic, are you?"

"Her psychic?"

Casey looked startled, but not startled enough, Mike thought. Great. "Just how well do you know my aunt?" he asked. "How'd you meet her?"

"Through some mutual friends," she said. "I teach at the University of Michigan."

"And burgle houses on the side?"

"I didn't break in," Casey protested. "The cutest little boy unlocked the door for me. He said he lives next door."

Mike's suspicions came flooding back, along with an irrational irritation. Dubber was a gangly kid with giant feet, a buzz cut and crooked teeth that only an orthodontist could love. Even his own mother wouldn't call him cute.

"He had no right to let you in."

"Mrs. Jamison told them to. She said if you weren't home, I should go see your neighbors, the Randalls. That she'd notify both of you that I was coming."

This was getting more and more bizarre by the minute. Yeah, he was taking care of the house for his great-aunt, fixing up the place a bit in lieu of rent, but she'd never interfered in things before. She'd always treated the place as if it was his, even though he kept insisting it wasn't. She wouldn't just send someone over without discussing it with him first.

He looked at Casey in her stocking feet and the sweat-shirt that fell ever so gently over her curves and the jeans that clung as close as a caress. Breath was hard to come by.

"You never answered my question," he stated. "How did you meet Myrna?"

"What's to tell?" the intruder said with a shrug of her shoulders. "She came to the university for a lecture. Some friends introduced her to me when they found out she wanted to have a family history written. I've written several for people in the Ann Arbor area."

"Myrna wants you to write a family history?" This made no sense. "Myrna prides herself on ignoring the whole family. She routinely sends us all notices that we're out of her will."

"Well, maybe she only likes dead family members."

"Or maybe this is all a hoax," Mike said. "She wouldn't have sent you here without telling me."

"So check your mail or your answering machine," the woman said.

She probably thought that would make him go into the other room, and she could escape. And maybe that was what he should let her do. But he just waved her back to the stove with his gun while he went over to the kitchen phone—the one that had the answering machine. He glanced at it. Lights were flashing. He pressed the Rewind button, then Play.

"Mike. Dave, here." The voice seemed to shout into the silence of the kitchen. "You back from that trip yet? Give me a call." There was a click and a whir.

"You've been away?" Casey said. "No wonder your aunt couldn't get in touch with you."

Mike glared at her briefly. "I wasn't totally unreachable."

The next message started. "Hey, Mr. March, it's Joe. The calendars are in. I sent a couple to the station for you." Click, whir.

"Mr. March?" Casey asked.

"It's a fund-raising thing," Mike snapped. These messages were personal. Hadn't she ever heard of privacy? Or at least the pretense of privacy? "It's the Kops for Kids Kalendar."

"I've never met a Mr. March before," she said. "This is so thrilling."

He gave her a glare, the one that made even the toughest perp zip his lips in less than three nanoseconds. It had no apparent effect.

"I've met a Mr. January, but January's not a very exciting month. Not like March, with those winds roaring in."

Gritting his teeth, Mike turned back to the machine. *Come on, Aunt Myrna. Where are you?* "Mike? It's Tammy. Hon, I sure don't want you to find out the wrong way. Darcy and her doctor are back in town." Click, whir.

Damn. Tammy'd always been a busybody.

"Who's Darcy?" Casey asked.

"Nobody."

"Mike, it's Mrs. Kinder from down the street. I thought you should know that Darcy and her husband bought a house in that new subdivision on the east side. Just so you won't be surprised if you see them in town." Click, whir.

Great. Like he cared. Darcy was the past. Finished. Been there, done that.

"Your ex?" Casey asked, her voice softer.

"No," Mike snapped. Right. The old pity machine. Mr. March had no effect on her, but thinking that he'd been dumped made her all sweet and sympathetic.

"Mike, it's Ben. Susie said I should tell you something. Give me a call—"

Mike hit the Stop button. Damn, listening to this thing in public was like standing out in the street in your long johns, back flap down.

"There's a faster way to solve this mystery," he said, and grabbed up the phone. He dialed his great-aunt's number and heard her answer in a moment. "Aunt Myrna?"

"Michael," she snapped. "Where have you been?"

His heart sank into his shoes. She'd sent this woman, no doubt about it. He slipped his gun into the holster with a sigh. And what a royal fool he'd made of himself.

"Is Casey there?" his great-aunt asked. "Now, you be nice to her. She's just the sweetest thing around."

"Yes, she's here, Aunt Myrna." Mike paused, letting the rest of her conversation drift by him. "She said you want her to write a family history."

"Oh, don't sound so forbidding, Michael," his great-aunt scolded. "I had to come up with something to get her there."

"You had to—"

"Hush, I don't want her to know I've told you," she said quickly.

"You haven't told me anything."

"I had to get her away," his great-aunt told him. "And what's safer than living two hours away with a big, strong cop?"

"You mean..." She was in danger? He stopped and looked over at Casey. She'd stooped to pet Gus, while the cats milled around them both. There was something so gentle, so fragile about them all it almost scared him.

"Michael?" his great-aunt said.

"Yeah, fine, Aunt Myrna," he said wearily. "I'll take care of things."

"You'll watch out for Casey?"

"As long as she's in my jurisdiction. That's my job."

"Maybe that's your problem." She hung up the phone. Casey stood up. "Well, have I been cleared?"

"For now," he said.

"Uh-oh, that sounds ominous." Those green eyes sparkled with laughter, drawing him closer in spirit if not body. "And—"

The broken back door swung open as two Berrien Springs cops pushed it in. Oh lordy. Mike had forgotten all about his call for backup. And of course the cops had to be Ben Williams and Ed Kramer—guys he'd served with in the army. If they found out he'd thought Casey and her cats were part of a burglary ring, they'd never let him live this down.

"What's up, Mike?" Ed asked. "We got a call you had a break-in. Sure it wasn't the ghost?"

"Ghost? There really is a ghost?" Casey asked, looking from the cops to Mike.

"No, there isn't," Mike snapped. "It's just an old wives' tale."

"I don't know. Some old stories have a lot of truth in them," Ben said. "And it is getting close to Christmas. Maybe old Simon's out looking for Priscilla, like he always does this time of the year." He turned back to examine the door. "Although I don't think he did this. As I understand it, ghosts float through walls and stuff."

"Mike did that," Casey explained. "Who's old Simon?"

"Just someone who lived here years back," Mike told her quickly, hoping to get the two officers out before they got too curious.

"Mike did that?" both cops chorused, bewilderment filling their faces.

Damn. It was probably too late. "Look, the whole thing was a mistake. It was nothing. Get out of here and go back to serving and protecting."

"Mike just thought I was a burglar—me and my cats."

Ed smirked at Mike. "A ring of cat burglars, Mike?"

"They do look purrty dangerous," Ben said.

"You guys are really funny," Mike snapped. Yeah, it had been dumb, but did they have to make sure she realized just how dumb? He introduced Casey to the two officers. "I wasn't expecting anyone and I saw Gus pinned down by these cats...."

"Gus was pinned down?" Both cops graduated from smirk to loud laughter.

Dammit, he didn't need this, Mike thought. Not when he was falling asleep on his feet. "Gus hates cats," he insisted.

The cops only laughed more, while Casey turned to frown at Mike.

"That's nonsense," she said. "He's a great big fuzzy bundle of love. He wouldn't hate anybody." She blew a kiss at the dog.

A flash of pure annoyance washed over Mike, taking him unawares and making him nauseated and sweaty. This was absolutely nuts. It was his cold. It was exhaustion. It was the pure-and-simple fact that this woman didn't belong here. He and Gus lived alone, always did, always would. There had to be another way to protect her from whatever mysterious danger was threatening her.

"Well, I guess we'd better get going," Ed said, once he could stop laughing. "Be sure to call us if either you or Gus gets pinned down by your burglars again." More hysterical laughter as they went to the door.

Ben turned before he followed Ed out. A frown had replaced the humor on his face. "Uh, Susie wanted me to tell you—"

Mike just waved him off. "I know about Darcy."

Ben's expression cleared as if a weight had been lifted

off his shoulders. He glanced from Mike to Casey and back again. "Looks like it don't matter anyhow. Later, man."

He left, though he didn't close the door too solidly. It swung open and let in a blast of cold air seasoned with wet snow. Mike picked up a chair and, fighting the urge to throw it at the door, just wedged it under the knob to hold the door closed. At least the draft stopped. The knowledge that he'd acted like an idiot continued to eat at him, though.

"You look awful," Casey said. "Sit down and I'll get you some dinner. We can talk about all this later."

He was exhausted and had a doozy of a cold, but her words lit a fast-burning fuse. He wasn't some little kid who had to be coddled; he was a man, a cop, someone who did the taking care of. Someone his great-aunt had assigned to protect this intruder.

"You don't need to get me anything," he said as he took his jacket off. "I called in a pizza order when I was just outside of town. It should be here any minute."

"Oops." She looked worriedly at him. "I sent it away."

She'd sent it away? Mike put his jacket on the table and slowly sat down, hoping against hope that he'd misunderstood what she'd just said. "You sent my large cheese, sausage, hamburger, green peppers and onion pizza away?"

"How was I supposed to know you'd ordered it?" she asked, hanging his jacket over a chair. "Besides, soup will be better for you. It'll give you a good dose of liquids and it's full of vegetables."

He just stared at her, the scent of the soup penetrating his cold. "It smells like herbal tea," he muttered darkly. The day was going from bad to worse to disaster.

Casey sniffed the air for a moment and then turned back, smiling. "You're right. It does."

And herbal tea smelled like boiled sweat socks, he wanted to scream. But he didn't. His mother had raised a gentleman, so he just looked grimly down at the noxious mess Casey was putting before him. She set a plate of warm bread on the table, and then another bowl of soup, before sitting down herself.

Mike transferred his frustration to Gus, who still had that stupid grin on his face, as if the two cats were his long-lost siblings.

"Damn it," Mike snapped. "He really does hate cats. He always has. What did you do to him?"

Casey just laughed. "Nothing. I think it's the cats. They have that effect on everybody. They carry an aura of harmony with them wherever they go."

Mike sipped at his soup. It didn't taste nearly as bad he'd expected. With the fresh bread, it was almost good. "So where do you find cats that ooze harmony into the atmosphere?" he asked. "This some special kind of breed?"

"I got Snowflake from the shelter I worked at," Casey said. "And I found Midnight out in a parking lot one night a couple of years ago."

"Oh." Mike looked back down at his dog. "I found Gus running loose on I-94 about a year and a half ago. I think somebody just dumped him there."

Casey was suddenly reaching across the worn table to take his hand. "We're both old softies. I knew you were a kindred spirit."

The touch of her fingers on his felt too soft, too warm, too wonderful. He pulled his hand away abruptly and got back to the business of eating. He wished his great-aunt had given him some specifics about the danger Casey was in. He had the feeling he wasn't supposed to talk about it, but in most of these cases, it was a husband or boy-friend—ex or current—that was the threat. Maybe Mike could get a hint from her.

"So tell me about yourself," he said. "What are you studying?"

"I'd much rather talk about the ghost," she said. "Have you ever seen him?"

"There is no ghost. It's just a stupid old story that's been around forever."

"But all stories, especially old ones, have some foundation in fact."

"From people who want an explanation for a house that creaks and groans and has doors that pop open by themselves. Anyway, how are you going to go about writing this family history?"

"There has to be more to the ghost than that," she said. "Hasn't someone seen him?"

Mike grimaced. He thought this ghost rumor was idiotic. Why was everyone so drawn to it? "There's no ghost," he said. "Cold drafts aren't all that rare, even in the summer. Lights reflect off mirrors and windows and end up in odd places. And so can sounds."

"You're a pragmatist."

"I'm a realist," he corrected. "Give me cold hard facts and I'll believe."

"You only believe in what you can see?" she asked. "What about stuff like truth and beauty and love?"

How had they gotten on this road? And how was he going to get the conversation back to the danger she was in? "Truth is fact. Beauty is totally dependent on a subjective standard," he said. "And love is nothing more than a hormonal reaction."

She looked as if she'd picked up a live electrical wire. "Does your girlfriend know you define love that way?"

"I don't have a girlfriend."

"I'm not surprised."

"But I suppose your boyfriend has a better definition."

"He wouldn't be my boyfriend if he didn't." She went back to her soup, not volunteering any more information.

Mike ate for a few minutes, stewing silently—but over her lack of information, not over the fact that she had a boyfriend. And he could just picture him....

"Let me guess what he's like," he said suddenly. "Big, hulking guy. Ex-football player with a smooth line and a fast car. And a quick temper."

Casey burst into laughter. He might have enjoyed the

sweet, soft sound of it if he wasn't so sure she was laughing at him. "Hardly," she said after a minute, once she could talk again. "Melvin's only a little taller than me and very thin. He doesn't drive and I have never seen him impatient, let alone angry."

Mike just stared at her. At the fiery color of her hair and the dancing light in her eyes. At the soft curves her sweatshirt enhanced. And he felt his blood boil.

"That's what you like in a man?" he scoffed. "Although that may be stretching the definition of *man* a bit."

Her laughter fled. "You have no right to say that! Melvin's sweet."

"Sweet?" Mike spat the word out. "A real man's not sweet."

"Have you asked Darcy about that?" She looked stricken even as the words echoed in the air around them, and she reached over to cover his hand with hers. "I'm sorry. I shouldn't have said that."

He snatched his hand back as if her touch burned. "It's all right," he said, and went back to his soup. "As I said before, Darcy's not anybody that matters."

"I still shouldn't have said it. I do that all the time—say stuff without thinking, I mean. Then I end up apologizing all over the place. I can't believe how often I've hurt Melvin's feelings accidentally."

"Melvin's a jerk," Mike snapped.

"Boy, have you got your jeans in a knot," Casey said, sitting back with a frown. "I'm glad that I'm staying in the apartment over the garage."

"You're what?"

"Your aunt said there was a nice little apartment over the garage where I could stay."

He sighed and for a brief moment considered letting her stay there, along with whatever other critters had taken up residence in the apartment. It would be better for him in the long run. But he couldn't do that. She needed his protection, and that meant she needed to be here.

"No one's lived there for ages," Mike said. "It's in horrible shape. As in unfit for human habitation."

"I've probably slept in worse."

"I doubt it."

"So I'll just unroll my sleeping bag in a spare bedroom for tonight," she said. "Tomorrow we'll look at the garage apartment."

"Tomorrow you'll see that I'm right."

"I'm beginning to get a clue why you're girlfriendless."

"I'm alone because I like it that way," he said. "Now would you make your cats release my dog?"

"Maybe old Simon has him in a trance." But Casey bent over the cats. "Snowflake, Midnight. Come on, let the puppy up."

"He's not a puppy," Mike said wearily. "He's a big…dog." He wanted to say "big, mean dog," but what was the use? Nothing was what it was supposed to be tonight. Gus was suddenly a pussycat; Mike was turning into one himself.

"Want another bowl of soup?" Casey asked.

"No, thank you," he said firmly. "I've had a long day and I'm going to hit the sack."

Aunt Myrna wanted him to protect this woman and he would. He'd even protect her cats. He'd protect Gus. In fact, he'd protect the whole damn world. But he had to get away from her so he could think.

"So what do you think, Snowflake? Feel any ghostly vibes?"

Casey and the cats were in the spare bedroom, down the hall from Mike's room. The white cat was stretched across the foot of the sleeping bag, watching Casey, while Midnight was curled up asleep on her lap. "I'd be willing to bet there is one. I've never felt a house with so much unhappiness in it."

Of course, that could be due to the present occupant, not a former one who'd hung around for a few extra decades.

"I don't think Mike would have been pleased if he'd known I met his aunt at a lecture I was giving," she told the white cat. "Or that it was about family ghosts. I suspect he's a firm nonbeliever."

Midnight sat up suddenly, staring off toward the closed door. Casey took advantage of the chance to stretch her legs under her flannel nightgown. This was her fourth family history, and like the others, it included rumors of a ghost. She'd taken on the first project as something to do over a summer after she'd broken up with yet another boyfriend, preferring the stories of people long gone over the messiness of present relationships.

Maybe it was that newspaper clipping in her wallet, the one she'd found back in her high-school days while researching a report. One of these days she was going to have the sense to throw it out, or the courage to see it through. If she could dig into other people's families, why her reluctance to dig into her own? Dad had always been open about her adoption; he wouldn't mind if she looked for her birth mother.

Midnight walked over to where Snowflake lay and began to groom the other cat, so Casey leaned back against the wall. It was stupid to let the little piece of paper get in the way all the time. But every time someone wanted to get close, all she could think of was that clipping and what it said about her mother. And in turn, about herself. What if—

Both cats stiffened suddenly, then shot over to the bedroom door just as Casey heard a shuffling in the hall, along with a low moan. She was right behind them, pulling the door open. The hallway was empty, except for Gus sitting in Mike's open doorway. It was also dark, despite the light spilling out from her door.

The cats moved off into the shadows, with Gus following them, as Casey glanced back at Mike's door. It was open, and she could hear his steady, even breathing coming from it. She hurried back into her room for her thick woolly robe and slipped it on as she went over to Mike's room.

"Mike," she whispered. He would know if it was the ghost.

The even breathing stopped suddenly. "What? What's the matter?" he asked quickly. "Is something wrong?"

"It's probably nothing," she said. "But I heard this noise...."

There was a muttered expletive and some rustling, then suddenly he was at the door. Sweatpants covered his lower half, leaving his muscled chest uncovered. And leaving no doubt in Casey's mind as to why he was Mr. March. Hell, with those biceps, he should have been Mr. All Year, or Mr. Decade.

"Stay here," he said brusquely, and slipped silently toward the stairs.

She forced her eyes away from his body to discover he had his gun in his hand. "What are you doing?" she asked, rushing after him. "The ghost was up here."

"There is no ghost," he hissed, and paused at the top of the stairs to whisper his dog's name. Gus was at his side in a second. "Now stay up here!" Mike ordered. He and Gus crept down the stairs.

This was absolutely nuts. She hurried down after Mike, almost running into him in the dark on the landing. "But the noises were up here. A scuffing noise and then a kind of moan."

"Will you stay upstairs?" he hissed again.

Light from the streetlights spilled in through the landing windows, showing a scarred patch on Mike's right shoulder when he turned. Even in the dim light it looked angry and red—a smoldering fire amid the snow. Without thinking, Casey reached out and touched it lightly.

"What happened?" she whispered.

He flinched away from her touch as if it was painful. "Nothing," he snapped. "It came that way. Now, will you go back upstairs?"

She hadn't hurt him, not with her touch, she was sure of that. But she'd felt pain under her fingertips nonetheless. Not about to make matters worse, though, she turned and climbed back up to the second floor, where she sat on the top step. The stairway was open, with just an oak banister on her right, but she could see nothing on the first floor, only darkness.

Snowflake came over and butted Casey's hand with her head until she began to pet her. Midnight climbed into her lap, stretching up to place her head under Casey's chin.

"Why can't I keep my big mouth shut?" she whispered into Midnight's fur. From down below, she heard the sounds of Mike checking out the house. "I'm always saying the wrong thing."

Snowflake purred loudly enough to chase away any spirits, but not enough to make Casey's gloom disappear. She was here to write a family history. She didn't need to know anything about Mike's scars or his life or who Darcy was.

Mike was coming back upstairs. Gus raced ahead of him to sniff at the cats, then give Casey a big sloppy kiss on her cheek. By that time, Mike was standing in front of her. She didn't need to see him to feel his frown.

"Everything looks snug downstairs," he said.

"I told you the noise was up here," she said. "I think it was Simon."

"The day Simon shows up is the day I win the lottery."

"Better check your numbers then," she said, and got to her feet. "I think he's here and so do my cats."

"Your cats see ghosts?" He was laughing at her.

"So did Gus."

"Gus did not." Mike wasn't laughing anymore. "He doesn't believe in such things."

"Oh, just because you don't, he's not allowed to?" Casey started back to her room. "Interesting."

"He doesn't believe because he's got some sense."

Casey spun around to face him at the doorway to the

spare bedroom. "And believing in the possibility of ghosts means I don't?"

"That remains to be seen." He frowned suddenly and glanced down the full length of her. "Is it that cold in there? I've got extra blankets, you know."

She followed his glance, taking in her woolly robe, her flannel nightgown peeking out below and her feet encased in thick socks, then took in his bare chest and bare feet. All right, so he was very macho and impervious to cold. Big deal!

"I'm just fine, thank you," she said with a haughty little sniff. "My sleeping bag is very comfortable."

"Probably warmer than Melvin would keep you anyway, eh?"

What was with him and Melvin? He had no reason to be so irritated. Besides, she and Melvin didn't have that type of relationship. They had the type of relationship that was the norm for her: something—cat, dog or human—was hurt and needed her care. So she was there. Simple. Uncomplicated. And little risk to her heart. Not that she was admitting that to Mike.

"I couldn't begin to describe the way Melvin makes me feel," she told him. "Because you couldn't begin to understand."

He just looked at her, then turned away. "Let me know if you hear any real noises."

"Those were real ones," she called after him. "Some of us aren't so narrow-minded in our definition of real."

But he just went into his room without saying anything else. Casey stomped into hers. This was not going to work. She should just pack up and leave.

"But I promised Mrs. Jamison I'd do this and I always keep my promises," she told Snowflake. "I'll just ignore everything about him, except how his behavior relates to the ghost."

But it was Mike's broad shoulders that lingered in her

mind as she drifted off to sleep, and there was nothing ghostly about them.

Mike turned over and punched the pillow into submission. It didn't matter. He was still wide awake.

He was not narrow-minded. She had no right to call him that just because he was too smart to believe in a ghost. But wasn't that just like a woman? Bring out a string of names to call you when you didn't exactly match up to her idea of what a man should be?

Mike turned over again and stared at the strips of pale light coming around the blinds in the window. He didn't like that back door downstairs. He'd wedged it shut with a piece of wood, but anybody wanting to break in could do so with no effort at all. Maybe he'd better check it again.

He'd left his sweatpants on after Casey's false alarm, so he just got out of bed and went softly down the stairs. Alone, since his good friend Gus had abandoned him. Not that Mike cared. Some people liked relationships; he could take them or leave them. No sweat either way.

The back door was fine, still closed tightly, so Mike had no reason not to go back to bed. No reason at all to stand at the kitchen window and stare at the falling snow, except that he was glad to be home and not driving in it. There was a chill in the air, even in the house, that he hadn't noticed before. If Casey had been cold before, she must be freezing now. Maybe he ought to give her a blanket.

On the way back to bed, he grabbed a blanket out of the hall closet and stopped at the door to Casey's room. It was slightly ajar, as if Gus had pushed it open. In the light filtering in from outside, Mike could see her. She'd taken the mattress from the old roll-away bed and put it on the floor, laying her sleeping bag on top. She was sleeping on her side, with Gus stretched out along her back. The black cat was sleeping by her stomach, while the white cat had crawled inside the sleeping bag and was cuddled by her chest, the cat's head resting on Casey's arm. She looked peaceful, contented…and warm.

Mike looked down at the blanket in his arms, feeling stupid for thinking she'd need it. She had everything she needed already. All those furry bodies were taking good care of her. Better than he could. He turned and went back to his own room.

It had gotten chillier in the house. Even his room seemed cold now. Cold and empty.

Chapter Two

Casey awoke to the sound of knocking. She sat up, trying to get her bearings, and discovered she was alone in the spare bedroom. Sunlight was streaming in through the thin drapes. The cats were gone, and Gus, whom she was sure had been there for most of the night, wasn't around, either. The knocking came again, from downstairs, so she climbed out of the sleeping bag and grabbed her robe.

Gus came bounding up when she was halfway down the stairs. "Where's Mike?" she asked the dog. "He went in to work, didn't he? Half dead with the flu, but he had to go to work. I've met that type before."

The knocking sounded again, and Casey hurried into the kitchen. The boy who'd let her into the house last night was at the door. "Come on in, Dubber."

"I came over to take Gus for his walk," the boy said, glancing at the door as he came in. "What happened?"

"Uh, it got real windy last night."

Dubber didn't let skepticism show on his face for more than a moment. "You're gonna need to get it fixed."

"I'm sure Mike will get to it."

"Mike doesn't do big stuff like doors," Dubber replied. "Mr. Slocum does. Want me to tell him?"

Casey nodded. "Thank you, Dubber. That's very nice of you."

A flush crept into the boy's face. "No problem," he replied after a long moment. "Mike's gone a lot, so I'm always looking after the place."

"Does that mean you know where the key to the apartment over the garage is?" she asked.

"What apartment?" Dubber looked confused. "There's just a big room and a little bathroom up there. And it's really pretty gross. A pig wouldn't live in it."

"Oh." Casey had gotten the impression from Mrs. Jamison that the quarters above the garage were suitable. Maybe the older woman hadn't been there in a while. Or maybe Dubber just had a hyperactive imagination. "I guess I'll have to clean it then."

"I can do it," Dubber quickly volunteered.

"You sure are a gentleman, aren't you?"

Dubber flushed a bright red. "Come on, I'll show you where Mike keeps the keys," he said, leading her into the living room. "He's got them upstairs. In his room."

"In his room?" Casey's feet slowed. "Maybe I should wait here."

Dubber frowned at her. "What for? Then you won't know where they are for next time."

"Yes, but…"

"Come on. Mike don't care."

Casey slowly followed Dubber upstairs. She had absolutely no interest in seeing Mike's bedroom, but the young boy was right. She should know where the keys were.

Dubber opened the door and led Casey inside. Mike had to have been in the military. His double bed was precisely made, the blanket stretched tight. A throw rug was precisely centered on the floor between the head and the foot of the bed, and every surface was polished and uncluttered. An easy chair stood in the corner by a window. The only thing that might be considered a decoration was a bulletin board on the near wall, with a row of hooks running across the bottom, each holding a key. She was more interested in the ribbons, citations and newspaper clippings that were on display. She walked over for a closer look.

"Mike's a real hero," Dubber said, and pointed to a newspaper photo of Mike with two small children, all three surrounded by rescue personnel. "He rescued these kids from a burning car."

"Really?"

"Yeah, the governor gave him a medal, and he's been nominated for some big police award."

"How come he's wearing a tux?" she asked.

"He was on his way to church to get married, but he stopped anyway."

Going to his wedding? "Was he marrying Darcy?"

"Yeah." Dubber nodded.

"But she married a doctor instead." Casey had gotten that much from the answering-machine messages last night.

"Yeah," Dubber said. "Mike's doctor."

"Gracious." Casey didn't know what else to say.

"Me and Gus didn't like her much, but I guess Mike did. He was pretty grumpy for a while after that."

"I would think so," Casey said. "She didn't dump him because he was late for the wedding, did she?"

Dubber just shrugged and started looking at the tags on the key hooks. "My mom said Darcy liked all the publicity and everybody fussing over her because Mike missed the wedding. But Mike hated it all. He just wanted everybody to leave him alone and for things to get back to normal."

"I can understand that," Casey said.

"Well, some TV show wanted them to have the wedding on the program," Dubber continued, pulling out another key tag to look at. "And then have this crew go with them on their honeymoon. You know, to film stuff for the show. Darcy thought it'd be so romantic. Mike thought it was dumb.''

"A wedding on TV?" Casey made a face. "That doesn't seem too personal."

"I think it'd be cool to be on TV," Dubber said. "I wanna be on *American Gladiators*."

Casey smiled. "That's a bit different from a wedding."

"Better," Dubber agreed, and stepped back. "I can't find a key to the apartment here. Maybe he doesn't have one."

"Maybe it's not locked," she said.

"Or maybe the mice have eaten through the door."

"No problem. I have cats, remember?" But would the cats remember how to catch mice? Or was it instinctive, like feeling your heart lurch with pain for someone who was hurting? Or was the instinctive part knowing how to feel for someone and still keep your heart safe?

"Take a couple days." Mike's sergeant's voice rumbled from deep within his barrel chest. "Help Berrien Springs out with their festival. I don't want you on the road until Sunday at the earliest."

"I'll take the afternoon off and see how—" Mike said.

"See nothing," the sergeant snapped. "You look like death warmed over. Get out of here and don't come back until next week."

"Come on, Sarge. I just have a little cold."

"Don't give me any lip, Mike. You could have a life-and-death situation pop up in your face anytime you're out there on the road. It ain't like you're a cashier down at the five-and-dime."

Mike didn't think there were any five-and-dimes around anymore, but didn't bother to start a discussion. Maybe taking a few days off was a good idea, since he needed to keep an eye on things around Casey, anyway. And his cold gave him a good excuse.

He finished up the last of the extradition paperwork and went on home. Mr. Slocum's van was parked in front. Good, the handyman must be fixing the back door. Mike pulled into the drive as Dubber and Gus rounded the corner.

"You call Mr. Slocum?" Mike asked when the boy got close.

"Figured you wouldn't get to it until later," Dubber said, and bent down to scratch Gus's head.

"I appreciate you calling. You're getting to be quite responsible."

"Casey said I was a gentleman," Dubber mumbled, his face turning a bright red.

Mike tried not to stare at the boy's sudden discombobulation. Casey and her cats could mesmerize dogs, but kids, too? And what was Dubber doing here this time of the morning on a weekday? Mike hoped he hadn't skipped school to hang around Casey.

"Don't you have school?" he asked.

Dubber nodded. "We had a late start today because of the icy roads. I was just gonna put Gus inside, then I was going."

"I'll take him." Mike held out his hand for the leash. "That'll save you a little time." And minimize the boy's risk of further exposure to Casey's mesmerizing rays.

Dubber seemed to understand all that was entailed in giving up the leash. His face fell slightly, but he handed it over. "Okay. Thanks." He turned toward his house, but looked back. "I'll be over to walk Gus after school."

"You don't have to," Mike said. "I'll be here."

"I don't mind." Dubber's face started to flush again. "Me and Gus, we're pals."

Mike just nodded and led Gus around back. He had the sneaking suspicion that if Gus could blush, he'd be blushing every time Casey's name was mentioned, too. Good thing someone with immunity was around.

Mike climbed up onto the back porch. The kitchen door was standing wide open.

"Yo, Mike." Barry Slocum straightened up and smirked at him. "Looks like you were right anxious to get in last night."

Mike frowned at him. Now what? "You must be getting a lot of exercise, jumping to conclusions like that."

"Hey, it ain't like I'm criticizing." The handyman's grin grew even more disgusting. "A young man, living alone like you do. It wouldn't be natural if you didn't get a little anxious at times."

Mike couldn't believe what he was hearing. Barry was standing there and cheerfully congratulating him, as if he'd busted the damn door on purpose. Mike pushed by him without another word, although he did pause a moment to exchange glares with that woman's ghost-seeing cats, sitting on top of the refrigerator.

"She's upstairs," the handyman called after him. "Taking a bath."

The words were still bouncing off the walls when Gus lurched forward, tearing the leash from Mike's hand as he raced into the living room. Mike frowned after his dog.

"Where's the fire?" he called, and was about to go check his answering machine when it hit him— Barry had said Casey was taking a bath. Oh no.

"Gus," Mike bellowed, running into the hallway and taking the stairs two at a time. "Gus, come. Sit. Stay."

But it was too late. The sound of a door popping open and slamming back against the wall echoed through the house. Then there was a piercing shriek and a lot of splashing.

"Gus," Mike shouted. "Gus, get the hell out of the tub."

But when Mike reached the open bathroom door, Gus was still in the old-fashioned, footed bathtub, dripping wet with a stupid grin on his face. Casey, on the other hand, was on the tiles next to the tub, holding a towel—a rather small towel—in front of her.

Mike wanted to order the dog out of the water. He

wanted to reprimand him severely and send him out of the bathroom with his head hanging in shame. He really did. In fact, his mind had the words all formed, but his vocal cords were paralyzed.

He had never seen a woman so completely, entirely beautiful. Her hair was wet and pushed off her face; her soft skin gleamed with wetness and her eyes flashed with a fire that threatened to scorch him. He felt his mouth go dry and his heart start to pound.

Casey pulled at the towel, trying to wrap it around herself. "What is going on? Don't any of you Burnettes know how to enter a room?"

Sweat beaded under Mike's hairline as he stared at her. Damn. She had more curves than a mountain road. Curves sharp enough to warrant guardrails and warning signs.

"Gus likes to take baths," he said. "He knows how to pop the door."

"He knows how to pop the door?" she repeated. "Maybe you should get it fixed."

"I have," Mike snapped. A drop of water was making its way down Casey's neck. It slid across her chest to disappear into a shadowy valley the towel was hiding. He found it was suddenly harder to breathe.

"You have?" Casey said. "Then how'd he get in this time?"

"I mean I've tried to get it fixed." Mike took a deep breath and tried to force his eyes away from that velvety skin. They refused to obey. He concentrated instead on forming coherent sentences. "I had the lock changed and it didn't help. I even had the door changed."

"Right." Her voice dripped with more sarcasm than Gus was dripping water. "I suppose he must know how to turn the knob."

"Maybe it's the frame," Mike said. "I'll have Barry look at it again."

"That would be nice."

Aunt Myrna had sent Casey here in order to protect her

from something, but if Mike wasn't careful she was going to need protection from him. Damn, but he wanted to go over there and see if her lips tasted as sweet as they looked, feel if her skin was as velvety as it appeared.

He grabbed up a larger towel near the door and tossed it to her. "Gus," he called sharply to the dog. "Out!"

"Don't talk to him that way," Casey scolded, as she wrapped the towel around her. "It's not his fault he's been allowed to develop bad habits."

"Do you want him out or don't you?"

The bigger towel didn't make a bit of difference. He could still see the gentle curves of her calves, which led his eyes up to her knees and then her thighs, and above that, the beginnings of the sweet fullness of her buttocks. Oh, man, he needed to leave.

"Gus, out!"

Casey went over to the tub. "Sweetie," she said to the dog. "Come out, baby. It's Casey's turn in the tub."

Gus clambered out, then shook himself vigorously.

"See how easy it is when you ask nicely?" she said.

Mike just stared at her, refusing to let one single word come out of his mouth. The way his stupid mind was acting, he'd start asking nicely for all sorts of things. All sorts of—

"Casey?" Dubber's voice rang out. It was loud—and close.

"Oh no," Casey murmured, glancing down at her towel-clad body. "Close the door."

Mike shut it instantly.

She frowned at him. "I meant with you on the outside," she whispered harshly.

"Be specific, will you?" He took a deep breath, then casually sauntered out into the hall, carefully closing the door behind him. Dubber was at the top of the stairs, looking around.

"Oh, hi, Mike," the boy said. "You know where Casey is? I wanted to ask her something."

"Uh, actually..." Damn. Mike took a deep breath. "I can give her a message if you'd like."

Dubber's face fell. "That's okay. It wasn't anything important. I gotta get to school." He trudged back down the stairs.

Mike watched him go, feeling that he and the boy had something in common. So much for the immunity he'd thought he had to Miss Casey Crawford's mesmerizing rays. The difference was that he wasn't giving in to them. Hey, if Darcy's defection hadn't gotten to him, then Casey wouldn't, either.

"Is he gone?" Casey whispered. She'd opened the door a crack.

Mike nodded.

"I've got it all figured out," she said, opening the door wider.

A sopping-wet Gus came out, looking very pleased with himself. Mike was less pleased— Casey had traded her towel in for a robe.

"It must be Simon."

"What must be Simon?" Mike asked. He was feeling weary all of sudden, like he really did have the flu and should be off in quarantine.

"Who pops open the door," Casey said. "What was Simon like? Did he have a habit of peeking in at naked ladies?"

"Simon died years ago," Mike said carefully. He was too close to her; he should move back a few steps, if he could only find the strength. He tried. He tried hard, but couldn't get his feet to move. "I have no idea whether he liked surprising ladies in their bath or not, but he's not opening the door for Gus."

"He could be."

Mike had had enough. He was strong. He was up for State Policeman of the Year, for heaven's sake. Some little slip of a woman wasn't going to weaken him like this. He took a step—a giant step—away. "Why would a ghost who can walk through walls need a dog to get into the bathroom to look at naked women?'' he snapped. ''It doesn't make any sense.''

''No, it doesn't, does it?''

She was purposefully misunderstanding him. She was trying to drive him crazy with her nearness and to tease him with her word games. ''I have to go dry Gus off,'' he said, and dragged his dog into his bedroom. He shut the door firmly.

The walls were massive, plaster on each side at least an inch thick. The door was solid oak; the hinges and clasp were old and sturdy. Yet he could feel her presence in the next room as if they were all tissue paper. He sank onto the bed and let his head drop into his hands.

''It's the flu,'' he told Gus. ''I've just got a doozy of a flu bug and I'll be fine in a day or two.''

Gus put his head on the bed next to Mike and whimpered in sympathy.

Casey got dressed, then leaned against the edge of the window looking out over the street. Mike's house was just a few blocks from downtown Berrien Springs, but it was quiet and peaceful. Nothing like downtown Ann Arbor or downtown Fort Wayne.

All the houses around here were big, old Victorian ones. Probably built around the turn of the century. The lots were large, with massive trees, and Casey could imagine wonderful gardens beneath the thin coating of snow that had fallen last night. What kind of stories had been played out over the years in these houses? How many tears had been shed in this room alone? She could suddenly see herself raising a family here, filling the large rooms with kids and cats and dogs, all waiting for when Mike—

She pushed herself away from the window. Where had that daydream come from? She glanced around, almost expecting to see a spirit fleeing the scene.

"Well, it certainly didn't come from me," she said aloud.

It was definitely time she moved into the garage apartment. Things were getting a little out of hand here. Not that she couldn't handle them, but there was no reason to push things. Mike was obviously hurting over this thing with Darcy, and Casey knew she was a sucker for anything hurting. Snowflake and Midnight were proof of that, but so were the two dogs that lived with her father and her stepmother, Val, and the cat that her brothers had taken in. No, better to be safe than sorry.

Casey found Mike in the kitchen, going over what she assumed was the mail that had accumulated while he'd been gone. "Have you got a key to that garage apartment? I want to get started cleaning it."

"You aren't still thinking about moving up there, are you?" he asked, frowning at her. "There's plenty of room here."

And a guy more needy than Snowflake. "I think it would be best if we had our own space."

"You're thinking about that bathroom thing," he said. "All I have to do is put a hook on the inside. Gus can't pop the hook out of the eye."

"It's not that at all," she insisted. "Mrs. Jamison said I could use that apartment, and that's what I want to do."

"It's not safe," he snapped.

"From what?"

"From anything."

"Come on, we're in Berrien Springs."

"No place is safe anymore."

"That's for sure," she said, getting a bit irritated herself. "Including right here. Not if you like closed doors, that is."

Mike glared at her for a long moment, trying to get her to back down, but she refused. She thought with her heart all too much, but this time she would be strong.

He looked away. "Fine," he said, and got to his feet.

"I'll show you the place and then you can admit I'm right."

"When hell freezes over," Casey vowed.

"It does that a lot up here in the winter," he stated.

Not saying another word, she followed him out to the garage. The stairs to the apartment were inside, and she saw that her worst fears could soon be realized. Boxes, broken tools and other junk littered the stairway.

"I don't think upstairs is going to be any better," Mike warned.

"Don't worry." She waved her hands, shooing him upstairs. "I have time. I can clean up."

But her heart was rapidly sinking into her shoes as she climbed over the junk on the stairs. Mike was all too likely to have been right; this place was unlivable. She was going to have to stay in the house, right alongside Mr. March. She wasn't going to have a choice.

"Hnnh." Mike grunted. He'd fiddled with the lock and pushed against the door, but had to slam his shoulder into it several times before it popped open.

Casey hurried into the room, anxious for it to prove her fears wrong. She came to a quick halt. The room was piled high with boxes and old furniture, several of the windows were cracked and there were two huge spiderwebs in the far corner. But the absolute worst was the smell.

"Something died in here," she said.

"Probably more than one something."

She wanted to respond with something positive, but no matter how her brain scrambled, nothing came.

"This doesn't look good," Mike said.

"I wonder if Mr. Slocum has some free days this week," Casey said.

"He'll need some free weeks to fix all this up properly."

Mike flipped the electric switch by the door, but nothing came on. Shaking his head, he clumped back down the stairs. Casey went into the bathroom.

It was as bad as the main room. Everything was coated

with dirt, and turning the spigots in the sink produced no water. Cobwebs hung from every imaginable surface, while a dark water stain added distinction to the far wall. Things didn't look good. Not at all.

Mike came back upstairs. "Wires are all shorted out."

She nodded. "The water's either turned off or the pipes are broken."

He leaned against the doorway, arms across his chest. "I believe I feel hell freezing over," he said.

Casey would have kicked him if she hadn't thought it was a bad way to start their landlord-tenant relationship. "I thought you were supposed to be taking care of things for your aunt," she said. "You aren't doing a very good job of it."

"I'm taking care of the house," he said. "And that was in terrible shape before I started."

"The bathroom door doesn't close tightly," she retorted.

"It will once I put a hook on it."

"Unless you kick it down."

He stared at her, his blue eyes seeming to measure her. "Lady, you are one beautiful woman," he finally said. "But I am not so desperate for female companionship that I have to kick in bathroom doors."

His words should have relieved her, but they left traces of irritation instead. He didn't have to be quite so positive about it all.

"Can I have your promise on that?"

He straightened up from the door. "You've got my sacred vow," he snapped.

"Until hell freezes over?"

"I told you, that happens almost every winter here. You're safe until your cats explain the meaning of life to me."

"My cats don't explain anything."

"So you're really really safe then, aren't you?"

Somehow, she wasn't too sure.

Chapter Three

"Come on, Aunt Myrna." Mike glanced over his shoulder as he spoke into the phone, but Casey was still upstairs. "How I am supposed to protect her if I have no idea what she's in danger from?"

"I'm not sure I ought to be talking about it," his great-aunt said. "She has a right to privacy, you know."

Mike tried not to scream in frustration. The last thing he wanted was for Casey to come down now, and she surely would if she heard his primeval scream echoing through the house. Though he probably could claim it was the ghost and she'd buy it.

"I need an idea, Aunt Myrna. A hint. Is she on the run from the mob? Did she blow the whistle on some government scandal?"

His great-aunt just laughed. "Oh, Michael. What a sense of humor."

"I gather that means it's none of the above," he said. "So that leaves a boyfriend. Her current or an ex?"

"Maybe you should be asking her these things."

"I thought she wasn't supposed to know that I knew she was in danger."

"But maybe you could get her to talk about things. You know, over dinner one evening."

Suspicions were rapidly building. "Aunt Myrna," he said. "She's *not* in any danger, is she? This is all some matchmaking scheme. I am not—repeat *not*—looking for a new girlfriend."

"Matchmaking? Me?" The woman was sputtering with anger on the other end of the phone line. "You've put your brain next to the radar detector one too many times, dear nephew. I am truly concerned about poor Casey. She could be married and I would still be concerned about her."

That was a new fear. An irrational one. "Is she?"

"No, of course not. But if she was, I'd worry about her."

"If you're so worried, why did you say she could live in that garage apartment?" he asked. "How was I supposed to protect her there?"

"I knew she wouldn't end up there," his great-aunt said. "That apartment's got to be in terrible shape and you wouldn't let her."

Mike just closed his eyes. "Is there anything else I'm supposed to be doing or not doing?"

"Just take care of her, Michael. Is that too much to ask?"

He heard Casey on the stairs and stepped farther into the kitchen. "I'll do my best," he said quickly. "Though I'm not fond of guessing games."

He was hanging up the phone when Casey came into the kitchen. The room seemed brighter all of a sudden, and warmer, like spring was just around the corner. A crazy idea, since it was the beginning of December and winter was looming ahead. Was he going to have to erect massive barriers every time she came into the room? He went back over to the mail he'd been sorting ages ago.

"So you settled in?" he asked, as he ripped open an envelope. An ad. He tossed it aside and picked up another.

"Pretty much." She sat down at the table, too, leaning on her elbows and resting her head in her hands. "I found the sheets okay and got my bed made. There was plenty of room in that dresser without moving anything."

He looked up. "I can get those boxes out of there."

She was wearing a plaid flannel shirt, open at the neck, and his gaze somehow got stuck on the soft expanse of skin peeking out. He remembered that water droplet that had rolled down there this morning and felt his mouth go dry.

"No, it's okay. I don't want to bother you in any way."

He started, wondering if she could read his mind—or his body—then realized she was talking about the room. He went back to his mail. "Whatever you want."

"No, I really mean it," Casey continued. "I had thought when I took this job that I'd be in my own place and not imposing at all on you, but it hasn't turned out like that. I just want you to know that I'll stay out of your way as much as possible."

"I'm not around all that much normally, anyway," he said. He put the envelope down and sat back in his chair. Her green eyes were troubled; they looked darker and more serious, and he thought he knew the reason. "Not that you'll be alone. Gus is a great watchdog. Anybody tries to get in the house and he'll tear them apart."

He was sure he saw skepticism in her face.

"No, really," Mike continued. "He only let you and your cats live because Dubber let you all in."

Casey shook her head, and the sunlight streaming through the window behind her set flecks of gold dancing in her hair. Mike had the urge to touch it, to see if it was as fiery as it looked. What was happening to him? Darcy'd never had this effect on him.

"I'm more worried about getting in your way," Casey was saying. "I'll fix my meals when you're done and stay up in my room if you have guests over. I'll be working up there on my laptop most of the time, anyway."

That would be fine, best even. The less he saw of her, the less power she had over him. "I never have guests," he said. "Remember? I have no girlfriend."

"But you might get one," she said. "Or have the guys over to watch football. I just want you to know that—"

"You'll stay out of my way." He nodded. On the other hand, maybe the opposite would be better—see a lot of her and truly build up an immunity. "And I just want you to know that that isn't necessary. Make yourself at home. Feel free to spread out your stuff on the dining-room table. I never use it."

She looked less worried, less serious. "Well, if you're sure."

"Positive."

"I'll be quiet as a mouse, though."

"Aren't you afraid your cats will eat you?" he asked.

She looked surprised by his joke, then her lips slowly curved into a smile and it was like the sun coming out after a rainstorm. The world, the kitchen, lit up. She reached out and put her hand over his.

"This may work out, after all," she said, and squeezed his hand slightly before releasing it. Then, humming lightly, she went back into the living room.

Mike stayed still. He couldn't have moved if he tried. If he believed in ghosts and spirits and things like that, he'd vow that someone was still holding his hand. That the fire that had traveled up his arm, rendering him helpless, was not his reaction to Casey's touch, not something of his doing. He just wanted to be left alone, by everybody. Was that too much to ask?

He pushed aside the mail, having gotten nowhere with it. He'd do it later. Right now, he needed to be active. Pound nails, chop wood. Seal up those dormers in the attic—that would be just the thing. He got his tools and his jacket and hurried up to the second floor, where he let a staircase down from the ceiling.

"Oh, is that how you get up into the attic?" Casey asked. "Cool. Now I can look for all those diaries and letters Mrs. Jamison said were there."

"Great," Mike echoed weakly.

Casey looked around the attic with wonder and excitement. It was a real old-fashioned attic, like something out of a 1940s horror flick. Dark and dusty, with cobwebs hanging from the ceiling. With bat and mouse droppings decorating the far edges of the dirty plank floor. Light came from a single bare bulb hanging from the rafters above, as well as a louvered dormer window, which Mike was presently cleaning.

"Where do you suppose the letters and stuff are?" she asked.

He shrugged, not bothering to pause in his work. "Beats me. Just poke through the boxes all you want. No secrets up here."

No? Didn't all families have secrets? Casey went over to a pile of boxes in the far corner. Had she been a secret? Was that why her birth mother had abandoned her that way?

"I think someone's trying to tell you there's a family of ghosts under those boxes."

Casey started at Mike's words and looked down to find Snowflake and Midnight staring at the bottom of the pile. They were alert but not paranormal hyper.

"I think they're really telling me a family of mice is living under all these boxes," Casey replied.

"Don't worry about it," Mike said. "I'll protect you."

"My hero," Casey murmured, putting a hand to her heart.

Mike made a face at her before turning back to the dormer window he was covering for the winter. Casey just stared at his back for a long moment. Two jokes in less than an hour. Must be some kind of record. But then her attention wandered slightly farther afield—to his tall, broad shoulders and slender hips. To his craggy, outdoor kind of face and his blond hair, cut short. He was dressed in jeans, boots and a leather jacket. Macho chic with an outdoorsy accent. A lot of women would probably vote for him as a hero.

But not her. He was stiff and overbearing. Although she could see him in a gothic novel, standing side by side with Heathcliff, staring out over the moors.

Casey shook her head and tore her eyes away. She didn't know him well enough to decide if he was stiff and over-bearing, or gentle and considerate. For all she knew, Darcy had destroyed all sorts of gentleness in him. Destroyed or caused it to be hidden?

Stop it, she ordered herself. She could feel the symptoms—sympathy, curiosity, finding excuses for his curt-ness. If he was a cat, she'd be taking him home and think-ing up reasons why she just had to keep him.

She opened a box and found old clothes. Just old clothes, a quick rifling through the contents assured her. She moved the box over to look in the next one. More of the same. She moved the bottom box slightly, but not enough to see if anything was underneath.

"Cats are sensitive to a lot of things," she said. "So you can't really tell what might be under the boxes."

"If you want to know, you look." Mike paused to clean some of the debris around the louvers. "That's what a guy like me, who's not sensitive to anything, would do. Hey, leave those alone."

Casey turned to see Midnight sitting in front of Mike.

"That little bum wants to steal my gloves," Mike said.

"She likes to pick up anything small and soft," Casey explained. "She was pregnant when I found her, but her kittens were stillborn. Since then, she seems to always be looking for a kitten substitute."

"Why don't you get her a little stuffed cat?"

Casey grimaced. "She has about ten of them. She loses interest once they're hers."

"Ah," he said, and turned back to his work. "Sounds like some women I know."

Don't ask, she told herself. *Don't ask. Don't ask.* For once, Casey obeyed her orders and just opened another box. It was filled with old Christmas decorations. Interesting, but not the right kind of interesting.

"Hey, come back here," Mike shouted.

Casey looked up in time to see Midnight streaking toward the stairs with Mike's glove in her mouth. Mike was right behind her.

"Gus," Mike called out. "Stop that thief."

Gus had been sitting at the bottom of the stairs, but from the pained look that came over Mike's face, she guessed that the big dog had done nothing to apprehend the culprit. Most likely, he was now wagging his tail and grinning up at his master.

"I guess he doesn't want to be a police dog." Mike turned away from the stairs and fixed his gaze on Casey. "Does that cat hide the things she steals?"

"No, I'm sure we'll find it in my bedroom."

"Okay." He walked back to the attic window. "If I get my glove back, I won't press charges."

"Wow," Casey mocked. "Three jokes in less than an hour. You're on a roll."

"Hey, I'm a very humorous guy," he said.

"True. Kicking in doors, waving around guns, a laugh a minute."

"Watch it, lady, or I'll have your cat arrested yet."

She just smiled at him, the smile staying warm in her heart even as she turned back to the next box. This was great. They could laugh and joke around without her rescue hormones kicking into overdrive. Or without her female hormones going gaga over his biceps. She opened the box; it was filled with old photo albums.

"Oh, wow, look at these." She heard his footsteps come

closer and felt his nearness. Down, hormones, she ordered. "You know who any of these people are?"

"Nope."

She looked up at him. His blue eyes were distant, like they were shut behind a hundred doors. "None of them?"

"I doubt it," he said, and shrugged. "Look, I was adopted, okay? These folks are all part of my birth father's family, and I've only started to get to know the living ones. I don't know a thing about the dead ones."

There was so much in his voice—pain, fear, longing. All the things she could relate to. He turned, going back to the dormers, but she felt he was going farther away than that.

"I'm adopted, too," she said, hurrying after him.

"Is that so?" He picked up the plastic sheet and the staple gun.

She felt as if he was going to staple that stupid sheet between them, to shut himself off from her if he could. "How'd you find your birth father?" she asked.

"One of those registries," he said.

He was trying to hold the plastic sheet in place while positioning the staple gun. The plastic slipped once, then twice. She went around to his other side, brushing aside the major cobwebs in the way, and held it in place. Their shoulders touched; the tiny space between the side walls of the dormer was barely big enough for one.

Mike seemed not to notice her. He put a staple in each of the top corners, but then stopped with a sigh.

"I joined the army after high school," he said, the words coming slowly as if they had to travel a long distance or fight to come out. "I was in a unit with two guys from here—those two cops that came yesterday, actually—and they kept talking about how I looked exactly like a kid they went to high school with. It got me thinking. My mom— my adoptive mother—had told me that my birth parents were from this area, so it wasn't inconceivable that that kid I resembled was a relative. I found Stephen, my birth father. That kid turned out to be a cousin."

"Wow, what a great story," she said. "So now you have two families."

He went back to stapling. "My adoptive parents are both dead. Dad died when I was ten, Mom when I was twenty."

"I'm sorry."

He smiled at her. "So am I. They were good people. They didn't deserve to die young." Then he frowned. "That was a dumb thing to say. Nobody deserves to die young."

"My mom died when I was twelve. Dad remarried a few years later and I really love Val, but I still miss Mom."

"I know what you mean."

She took his hand in hers, needing a bond between them, an anchor if the storm got strong. "Can I ask you something personal? How did your birth mother give you up?"

"How?"

"Yeah, did she go through an adoption agency or leave you in a church or give you to friends, or what?"

"Oh." He nodded. "Through an agency, but it was a pretty open adoption. I guess Mom and Dad got to meet her."

"That's nice," Casey said. And it was for him. He didn't have any of the doubts or fears that came with finding out you'd been dumped in a Benton Harbor church basement in the dead of winter. Or with reading self-righteous quotes from the priest who'd found you.

"Why did you want to know?" he asked.

She just shrugged and let go of his hand, smoothing the plastic sheet out against the window. "No reason."

He took her hands in his this time, pulling on them to turn her. "No woman I have ever met asks a question like that for no reason."

His touch was so safe, so secure. It was like she could trust him to take care of her, to not let the fears get anywhere near her. But that was her crazy imagination going wild, as it liked to do. She tugged her hands free.

"So we're turning it into a sexist thing, are we?" She

tried for a teasing tone. "And just how many people, male or female, have actually asked you that question?"

"You're avoiding the issue."

"No, I'm avoiding my research. I should get back to those boxes so we can bring down the ones I want and not leave the attic open all day."

But before she could move, he put his hand on the other side of her, trapping her in the dormer's narrow space. "Hey, I'm a cop. I know when someone's concealing evidence."

"Well, this someone's not concealing anything," she said.

"No?"

It suddenly got very still in the attic, as if even the cobwebs were listening and holding their breath. Mike's eyes looked straight into hers, and it felt as if he was reaching into all the hiding places in her soul. Her eyes left his but stopped at his mouth, noting the fullness of his lips. She wondered what they would feel like pressed against hers, knew that her heart would race as it never had before.

Realized that they were playing with fire. She ducked down to slip under his arm.

"Hey, guys. You up there?"

It was Dubber's voice, Casey decided, though it sounded deeper than it had the last time they'd talked. She hurried over to the stairs to look down.

"Hi, Dubber," she said as the boy came up the stairs.

"Hey, Dubber," Mike said. "What's the matter? Caught a cold?"

Dubber studiously turned to Casey, ignoring Mike. "You coming to the Pickle Festival this weekend? I'm marching in the parade."

"The Pickle Festival? What in the world is that?"

"Well, actually, it's the Berrien Springs Christmas Pickle Festival," Dubber said, as if that cleared things up. "We have it every year in early December. There's a parade, pickle tasting, a Christmas-tree display, a craft show. Stuff like that.''

Casey felt lost and looked over at Mike.

''Berrien Springs used to be the pickle capital of the Midwest,'' he explained. ''And there's some old German tradition about hanging a pickle on the Christmas tree. Since there's a lot of German people in the area, it seemed like a good theme for a local festival.''

''A pickle on the Christmas tree?'' she repeated. Things were not getting clearer.

''That's the best part,'' Dubber said. ''A pickle's hidden on the tree, and if you're the first one to find it, you'll get your most favorite wish in the whole world.''

Mike grimaced. ''Yeah, assuming your parents can afford it.''

Dubber gave him a dirty look. ''It's not like that at all,'' he said. ''Joey Kovacs found the pickle on his tree last year and then he won his mountain bike from Outpost Sports. So it had nothing to do with his parents.''

''Coincidence then,'' Mike said.

''I think it's a nice story,'' Casey said. ''Coincidence or magic, though I personally like the idea of magic myself.'' She grinned at Dubber.

He smiled back, then turned bright red. ''Need any help moving boxes?'' he asked her.

''I'm right here,'' Mike said. ''If she needs any help, I can do it.''

Casey gave Mike a pointed look. ''There are a lot of boxes up here,'' she said. ''More than enough to keep a Boy Scout troop happy.''

She could see that both of them were about to say something, but Midnight returned, padding lightly up the stairs and across the plank floor. Straight over to Mike's other glove, still lying on the floor. The cat gave him an I-dare-you look before snatching up the glove and running for the stairs.

''Damn it,'' Mike snapped. ''Your cat's at it again.''

Casey struggled not to laugh. "Maybe he thought they belonged together."

"Yeah," Dubber snickered. "Like Romeo and Juliet."

"Or a pickle and a Christmas tree."

Mike glared at both of them for a moment, before stomping over to the stairs. "Come on, Gus," he said gruffly as he clumped down the rickety, pull-down stairs. "You've been sitting on your butt enough. Let's go outside and get a little exercise."

"Why don't you wait a minute?" Casey called down. "Let me see if I can find the gloves Midnight took."

"She can have them. I have more."

"It's no trouble, just wait a minute and—"

"But if she wants boots, go out and buy some for her. I only have one pair."

The fading sound of heavy footsteps told Casey that Mike wasn't waiting around for any kind of an answer. Shaking her head, she turned from the stairs and picked Snowflake up.

"Come on, sweetheart. It's warmer on our bed." Casey turned to Dubber. "Can you bring that box of photo albums down?"

"Sure." He followed her down the stairs, then closed up the stairway. "You know, Mike's a good old boy, but he does tend to be grumpy."

"I guess he's still a little under the weather," Casey said.

"Nah." Dubber shook his head. "He just doesn't know how to act around you."

"Me?" Casey scratched the purring cat in her arms. "What did I do?"

"Nothing," Dubber assured her. "Mike just ain't what you'd call a ladies' man."

Casey pulled out the family tree Mrs. Jamison had given her and spent the rest of the afternoon matching up names and pictures, weddings, christenings, birthdays and holidays. Little by little, the people started coming alive for her. She found an old group shot with a man in the back labeled as Uncle Simon. Was he the same one as the ghost?

At the bottom of the box was a stack of letters, and she delved into them eagerly. Simon Van Horne had had two brothers—Joseph, who'd lived in the area, and Timothy, who'd moved out west—but, it seemed, no children of his own. Joseph apparently had had three children—two boys and a girl, all of whom were close to Simon and his wife, Stella. There was no mention of a Priscilla, but there was mention of Stella's much younger brother, Robert Schmidt, who'd come to live with them after his parents died.

Casey surfaced when she noticed it was getting dark. It was almost five o'clock already. Mike was still out on his errands, which was just as well.

Things had gotten a little tense up there in the attic. She didn't know why she had reacted to him so strongly; she'd been around hunks before. It must have been the confidences, the talk about adoption that had forged some immediate bond between them. Or set off some immediate sparks. Whatever, they were over now, and all she was feeling was hungry. Maybe she'd make a pizza for dinner. If Mike came back in time and hadn't eaten, he could share it. If not, it would be her dinner for today and tomorrow.

After a quick trip to the local grocery, she whipped it up—one superhealthy, deluxe vegetarian pizza: fresh green peppers, fresh mushrooms, fresh onions, fresh alfalfa sprouts, even fresh tomatoes sprinkled over freshly grated cheese.

"So do I put it in now or wait?" she asked herself, frowning at the clock. "If I wait, then it seems like I want him to eat with me, which isn't exactly being as unobtrusive as a mouse."

So the pizza went into the oven. It wasn't in for more than fifteen minutes, though, before Mike and Gus came in. Casey felt her stomach tighten for just a moment. Was she going to feel that rush of hunger for his lips, that need to feel his arms around her? Had she been fooling herself into thinking it had been a temporary aberration?

"Hi." She busied herself drying the dishes that she'd used while making the pizza. "Got all your work taken care of?"

"Yeah, everything's shipshape."

Mike went to hang his coat up and Casey breathed a sigh of relief. No hormonal surges. Well, no major ones. She had noticed how the light in the kitchen caught his eyes and turned them a deeper blue, but that wasn't any big deal.

She bent over to pet Gus as Mike came back in. "Snowflake and Midnight are in the living room," she told the canine.

"You can't talk to him like a regular person," Mike said. "He's a dog."

"He's a sweetie pie," she replied, as Gus dashed into the other room.

"And he hates cats."

"With a passion."

"I'm glad you noticed."

Mike's face lit with a smile, and it seemed to touch a chord in her heart. She felt like she'd stumbled into a field of wildflowers. She smiled back; she couldn't help it. But she only let it linger on her lips a few seconds before she went back to her dish drying.

"So," she said briskly. "Are you working tomorrow?"

"Not exactly." Wrinkling his forehead, he looked around the kitchen. "I'll be back on the road Sunday. I've got to work the parade tomorrow."

"Ooh." She flashed a quick grin at him. "So I get to see both you and Dubber in it?"

"If you look quick." He leaned against the table, his face serious suddenly. "Hey, I'm sorry I was gone for a while. Here I assured you that you'd be safe here, that Gus would be here if I wasn't, and then I go off and take him."

She just shook her head slowly, not having the slightest

idea what he was talking about. "I was fine. I don't need a baby-sitter."

"Well, it won't happen again. Gus'll be here while I'm at work, and I'll have the local guys keep an eye on the place when they're on patrol."

"Are you expecting trouble?"

"Well, you never know." He shifted his position. "I was thinking about this whole arrangement. It's crazy for us to live in the same house and duplicate chores. Want to order in some pizza for dinner?"

"Actually, I've got one in the oven."

"You know how to make pizza?" The tone was more cautious than disbelieving. "Did you work in a joint in high school?"

"No. I learned when I was a college student."

"Where did you go to school?"

"The University of California at Berkeley."

"Berkeley?" Horror filled his face. "What's on it? All kinds of sprouts and stuff?"

"Let me get it out of the oven," she said quickly. "Before it burns."

"Oh, we wouldn't want that."

Casey ignored the insincerity in his tone and busied herself with getting the food out of the oven and onto the table.

"That pizza smells like that soup you made me eat."

"I made you eat?" The words came out fast. "I don't make people do anything. Besides, it helped you get over your cold."

"Oh, it did. It certainly did."

She glared at him. If he was patronizing her, even the least tiny bit, he was going to have another scar—this time on that manly face of his.

"And it was delicious."

"I'm glad you liked it," she said. "That's why I made this vegetarian pizza for our dinner."

"And I'm glad you did." A tight smile came across his

face. "I wanted to ask you to make one, but it seemed like so much work I didn't think it was fair."

They traded stares for a long moment, then both burst out laughing. The threat of a storm had passed, leaving behind sunshine and the promise of joy. Casey put the pizza on the table.

"Would you like some wine with the pizza?" she asked. "It's nothing fancy. Just one of those five-liter tappers you get in the supermarket."

"Hey, I'm not a fancy guy."

Suddenly the kitchen turned pleasantly warm. Casey didn't know any woman in her right mind who wanted fancy. She herself wanted funny. Solid. Friendly. Gentle. Passionate. Faithful. Strong, when the current was against them. She wanted—

She wanted to eat.

"We'd better get started or we're going to have cold pizza."

Mike got the wine from the refrigerator, and a couple of glasses, then they sat down. Gus came in to settle at their feet beneath the table. It left a homey feeling in her heart, a sense of belonging and rightness that took her by surprise. She and Mike would be housemates for a while, friends even, but that was all. There was no reason for her heart to feel satisfied. Or to feel that there was such a promise of more lingering in the air.

"So how'd your research go?" Mike asked.

"Great. I found a picture of Simon."

"I assume while he was alive, not in his haunting days."

She made a face at him as she reached for a piece of pizza. "Yes, while he was alive. What is the story behind him, do you know?"

Mike cut himself a large piece, apparently not as averse to vegetables as he pretended. "Only vaguely. The story goes that his fiancée left him and he never got over it, even though he married later."

Casey watched Mike's face, struck by the awful coincidence of both of them being jilted. "Who was Priscilla? One of the cops here last night mentioned her."

"His fiancée," he said.

Simon's Darcy. "And what happened to her?"

Mike just shrugged and took a large bite of the pizza. "That's not part of the story. Maybe she married his doctor. Hey, this is pretty good."

He talked about marrying a doctor offhandedly, like it didn't matter one way or another, but Casey knew that couldn't be true. It must still hurt. "Why is he haunting the place?" she asked.

"He's not," Mike answered. "He died about fifty years ago, at the ripe old age of eighty. He has not been around since."

She ignored his skepticism. "He built this house, didn't he? That's what your aunt said."

"Timing would be right. It was built in the 1890s."

She looked around her, as if feeling the presence of all the past inhabitants. "I wonder if he built it for Priscilla."

Mike took another piece of pizza. "I imagine he built it to have a place to live."

Casey knew nothing was that simple. And the sorrow she felt in the air confirmed it.

Chapter Four

Casey popped up in bed, her heart racing. The room was dark, with just a faint light filtering in around the drapes. Both cats were awake, energy pulsating from them as they stood at the foot of the bed.

Simon was up and about.

Snowflake let out a yowl, a deep guttural sound that reached into the far corners of Casey's soul, then was joined by Midnight's soft, singing whine. They jumped off the bed and raced to the door.

As they hurried—almost floated—out into the darkness of the hallway, Casey was right behind them, pulling on her thick fuzzy robe as she went. This was her chance to meet Simon, to get a sense of why he was still here. It would be the basis of the family history. The floorboards groaned beneath her while the whole house creaked, as if fighting a bitter wind outside.

Casey held her breath as she and the cats passed Mike's room, but both he and Gus seemed to be sleeping soundly.

Just as well. They'd had a good time at dinner last night, but there was no reason to push things. Her attempt to have a talk with the ghost might be a bit too much for him. She slipped by his door and went down the stairs, breathing once again when she got to the bottom. The cats turned left, leading her into the dark living room.

Casey slowed her steps and fought to slow her racing heart, as well. It was chilly in the room, with a skewed square of light lying across the rug. The high ceiling harbored all sorts of shadows, just as the house itself harbored secrets.

"Simon," she said, barely whispering. "Simon, are you here?"

The cats had settled at her feet, staring off toward the built-in bookshelves on the far wall. She could feel his presence. It was faint at first, like he was hesitating, but then seemed to be getting stronger. He was reaching out to her, she was certain. She got a whiff of a faint scent. Peppermint.

"Are you looking for Priscilla?" she breathed into the darkness.

Suddenly there was a flash, and a blinding light filled the room. She blinked and stepped back. Her eyes and thoughts cleared then, and she realized the ceiling lights were on!

"What in the hell are you doing?" Mike barked.

Casey spun to find him in the doorway, one hand on the light switch, the other holding his gun. "Don't swear at me," she said. "And I might ask you the same thing. What are you doing?"

Everything that hinted at paranormal was gone. No presence. No load of pain. No peppermint. Nothing. Just the empty cold of an old house and the anger of a young police officer. Casey wrapped her arms around herself, shivering. Was this house always so cold or was it just her?

"Why in the world do you go sneaking around in the middle of the night?" Mike yanked the clip from his handgun and ejected the round from the chamber. "You can get seriously hurt doing that."

"If you weren't so on edge," she snapped, "maybe we wouldn't have to worry about my getting hurt."

"Hey, lady. I hear these weird sounds and someone sneaking around down here," he said. "I'm responsible for this house, and you while you're in it. Just what the hell do you expect me to do?"

"Damn it, I told you not to swear at me."

"I'm not swearing at you," he replied. "I'm swearing with you."

There were more words that she wanted to throw at him, but that would just be playing into his game, and she wasn't about to give him the satisfaction. She clenched her teeth hard and just stood there, trying to keep herself from shivering.

Once they stopped shouting at each other, the normal creaky quiet of the old house surrounded them, wrapping them in an invisible, thick fog. The five of them—two people, two cats and one dog—just stood there staring at each other. Gus was the first to move, walking over to the two cats and sniffing at them. Snowflake ignored him, but Midnight touched noses—a big, black furry one going against a small, soft black one.

Casey felt the hardness in her heart melting. People talked about fighting like cats and dogs, implying how the two species hated each other. But looking at the animals here, she couldn't help wonder if the world wouldn't be a better place if people treated each other as well as they did. And a good place to start would be between herself and Mike. Sighing, she turned toward him and—

"Well, I hope you learned your lesson," Mike snapped. "And that you don't do anything this stupid for a while."

Casey's mouth fell open, and she could feel her anger return like a California brushfire. Just who in the hell did he think he was, calling her stupid?

"You are an insufferable pain in the ass," she shouted.

Her cats snapped around to stare at her, and she could hear Gus whimper a little. The hell with them all, she thought.

"Me?" he shouted back. "I'm not the one waking people up."

"I live in this house, too. I have a right to walk around."

"Fine, walk around," he snapped. "But turn on the lights like a normal person. Don't go sneaking around in the house like some nutcase."

"Oh, excuse me. I suppose you're an expert on nutcases."

"I know what's normal."

"Oh, right. You live alone in a big house with just your dog and a loaded gun by your bedside. I can see how you're an expert on normal."

"I'm a cop."

"That's no excuse.'

"I have it on the best of authorities that it's the best excuse to live alone there is."

"On the best of authorities?" she repeated, totally confused. It was hard to stay angry when she couldn't come up with a snappy retort.

"Sure, that nobody in their right mind would want to live with a cop."

She frowned at him. "Who would say that?" she asked.

He just glared at her, a mixture of annoyance and regret on his face. "Never mind," he said. "Forget I said anything."

"Did Darcy say that?" Casey demanded. "I'll bet it was her."

He looked like a man sorely put upon. She could see the indecision in his eyes.

Then he sighed. "Not that it's any of your business, but yes, she did. Not quite like that, though. She said she didn't think she could live her life, fearing that every time there was a knock at the door it was someone coming to tell her something had happened to me. Anything else you want to know that's none of your business?''

But before Casey could answer, Mike had already turned and left, stomping upstairs like a three-ton elephant, with Gus at his heels. If she didn't feel so badly for him, she'd say he was totally insufferable.

"Come on, guys," she called out softly. "We're done for the night."

She turned off the light and led the way back to their bedroom. No ghost in his right mind would come out now, not with all the negative vibes floating around the house. Hell, she'd be lucky if he ever came back, especially an uptight male ghost like her spirit appeared to be. It was easy to see that the ghost and Mike were related. The family resemblance was more than a little obvious.

Mike sat on the edge of his bed. It was morning already, but he felt as if he'd hadn't slept at all. Thanks to Casey's little stroll last night, he hadn't slept much.

Why had he let her bait him into telling about Darcy? It was that old mesmerizing trick of hers, that and being woken from a sound sleep. He was going to have to be more careful in the future. He could see all sorts of sympathies appearing in Casey's eyes. Just what he didn't need—someone feeling sorry for him.

Darcy had been right—fearing every knock on the door and ring of the phone would be a hell of a way to live. And if he needed proof of it, he just had to look at the divorce statistics for cops. No, he realized now there were some things a man had no right to ask for, some things that a man couldn't allow another to give. But it wasn't a cause for sympathy; he had chosen his path and continued to choose it each day.

"Something I may have to explain to the redhead," he said to the dog. "And to her cats."

Gus yawned and thumped his tail on the bed.

"I thought you hated cats," Mike said. "You're always chasing Mrs. Kinder's Dusty."

After giving Mike a quick glance, the dog stood up on the bed and shook himself, then jumped off and stretched his front paws. If Mike thought Gus was thinking anything—which he wasn't—he would have thought the dog was thinking that chasing a cat didn't mean he didn't like them.

Criminy, that woman was affecting everything he did. Now she was having him attribute thoughts to a dog. "I wonder if Aunt Myrna's going to tell us when the 'all clear' sounds and Casey's no longer in danger."

Speaking of danger, he needed to get himself in gear and check the place out. He showered quickly, got dressed and, after cautioning Gus to be quiet, went downstairs carrying his boots so that his steps would not make any more noise than the creaking floors already did.

If he owned this place, he'd have a bunch of rugs thrown around. Give the place a homey feel. Make it warmer, too. But he didn't own it and never would. Myrna had tried to give it to him, but he'd turned her down too many times to count. Darcy had taught him to beware of letting anything cling to his shirttails, even a house.

He and Gus went outside, into the brisk morning air. It was chilly, but clear. A good day for the Pickle Festival to begin. While Gus checked out the backyard, Mike walked around the house. Everything looked secure. No new scratches by the windows or doors. No—

He stopped. There were fresh footprints near the dining-room window. The snow was trampled just at the spot where the drapes parted slightly, but since the tracks led back to the snow-free driveway, Mike couldn't tell where the person had gone from there. He took a deep breath and stepped back. Damn. Slowly, cautiously, he walked out to the front of the house, looking down the deserted street.

"Hi, Mike," Dubber called. The boy was sitting on the

Randalls' front porch, packing newspapers into a canvas bag.

"Hi." Mike walked over. "You see any strangers around here this morning?"

The boy shook his head. "Nope, why? You looking for somebody?"

Mike shrugged. "There're footprints over by the dining-room window."

"Oh." Dubber's face turned red—his color these days it would seem. "That was just me."

"You?"

The boy shrugged self-consciously. "Yeah, I was seeing if you guys were up yet. I thought maybe you'd want your newspaper right away."

Him or Casey? "Well, that was nice of you," Mike said carefully. "Sure. I'll take it."

"Huh?"

"The paper," Mike said, holding out his hand. "You were going to give us our paper early."

"Oh yeah." He pulled a paper out of his bag, and as he gave it to Mike, his face lit up. "Hi, Casey."

Mike had known she was there from Dubber's face, but he turned slowly. She was in her fuzzy red robe, which should have made her look like a giant red bear, but instead made her look as cuddly and cozy as a kitten. Even her leather boots, peeking out from under the robe, didn't spoil the effect. Mike had the urge to go over and bury his face in her neck, to hold her in his arms and—

"You've got a phone call," she told Mike.

"Okay." She had to have been out here for a reason other than that she was looking to cuddle with him.

"Hi, Dubber," she called over to the boy. "You all ready for the parade?"

"Uh-huh." He ran across the yard, beating Mike by a few yards. "You want a newspaper?" he asked her, holding one out to her.

Mike frowned at him. "You already gave me one."

"This one's for Casey," he said, and turned back to her. "You know, in case you want to do the crossword puzzle."

Casey just smiled at him. "Thanks anyway, but I think we can share Mike's."

"You sure?" Dubber pressed. "I got extras."

"Yeah, I'm sure," she said.

"And she's probably also freezing," Mike noted. Dubber's eagerness was getting to be a bit much. As was Casey's ever-so-sweet reaction.

"Oh." Dubber looked deflated as he glanced at her robe. "Yeah. I'm sorry."

Casey flashed Mike a definite glare before she smiled back at Dubber. "No reason to be. My robe is warmer than my coat, but I don't want to keep you from your paper route. You've got a parade to be in."

"Right." He moved back toward the porch. "I'll see you there?"

"You betcha," she called, waving as she and Mike walked around the corner. "He was only trying to be nice," she said to Mike.

"He's got a crush on you."

"I know."

"Well, don't you think you should be discouraging him?"

She frowned at him. "What would you suggest? Slamming the door in his face? Telling him to bug off? Has it been that long since you were eleven?"

Mike let her go up the back steps first, a sudden thought taking hold of him and bringing a smile to his face. Of course, it all fit—short; didn't drive; not involved in a physical relationship. "Hey, how old is Melvin?" he asked. "He wouldn't be eleven, by any chance, would he?"

Casey turned, looking confused. "Melvin? He's in his early thirties."

Mike followed her up onto the porch. All right, so old Mel was an adult, but probably as irresponsible as an eleven-year-old. "Why doesn't he drive? Can't afford a car?"

"He could afford about a hundred cars if he wanted them," Casey said. "He developed some new computer chip that he sold for millions of dollars."

Hell. Mike pulled open the back door, fighting an irrational urge to kick it in instead. "What's he think about you coming here?" he asked. "Probably ticked off, right?"

She stopped on the porch. "He thought it was a great opportunity for me. He knows how much I like doing family histories."

"Fine. Great. He's perfect," Mike snapped. "So why don't you marry him?"

"Boy, you got up on the wrong side of the bed," Casey retorted. "Go answer your phone call. I'll stay out here and keep an eye on Gus."

"He doesn't need anyone to keep an eye on him."

"Go answer the phone before I slug you."

Casey smoothed her blanket out the best she could around a snoozing Snowflake. "So is he always this grumpy?" she asked Gus. "Or was he just needing his morning coffee?"

Gus was too busy to answer. He and Midnight were lying on their bellies, staring under the dresser. Casey was certain she didn't want to know what they were looking at.

"I suspect this is just your way of avoiding the whole subject," she told the dog. "You have lived with that guy too long. You are just like him."

Well, maybe not just like him. The dog was much more easygoing, did not seem to have a fixation with Melvin that set him off into dark moods and seemed quite delighted to be sharing living quarters with Casey and her cats.

"I'm going down for breakfast," she told the whole crowd. Snowflake was the only one who moved—she yawned. "Yes, I'll miss you all, too."

Casey went into the hall and down the stairs, glancing

through the balustrades to see if Mike was still around. No sign of him. Maybe he'd left while she was taking a bath—with the new hook securely holding the door shut. That would be fine with her. She had enough on her mind without having to deal with his mood swings.

She hurried down the steps, across the black-and-white marble foyer and down the hall to the kitchen. Mike was sitting at the kitchen table and she screeched to a halt.

"Something wrong?" she asked. "Was your call bad news?"

He shook his head. "No. It was Stephen, my father. He and his family are coming up for the day. They were just double-checking as to the time of the parade."

"Goodness, this festival draws out-of-towners? Do I need to stake out my spot along the parade route early? Maybe I should go down there now."

"No, there's always plenty of room."

He cleared his throat and then got to his feet. He seemed to fill up the kitchen with his Mr. March macho body, and she considered making up some excuse to go back upstairs until he had left. When had she become so chickenhearted, though?

"I want to apologize for this morning," Mike said. "You were right about Dubber. He's a good kid and I appreciate you being so nice to him."

She felt a tingling in her hand, as if it wanted to reach out and take hold of Mike's. She felt a weakening in her determination, as if it was saying to let him be a friend. She felt remarkably uncautious all of a sudden. However, she was strong enough not to let any of that affect her.

"That's all right," she said carefully. "I can get pretty grumpy before breakfast at times, too."

"Speaking of breakfast, the Pickle Festival starts off with a pancake breakfast at the firehouse. Want to go down there for some?"

A little voice whispered that it would be much safer to

send him down there and have breakfast here by herself. But then she'd have to make it....

"It's to raise money for the local animal shelter," he said.

"I'd love to go," she said quickly. As an animal lover, she had no choice. "Let me get my purse."

A few minutes later, they were leaving the house. Mike offered to drive, but when he said it was only four blocks away, Casey suggested they walk. It was a gorgeous day—a little nippy, but the sun was pleasant and there was almost no wind.

"This is a nice neighborhood," she said. It felt so warm and welcoming. About half of the houses were decked out with pine garlands and wreaths and red bows for Christmas. All it needed was a real snowfall to make it perfect. "So when are you putting up your decorations?"

"I don't go in for all that," he said.

"Oh." She understood that, she supposed. A single guy living by himself had other things to do with his time and money. Still, it was a shame. The house would so lend itself to holiday decorating. Garlands along the porch rail, twin wreaths on the double front doors and colored lights in the pine trees in—

"How's the research going?" he asked.

"Fine." She put aside her decorating schemes. "There's a lot of material in the attic. I suspect this history is going to write itself."

The four blocks passed as if they had been only one. Between telling him about the photos she'd found, laughing about the various pickle-shaped signs advertising festival events and ignoring the growing warmth from his nearness, she barely noticed the passing time until they got to the firehouse. Mike was jovially greeted from all sides, and Casey stepped aside slightly, not wanting to give anyone the wrong impression.

"So you're Myrna's author lady?" someone said to her.

"You writing about Simon?" someone else asked.

In the next five minutes, Mike must have introduced her to twenty people and she must have confirmed a dozen times that she'd been hired to write the family history. In the middle of a discussion with an elderly woman named Mrs. Kinder, Mike disappeared from Casey's side. She told herself she hadn't expected him to stay; this hadn't been a date, after all. And he certainly hadn't wanted to give anybody that impression. But then he was back again, with tickets to the breakfast.

"We'd better get in line before all those flapjacks get eaten up," he said, taking her arm. He gave the old lady a nod. "You come over and tell Casey all your stories some afternoon. You know more about the family than Myrna does."

"Ha, butter me up," Mrs. Kinder said with a wave of her hand. "I know some stories about you, too, young man, and don't think I won't tell them."

"But do you know the really good ones?" he asked.

"Who does know the really good ones?" Casey asked him once they got into the food line.

"Only me," he said. "So they'll be forever hidden."

"And you won't tell me even one for the history?" she asked. "How about one about your first girlfriend?"

"Somehow telling one for publication in a family history doesn't seem like a good way to keep it a secret."

After they each got their plate of pancakes and cup of coffee, they found places at one of the long tables set up where the fire trucks normally were stored. It was easy to see this was a community affair. Young mothers with babies sat watching older kids running up and down the aisles. One end of a table was filled with old men laughing and talking over coffee and sections of the newspaper, while a group of old women sat at the other end, talking over knitting. Casey wondered what it would be like to live in a place like this, where everybody knew you and was part of your life. She'd grown up in Fort Wayne, which wasn't large, but wasn't a small town, either. And now she lived in Ann Arbor.

She was perfectly happy with the way things were. She was. It was what she wanted. So why did this seem so appealing?

Mike was talking to someone at the next table, leaning back and discussing the local high-school football team, when Casey found herself listening to a nearby conversation.

"Why is she here?" the woman next to Casey asked.

"She's really got some nerve," another agreed.

The two women were glaring at someone now manning the coffee table. This woman was young, probably Casey's age, and average looking—medium height, medium brown hair pulled into a ponytail, but with a nice smile. Why wasn't she welcome here?

"Poor Mike," someone else said.

"That's Darcy," the first woman said, leaning close to Casey.

Darcy! She looked nothing like Casey'd expected. Somehow she'd thought blond and gorgeous and dressed in tight, slinky clothes. Darcy looked nice.

"She dumped him, you know."

Casey nodded and looked back at Mike. He was still laughing with the others, but as she watched, he finished up his coffee. His smile was bright and natural; he hadn't seen Darcy yet. Maybe he didn't have to know she was here. Maybe Casey could keep him laughing and having a good time.

"Want more coffee?" she asked as she got to her feet. "I was just going to get more myself."

He frowned at her cup, which was still more than half-full. "Don't be crazy. I can go and get—"

"No, I'll get it," the woman next to Casey said, grabbing Mike's cup from his hand. "Was it regular or decaf?"

Mike got to his feet and took it back from her. "What is going on?"

He turned to follow their guilty glances and looked over at the coffee table. As they watched, several other people were getting refills. And showing their loyalty to Mike, from their body language. Casey wanted to cheer, but another part of her couldn't. How horrible Darcy must be feeling.

"Aha," he said, and turned back to Casey and the others. "Hope you guys aren't planning a life of deceit. You're pretty bad at it."

He moved his folding chair out of the way and walked up to the coffee table. It seemed that all conversation in the hall died, that every eye in the place was on him. Two older women were getting coffee, and reeking disapproval from every pore. They moved slowly aside when they saw Mike coming, as if they were thinking of blocking his way.

Mike stopped in front of the table. Darcy's face was stiff; Casey could feel her uncertainty from across the room. But then Mike spoke and Darcy smiled, then laughed. She poured Mike his cup of coffee, then said something to make him laugh. He reached out—Casey thought for his cup of coffee—but took Darcy's hand instead as he continued to talk. Then he let go, leaned across the table to kiss her briefly, before taking his cup.

As soon as he turned around, so did everyone else. They all started talking and laughing, so loudly the place felt about to explode. Mike walked back through the suddenly animated crowd to his place across the table from Casey. She watched him approach, then turned her gaze to Darcy. People were stopping to talk to her. The smile on her face was surely enough to melt the ice and snow outside. Mike sat down.

"That was very nice of you," Casey said.

He shrugged and sipped at his coffee. "It was no big deal."

"Not everyone would feel that way."

"Not everyone knows what went on between us." He

pushed his cup of coffee to the middle of the table. "You ready to go?"

"Yes," she said. "But we can't. Not yet."

His eyes asked the question.

"If you rush out now, it'll undo all the good you just accomplished," she said. "If you want to be a hero, you're going to have to suffer a bit longer."

"Who said I wanted to be a hero?"

"Hey, you could have let me go get the coffee for you."

His eyes darkened as they locked with hers. "Why'd you offer to go?" he asked. "I know why everyone else acted that way, but why you?"

Good question, but she had no good answer. "I don't know," she said.

"You would have for Melvin," he said.

"Yes."

"I'm not sure I like being in the same category."

"I'm not sure why."

But he ignored her statement. "Why did Myrna send you?"

She was confused. "To write the family history."

"That all?"

Chapter Five

Mike's father, Stephen, with his wife, Joy, and three kids, Kate, Monica and Brad, arrived at the house just after Mike had left for the parade, so Casey made his apologies and gave them the map he'd left.

"I told you I should've driven the whole way," Kate said. "If we hadn't stopped to change drivers, we would have made it on time."

Stephen just smiled at the girl. "But we did make it on time," he said. "We've got a good twenty minutes to walk downtown before the parade starts, so we aren't late."

"Are you going to the parade, too?" Joy asked Casey. "Why don't you walk down there with us? Mike said you're new in town."

"New in town and new to pickle festivals," Casey agreed as she got her coat. "I'd like the company. Thank you."

"They have chocolate-covered pickles here," Brad told her as they walked down the front steps. He looked about five—just the age that would find the idea of chocolate-covered pickles appealing.

"I think I'll pass on them," Casey said.

"They're yucky," Monica agreed. She had to be seven or eight. "But they're fun to bring in your lunch and offer to friends."

Brad and Monica skipped on ahead toward the downtown area, followed by Stephen and by Kate, who was trying to convince her dad that they—well, she—should drive there.

"Let me guess," Casey said to Joy as they trailed after the others. "Kate just got her license."

"Kind of obvious, isn't it? She's even worse than her brother Rob was at that age." Joy grinned at Casey. "So how are you and Mike getting along?"

Casey gave the other woman a strange look as their feet crunched on the bits of snow on the sidewalk. "Fine," she said. "How should I be getting along with him?"

Joy shrugged as they crossed the street. "Hey, I'm just the messenger. Myrna called this morning and wanted a report."

"A report of what?" Casey asked. "How the family history is going? Pretty good, though I've really just started."

"I think Myrna was more interested in you and Mike."

"Me and Mike? There is no Mike and me."

"Maybe Myrna hopes there will be," Joy said. "How well do you know her?"

"Why does everyone ask me that?" Casey said with a laugh. "How well should I have known her before taking on this job?"

"Well, her psychic advises her every move," Joy said. "And she told us that Madame DeMarco saw great unhappiness easing with your coming here. So of course Myrna decided that had to mean Mike was going to fall in love again."

Casey thought of how Mike had gone to Darcy's defense this morning. She would have to guess that there was no falling in love *again* in his future. He was still in love. Not that it mattered to Casey. She had other goals. She shoved her hands into the pockets of her coat.

"Maybe it means I'm going to solve the riddle of Simon," Casey said.

"The ghost?" Joy looked eager. "Do you really think there is one?"

Casey nodded. "He's been around twice," she said, then frowned. "And Mike's chased him off at least once."

"What a party pooper!"

"That's what I say."

Ferry Street was already filling up when Casey and the Van Horne clan arrived. People were lining the sidewalks, and some of the older folks had brought folding lawn chairs to sit on, looking rather wedged into them in their bulky winter coats. In the middle of the block, a flatbed trailer was being used as a stage, with red-and-green bunting hanging from the edges.

"Let's take the other side of the street," Stephen said. "It'll be warmer in the sun."

It was also more crowded, but not unpleasantly so. People milled about talking while young children dodged around them on the sidewalk or chased each other in the empty street. The two youngest Van Horne children ran off to play while their parents were busy pointing something out to Kate.

Casey checked out the street. It was a postcard-perfect replica of a Midwestern small town, lined with small storefronts, none higher than two stories, and all festooned with Christmas decorations. The streetlights were hung with gold tinsel and stars; Christmas carols were being played over a loudspeaker system. It felt so safe, so much like home—though it was nothing like her home. She thought suddenly about what Joy had said—that Mrs. Jamison was thinking of something other than a family history when she'd sent Casey here.

Casey supposed the older woman could have been

matchmaking, but it seemed unlikely. Mrs. Jamison hardly knew her, and if she did, she'd know that Mike was not her type.

"Kids," Stephen called. "Get off the street, the parade is about to start."

Monica and Brad, along with scores of other children, scrambled off the street to join the older people lining the sidewalk. Sirens echoed from down the street, where Ferry dipped down to the river, and after a moment, Mike's state-police cruiser crested the bluff. After that came a large fire truck, followed in turn by a line of antique tractors. The townspeople all knew the people in the parade, waving to them and shouting good-natured insults.

A lawnmower precision drill team of elderly women came into view, followed by a herd of goats, and then Miss Michigan was striding down the street, a very tall, leggy young woman.

"I'll never be like that." Kate sighed.

The teenager, slightly shorter than Casey, was going to be a beautiful woman, but small like her mother. Right now, though, it was obvious she would sell her soul to be a six-foot beauty queen.

"Yeah, you're lucky," Casey replied. "You'll be able to wear heels to your senior prom."

Kate laughed.

"Casey! Hey, Miss Crawford!"

A group of young people in black vinyl jackets were marching down the street. Dubber lagged behind, waving enthusiastically at Casey.

"Hi, Dubber," Casey shouted.

"You certainly have a spirited young friend," Joy said, laughingly.

"He's a sweet kid," Casey replied. "He's always around to lend a helping hand. I don't know what I would have done without him." She returned his wave one last time as Dubber and his group marched on.

A line of antique cars came over the top of the bluff and

laid claim to her attention. Then there were groups of Boy Scouts, Girl Scouts and Campfire Girls, some 4-Hers leading animals and some little kids from a day-care center dressed as pickles. Proud parents walked along the sides, taking pictures. Casey smiled at an especially small pickle. This must be such a great place to grow up.

A rescue vehicle came next, and that was it. The parade was over. Casey sighed with a slight feeling of regret. She had enjoyed its unpretentiousness.

"We're going over to the historical society," Joy said to Casey. "Monica wants to see the Christmas-tree exhibit. Want to come along?"

"I don't know," Casey said. "I might just—"

"Miss Crawford? Miss Casey Crawford?"

Casey turned. A young girl dressed in the same black uniform jacket that Dubber had worn in the parade stared solemnly up into Casey's face. The girl's brown hair hung in a single thick braid down her back. Up close, Casey could see that the jacket was for a martial-arts club.

"My name is Tiffany. I'd like a few minutes of your time, please." The girl appeared to be about Dubber's age, ten or eleven, yet there was a certain adultlike quality in her voice. "Could we walk over to Panozzo's? I'll buy you a deep-fried pickle."

"A deep-fried pickle?" Just the thought of it was almost enough to spoil Casey's appetite. This place really went pickle crazy.

"You'll like it," Tiffany assured her. "Besides, pickles are healthy."

"All right." Casey had no idea who this kid was, but maybe she had stories about the ghost. She seemed a little young, but then everybody seemed to know who Casey was and what she was doing here. She hurried across the street after the girl.

"Take that table over by the window," Tiffany said as they entered the small restaurant. "I'll get our pickles."

Casey obeyed, but only because she was too curious not

to. She sat at the small, Formica-topped table and watched the crowd outside disperse slowly. Tiffany returned quickly with two small paper plates, each containing a breaded, deep-fried pickle. Casey's stomach curled up in a ball and whimpered when she looked at the green-brown wedges lying there, but she picked up a pickle wedge, closed her eyes and bit into it. She couldn't believe that people really ate these things.

"Well?"

Casey opened her eyes to find Tiffany staring at her. She chewed a moment longer and then, after swallowing, nodded and said, "It's okay."

"Just okay?" Tiffany asked.

"Just okay. What is it you want to talk about?" Casey asked.

"I want you to stay away from Jason Randall."

Casey put her pickle down. "Who?"

"Most people call him Dubber," the girl explained. "But what he's called don't matter none. What matters is that you stay away from him. He's my man."

"He's a little boy," Casey said.

"We're going to get married when we're old enough," Tiffany said firmly. "We're going to live on a big farm outside of town and raise horses, goats and llamas."

"Does Dubber know about this?" Casey asked.

"What do most men know about anything?" Tiffany replied.

Casey shook her head. "Tiffany, I like Dubber, but I'm not interested in him as a..." Jeez, how was she supposed to put it? Kids just seemed to grow up too fast these days. "...As anything but a friend."

"That may be so, but some men are excited by older women. You know, like that guy in *The Graduate*. The movie where this young guy was chasing this Mrs. Robinson, who was a whole lot older than he—"

"I know, I know," Casey explained. "I saw the movie. But I'm not encouraging Dubber in any way."

"Are you discouraging him?"

This was ridiculous. She'd just had this conversation with Mike. "I'm not rude to him, if that's what you mean."

"Why don't you just cozy up to Mr. Burnette?" Tiffany said. "He's not going with anyone right now."

"Tiffany, I don't think this is any of your business."

Tiffany was not listening. "And when you do, make it good. Dubber isn't that easy to fool. He's a pretty sharp cookie." The girl shrugged, a half smile on her face. "I mean, for a man."

Casey couldn't believe this conversation. She wasn't looking to cozy up to anybody. She had a full life, with plenty of opportunities for cozying up if she was so inclined—which she wasn't. She happened to like her freedom. She had things to do, places to be, as it were, and no time for cozying.

"It shouldn't be hard, Miss Crawford," Tiffany continued. "You're already living with him."

"I'm living in the same house, Tiffany. There is a difference."

The girl just shrugged. "Handle it any way you want, just handle it."

Maybe a small town wasn't such a great place to live. Not if everyone was going to butt into her business. "Tiffany, let me explain something to you."

"No." The girl shook her head. "Let me explain something. I'm the Region IV Tae Kwon Do champ in my age-weight class. I'm going to the nationals this summer. Do you understand what that means?"

"It means you're good at martial arts."

"I'm very good, ma'am. I can take big men down." Tiffany stood up; she wasn't much taller than when she was sitting. "And I could really hurt them if I wanted to."

"Tiffany, are you threatening me?"

"No, ma'am." The girl shook her head and smiled, sweet and cute like any little girl her age. "I'm just telling you."

"You and Dubber are much too young to be so serious."

"A good man is hard to find," Tiffany said, looking Casey straight in the eyes. "I've found mine, Miss Crawford. And like any woman worth her salt, I'm willing to fight for him."

Casey just stared as the little girl marched out of the diner. Life was becoming too bizarre. Maybe Casey should just go on back to Mike's house and work on her research. Ghosts were rapidly becoming the sanest part of her life.

Mike pulled his cruiser into the parking lot, then hurried into the old courthouse that now housed the historical society. The smell of chocolate mingled with the scent of pine needles, but that was all. The pickles here were all the ceramic kind.

"Mikey!" His half brother, Brad, came charging across the lobby and hugged Mike around the knees.

"Hi, squirt." Mike hoisted the five-year-old into his arms. "You see me in the parade?"

"Yeah. Can I ride in your car?"

"I'll have to arrest you," Mike said. "Only prisoners get to ride in it with me."

"Okay." He squirmed so that Mike put him down, then raced into the old courtroom, where the Christmas-tree exhibit was housed. "Mommy! Mikey's gonna 'rest me!"

Mike exchanged grins with the woman behind the pickle-ornament counter. "You've got a real fan there," she said to him.

"He's a good kid," Mike replied, and went into the exhibit room.

At times, Brad made him long for a son of his own. Someone to play with, to watch grow, to guide, to see life through his eyes. But that was just a dream and not likely to come true. Mike wasn't going to marry, and he sure as hell wasn't going to have a kid outside marriage, so he just enjoyed Brad and Monica as they were growing up.

He spotted Stephen and his family across the old courtroom, by a Victorian Christmas tree, and started over. Casey wasn't there, though, he realized with a frown. Maybe she was looking at one of the other trees. He glanced around, but didn't see her.

"Hi, Mike," Joy said, giving him a quick kiss on his cheek. "Nice parade."

"All due to my great leading, no doubt. Where's Casey?" he asked her.

She shrugged. "I don't know. She went off to have pickles with some little girl. I thought she was going to meet us here, but maybe something else came along."

Damn. How the hell was he supposed to protect her if she was always running off? "I thought she was going to stay with you all," he said.

"We invited her to come, but we could hardly hog-tie her and carry her with us," his stepmother explained, then frowned at him. "Is something wrong?"

He glanced around, conscious of the sudden tight knot of worry in his stomach. Monica was watching him. "Hey, kiddo," he said to the girl, making his voice light. "Did you see Santa Claus's pickle farm under that tree over there? He's got his elves picking the pickles and his reindeer putting bows on them."

"Reindeer can't tie bows," Monica said, but she skipped over to see it anyway.

"Mike?" Joy put her hand on his arm as she asked the question with her eyes.

Mike led her over to the old jury box, where they wouldn't be overheard. "Aunt Myrna sent her here because she was in danger," he told Joy as they sat on the hard narrow benches.

"In danger?"

He nodded. "Her boyfriend sounds like a nutcase," he said. "There's been no sign of him around, but I've been trying to keep a close eye on her."

Joy just shook her head. "Myrna didn't say a word about it to us."

That caught Mike by surprise. "She told you about Casey? When?"

"Oh, it was just in passing," she said quickly. "You know Myrna. Once she starts talking, she tells you her life story."

"She never tells me anything."

"No? It's probably a female thing. You know, woman to woman. Who's this boyfriend?"

Mike shrugged. "Some nerdy, whiney, wimpy guy."

"Melvin?" Joy sounded disbelieving.

"So she did mention him?"

"Uh, yeah. I guess she did." She bit her lip and glanced away for a minute, but her eyes were serious when she looked back. "And that he was a real threat to someone like Casey. Maybe you'd better go look for her. It seems for once Myrna knew what she was doing."

Mike got to his feet. "I'm probably worrying for nothing. She'll be at the pickle tasting."

"Better be sure," Joy said, and gave him a quick hug before sending him back toward the door.

Mike hurried out, then told himself he was overreacting. Casey would be around.

But she wasn't at the pickle tasting downtown. She wasn't anywhere around the samples of gherkins, dills and sweet pickles.

Mrs. Kinder stopped slicing up more pickles. "I haven't seen her since the parade. She was with your dad's family."

"You sure she didn't go with them?" another woman asked. "Maybe she's at the blacksmith demonstration."

She wasn't there, either. The forge was pleasantly warm, but had only a handful of people standing about.

"Your new young lady?" Dubber's grandfather asked. He was working the blacksmith exhibit, making bent-nail hooks for the visitors.

"She's just staying with me for a while," Mike said. "We're not dating."

"'Bout time you started going out again," the old man

continued, as if Mike hadn't spoken. "No reason to be a hermit 'cause you had a false start."

Mike just sighed. "Have you seen her?"

"Yesterday," he said. "Mighty fine looker. Good thing I'm not forty years younger, I'd give you a run for your money."

Mike just waved and went back to his car. She wasn't at the arts-and-crafts fair or at the community garage sale. He tried the library, the grocery store and the pet-food store. No one had seen her. He finally just drove home, not sure where to go next. Worry was eating a hole in his stomach.

And there she was, out in the backyard with Gus!

"What are you doing here?" he snapped. She was in her jeans and sweatshirt, looking all relaxed and comfortable in the wintery air and so damn sexy that it took his breath away.

"Haven't we gone through this already?"

Gus dropped a tennis ball in the small patch of snow by her feet. She reached down for it and Mike's eyes followed the tightened curve of her jeans. It didn't do his blood pressure much good.

"I've been looking all over town for you."

She tossed the ball and Gus raced after it. "Why? Were we supposed to meet someplace?"

Gus came charging back, tail wagging and ears flying and breath making little clouds around his mouth. He dropped the ball at Casey's feet and sat down, looking adoringly up at her. She laughed and, bending down, scratched his ears until he seemed ready to collapse in ecstasy. Mike just looked away.

The yard was all brown and bare, deep in its winter sleep. It should look dreary and dismal and ugly, but with her here, it looked like it was ready for spring. Like it was just about to burst into flower and song and warmth. How could she cast a spell on the yard?

"I just wondered where you were," he stated. "You are new to town, after all."

"What did you think? That I got lost?" Her laughter flowed over him, tugging at his black mood. "I don't think even I would be able to get lost in a town this size."

"Well, how was I supposed to know?" How could she mesmerize everyone and everything and not seem to care?

She threw the ball for Gus again, letting it roll into the dead leaves under the lilac bushes by the back fence. "You really are a worrywart, aren't you?"

"And you're never serious," he snapped. "Unless it's about a stupid ghost."

"Maybe you could learn something from that 'stupid ghost,'" she said. "You want to wander around for all eternity, looking for your lost love?"

He'd been working himself up into a good irritation, on edge and ready to be annoyed, but he found himself just staring at her, at a total loss for words. "What the hell are you talking about?"

"Simon and Priscilla," she said. "You and Darcy."

"Me and Darcy?" He frowned at her. "There is no me and Darcy."

"That doesn't mean that you don't wish there was."

He did not believe they were having this conversation. "I don't wish anything," he said. "Except that people would stop jumping to conclusions about me."

"You expect me to believe that you aren't still in love with her?"

"I don't expect anything," he said, as Gus brought the ball back, dropping it at her feet. "But no, I am not still in love with her."

Casey appeared not to notice the dog. "You won't even admit it to yourself."

"I'd admit it to anybody who asked, if it was the truth," he said.

"You aren't dating."

Gus was wagging his tail a mile a minute, looking from Mike to Casey. "How do you know I'm not dating?" Mike reached down for the ball. It was filthy, with bits of ice and snow and dead leaves clinging to it.

"You said you don't have a girlfriend."

"Maybe I've got several. Hundreds. Too many to count." He tossed the ball for Gus, but the dog didn't move. He just kept watching Mike, then Casey. Mike, then Casey.

"Maybe you've got none," she said. Gus got up and started to stroll around behind her.

"Maybe this isn't any of your business," Mike said.

"Maybe—"

He had a sudden glimpse of Gus jumping against Casey's back, and then she lurched forward, falling right into his arms. For a split second, Mike hoped she was all right. He was ready to curse out Gus for his clumsiness. But then the chilly air of winter turned to summer and his hands felt heat searing through her sweatshirt. Heat raced over him like a wildfire, consuming every rational thought in its way. There was nothing he could do but pull her in closer, to feel her softness pressed against him, and lean in to taste those lips.

But then she was out of his arms.

"Sorry about that," she said with a laugh as she stepped back. "I don't know what Gus was doing."

Or him, for that matter. "You okay?"

"Sure. Fine." Her voice sounded hoarse and her cheeks were bright. "I think I'll get back to my research, though. I found some fascinating letters from your great-great-grandfather."

"I should…" Hell, what was he supposed to be doing? "I should check on some things at the station."

"Those Mr. March calendars?"

"No, real stuff," he said, then thought how lame that sounded. "Gus, you stay here with Casey. I'll be back in a little while."

Gus just gave him that stupid grin.

* * *

Mike flicked through the television channels, but nothing caught his eye. Nothing that is, quite as strongly as Casey, who was standing in the kitchen doorway, talking on the phone. She was talking to a guy; Mike knew that much, since he had answered the phone. Melvin, he suspected.

Obviously she was engrossed in her conversation. Her head was bent over the phone, her only movement her right hand, idly running through her hair. Damn, but she'd felt good in his arms this morning.

He should have gone out tonight. Single guys were supposed to do that on Saturday evenings. He could have gone to the Pickle Festival concert and then the Pickle Festival square dance. Or to the movies, or even out for a beer. He should have sabotaged Stephen's car so that they'd spend the night.

Mike forced his eyes back to the television. No, he had to stay home with nothing to do but watch stupid ads for exercise bikes. He needed a life.

"So what're you watching?" Casey asked.

He looked up to find she had sat down at the other end of the sofa. Her black jeans and white blouse covered a lot of skin, but did nothing to hide her curves. He took a deep, steadying breath. "How's Melvin?"

Casey gave him a look that questioned his sincerity. "He's fine."

"Managing to survive without you?"

Her eyes narrowed suspiciously. "You've never even met Melvin. What do you have against him?"

Good question. "Nothing. Nothing at all." Mike turned back to the television. They were giving an in-depth description of the workings of the exercise bike, complete with a shapely female to point at the various parts in case someone didn't know what handlebars or pedals were.

Casey settled into the sofa, leaning back and putting her feet up on the hassock next to his as she frowned at the TV. "What is this?" she asked. "Some infomercial?"

"The secrets of a good body, a great social life and un-limited wealth," he said. "I'm thinking of getting one for Melvin so he'll stop bugging you."

She sat back up, obviously annoyed. "What is it with you and Melvin? Why should you care if he calls me? He didn't call collect."

"He whines."

"He does not," she protested. "Besides, how would you know if he does or not?"

"You feel sorry for him."

"Where are you getting all this from?" she snapped.

"You didn't look like you were glad to hear from him," he said. "No rosy glow of love in your cheeks after you hung up."

"Since when are you some expert on rosy glows?"

"I'm a cop. We're trained to be observant."

"Well, you aren't very good at it. I was quite glad to hear from him." She plopped back against the sofa, arms crossed over her chest as she stared at the television.

Mike's irritation doubled and tripled at her stupid de-fense of the guy. "He wanted something from you, didn't he? Let me guess. No one understands him. He's got a social function to attend, and with you gone, he doesn't have anyone to take."

Her glare told him that he'd struck close to home. "I'll have you know that I was happy to hear from him because I wanted his advice."

"On what, whining?"

She scowled again, then turned back to the television. "You aren't really watching this, are you?" she asked. "There's got to be something better on."

"Answer my question and you can change the channel."

The look she turned on him was one of pure anger. Sparks looked ready to shoot from her eyes, but he didn't care. He wanted to know why she'd turned to Melvin for help instead of him.

"Answer your question and I can change the channel?"

she repeated in astonishment. "I don't have to answer any-thing and I can still change the channel if I want."

Before he had a chance to figure out what she was talking about, she dove across the sofa toward him. In that split second, he realized she was going for the remote control on the arm of the sofa next to him, and he grabbed for it himself. A slight battle followed. She reached across him. He reached around her. But the device found its way into Mike's hands and he held it up above his head.

"Tell me what you asked him about," he said.

"I don't have to tell you anything," she snapped, and reached again for the remote.

Her hands closed over his hands, but then she came down on the edge of the sofa pillow and lost her balance. Her chest leaned against his arm, and sirens went off inside his head. She was all around him—her scent, her softness, the fire of her hair. He wanted to pull her against him, wanted to hold that sweetness close to him. Closer than it was possible to do and still breathe.

Mike felt his throat tighten up and his mouth go stone dry. "This has gone far enough," he said. "You can have the remote."

But her hands didn't release his. "You admit my con-versation with Melvin is none of your business?"

"I'm not admitting anything." He moved slightly, trying to put some space between them. "I don't want anybody to get hurt."

"Not willing to fight for your principles, eh?"

The world seemed to stand still at that. He looked into her eyes, still sending out sparks, but suddenly it didn't seem to be anger burning there. It was something else, something that took her by surprise.

With one easy movement, the remote fell to the side and they were kissing. Not one of those how-are-you, glad-to-see-you pecks on the cheek, but a full-blown, seriously be-ing without breath kiss. They were desperate for water and diving into a deep well. They were burning with a fever and the other held the cure. They were half of the other's whole.

His hands slid over her back, pressing her closer. He could feel the ridge of her spine and the soft curve of her lower back. He could feel her breasts, full and firm, crushed into him. And he could feel his heart about to explode. His lips grew more insistent, his breath nonexistent as she moved into him. Her hands, pushing against him, somehow pulled him closer yet.

He had never tasted such fiery sweetness. It was addictive; the more he kissed her, the more he needed to. It gave him strength. It gave him hope and wisdom and powers beyond belief. He wanted to run and dance and shout to the heavens, but he didn't want to let her go. Their hearts were racing, pounding in unison, until he wasn't sure which was his and which was hers.

Then suddenly she jumped away, as if he were on fire, and slumped to the floor. Closing his eyes, he lay back on the sofa. The room was filled with hoarse breathing, as if they'd run a marathon and sprinted the last mile.

Casey took a deep breath and let it out slowly. "Actually, Melvin and I never got around to my question," she said, her voice thready and weak. "He was too busy whining about not having someone to go to the computer-science Christmas dinner with."

Mike ought to feel a sense of triumph, but he was still having trouble breathing. "So maybe I can help."

She put her head back against the sofa, closing her eyes. "Do you know a Tiffany Kramer?"

It wasn't what Mike had expected. "You mean Ed Kramer's daughter? He's one of the Berrien Springs cops that came the other night."

"She told me to stay away from Dubber or else she'd hurt me," Casey said, a slight laugh in her voice.

Mike just stared at her. "You're kidding," he said. "Want me to talk to her? Or to her dad?" It would be pretty ironic if the only thing he got to protect her from was an eleven-year-old kid.

Casey sat up, turning to frown at him. "No. I don't want you to do anything," she said. "Except give me some advice. Should I ignore her or should I get Dubber to cool it? I'm not worried she's going to do anything. I know she's just afraid she's going to lose something important to her. But I don't want to hurt Dubber, either."

Mike just sat there, staring into those green eyes, which had grown thoughtful and troubled. Casey was being threatened by a little thug and followed around by a gangly, awkward kid who acted more like a puppy dog than anything else, but all she thought about was how to keep each from hurting. He reached over and touched her hand gently, running his fingers over the top of hers and fighting the urge to take her hand in his.

"Everybody hurts growing up," he said simply. "And everybody loses something. You can't keep the world from hurting."

"I'm not trying to save the world, just two kids."

Was it just two kids, though? There were her cats, and Melvin, Tiffany and Dubber. Not to mention Simon. Then Mike remembered how she'd tried to keep him from seeing Darcy this morning, and knew he was on her list, too.

It touched him, aggravated him and made him squirm all at the same time. He wasn't needy. He didn't need to be protected. He was the protector, the one who watched out for danger and kept everyone else safe.

"Well, since you're only going to be here a short time, I don't see where it matters," he said.

The harshness of his voice surprised him, and her also. She pulled back and looked once more toward the television, giving a short little laugh. "You're right," she said. "I'm a short-timer here. Why worry? Everything'll go back to normal once I'm gone."

But "normal" suddenly seemed bleak and unattractive. And lonely.

Chapter Six

Casey sat up in bed, alert and on edge. "What's the matter, Snowflake?"

The white cat went silent, but Midnight started his high-pitched whine; the spirits were up and about in the old house.

"Come on, guys," Casey said. "Let's pretend we didn't wake up."

The last time they'd gone out looking for Simon, they'd woken Mike up. And that was one person Casey was not ready to run into just yet. She liked him; she liked him a lot, but not *that* way. Yet she'd responded to his kiss last night like she was in love with him! What must he think?

Snowflake gave a grumbling yowl, then jumped off the bed with a thump, striding determinedly to the door with Midnight close behind. Since it was closed, all they could do was stop and look back at Casey. Even in the dim moonlight coming in around the drapes, Casey could see their glares.

"All right, already. I'm coming." She slipped out of bed. "Just quit your darn hollering."

Her feet were in the thick socks she always wore at night in the winter, but she took the time to grab her robe. "Okay, girls," she told them. "Here's the plan. We take a quick pass around the living room, but no noise. You hear?"

The two cats didn't bother looking at her. Sighing, she opened the door and followed as they slunk out into the hall. "I mean it, girls," she hissed. "I want us to be really, really quiet."

The hallway was darker than her room, but she sensed her feline buddies ignoring her words. She had a definite feeling that they were heading for trouble.

"Come on, girls," she pleaded. "You know what happened the last time we did this. You started yowling and Mike came storming down, ready to shoot all of us."

Midnight muttered something. It was obvious that neither of them cared what Mike did.

"Well, I care," she whispered. "I don't need any more hassle from that man."

Not that *hassle* was exactly the right word. That sounded as if she'd found him a bother, that she hadn't enjoyed that kiss. She had enjoyed it too much, that was the real trouble. And she wasn't looking for that kind of enjoyment.

She stopped, suddenly sensing that her cats were no longer in front of her. "Snowflake? Midnight?" She strained her eyes. "Where are you two?"

There was a low feline moan behind her, and she sensed more than saw them standing in front of the door to Mike's bedroom. "What are you two doing there?" she whispered. "Come over this way."

But they didn't move, not even an inch.

"Come on, girls," she murmured, bending down to pick the two cats up. They slid right out of her arms, though, and then there was a quiet thud.

Her heart stopped as she felt in front of her. The door

wasn't there anymore! Oh no, they'd opened Mike's door! Was every door in this household able to be opened by animals?

Casey got down on her hands and knees and felt around in the darkness for her cats. She touched nothing but Mike's rug, heard nothing but the even breathing that said he was still asleep. Well, the cats had to be in here someplace. She crawled a little farther forward.

Her eyes were getting used to the dim light and she could see the shape of the bed off to her left—with a lump at the foot that was rising slightly. Gus. Another movement there caught her eye. Damn. He was wagging his tail. Mike stirred.

"Gus, go back to sleep," Mike said, his voice groggy.

Casey held her breath and froze in place. Gus put his head down, but his tail was still wagging slightly. After an eternity, Mike began that even breathing again, and she could take a breath once more.

She crept forward another few feet and her hand brushed something. A sock. She tossed it aside. There was a slight movement up ahead of her. Snowflake! And next to her a shadowy shape that had to be Midnight!

"Come here, kitties," she whispered.

Neither cat was fooled by the sweetness in her voice. Neither cat moved. Instead, they both meowed in reply, telling her to come and get them. Casey started to crawl a little faster, when she suddenly stopped.

She'd felt something. Not with her hand, but with her heart. She sat back on her heels and looked around. Nothing looked different, but something had changed. Someone was here. There was a hint of peppermint in the air.

"Simon?" she mouthed. Of course, who else? "What do you want?"

She sensed so much suddenly. Unhappiness. Regret. A deep love that had never been spoken.

Simon was hurting, she was certain of it. All he needed was to make someone understand, keep someone from repeating his mistake. She looked around the large room. It was the master bedroom, so it must have been his room.

"The place you'd hoped to rest alongside your Priscilla," she breathed.

The pain was there again, so strong she could almost hear a silent cry echoing around the room, rattling the chambers of her heart.

"What the—" Mike shot up out of bed as if he'd been blasted from a circus cannon. Gus began to bark frantically.

Oh no. Should she make a run for it or try to stay hidden?

"Easy, Gus," Mike shouted, fumbling around on his nightstand.

Great, he was looking for his gun. Hiding wasn't going to work. "No, Mike. It's just me."

Mike flicked on the light and blinked at her. "What the hell is going on?"

But Casey couldn't answer. All she could do was stare at him. "You're naked," she gasped.

"It's my bedroom." But he grabbed a pair of sweatpants.

"You aren't even wearing shorts."

"I wasn't expecting guests," he replied, as he pulled the sweatpants on. "What are you doing in here?"

"I came after my cats." As soon as she said that, they began to walk nonchalantly over toward the door. Little creeps. "Why else would I be coming in here in the middle of the night?"

"I have no idea. Chasing a nonexistent ghost, hiding from Tiffany, or maybe you just wanted to check what I wore when I slept."

She wanted to tell him to dream on, but unfortunately her gaze drifted back toward him and her tongue got tied up. She'd always thought he was a good-looking, handsome man, but she realized that describing him that way would be like describing the Mona Lisa as a nice picture.

Mike was on the slender side, but athletically built, with long legs, broad shoulders and narrow hips and waist. Well-defined muscles made him look as though he'd been chiseled out of stone. The man was so beautiful he was breath-taking.

She forced herself to look away. It was high time she got out of there before she lost all sense. That kiss was bad enough; she didn't need to complicate matters even more.

Her cats had stopped by Mike's bed, eyeing Gus, who was eyeing them back. "Come on, girls, let's get back to our own room," she said to them.

As soon as she spoke, her cats leaped onto the bed and dived under the covers. Gus let out a howl, plunging after them so that the bed became a tangle of sheets, blankets and animals.

Mike just gave her a look that said this was all her fault and tried to grab Gus's collar. "Gus, off!" he ordered.

The dog let out a mock growl and dived in farther.

Casey took a few steps toward the bed. It wasn't like she was afraid to go closer, but maybe it wouldn't be necessary. "Snowflake, Midnight," she called. "Come, girls." They responded the way they usually did—they ignored her.

"Gus, enough of this," Mike snapped, and flipped the covers back to grab hold of his collar. He pulled the dog off the bed, then stepped back, waving Casey over to get her cats.

With a wary look his way, Casey came closer. Lumps on the bed pointed to where her cats were, but she wasn't sure under which layer of covers she'd actually find them. She felt around under the sheets, still warm from Mike's body—from that body that her all-too-active imagination was willing to picture for her.

"Come on, girls," she said with a bit of hysteria. She needed to get out of here. "Where are you?"

She moved over a step and her arm brushed against Mike's chest. Between the fabric of her nightgown and the thick fuzziness of her robe, she shouldn't feel a thing. But she did! She felt the heat of his skin, the hard steel of muscle just beneath and the racing of his heart. She jerked back, afraid he would feel the same response in her.

"I don't bite," he snapped.

"I know." One lump moved, and she realized the cat was on top of the sheet, not under it. "It wasn't that at all." She was more afraid that she might bite him!

"And I'm not exactly a sex-starved maniac, you know."

She found Snowflake and pulled her out. The cat plopped down on the bed and proceeded to give herself a bath. Now Casey just had to get—

"And that outfit's hardly the type to drive a man wild with passion."

She stopped her burrowing to glance down at herself. Woolly robe, flannel nightgown and thick socks.

"What's wrong with all this?" she asked, and made the mistake of looking at him again. Of letting those broad shoulders capture her gaze; of allowing her eyes to linger on those muscles that her hands so wanted to touch. She took a deep breath and pulled her gaze away. "It keeps me warm."

"Good thing," he said. "No one else would be tempted to."

"Not everybody equates sheer and lacy with sexy, you know," she told him. She was glad that this outfit didn't appeal to him. That made it all the easier to fight her wayward thoughts. "Some people see beyond such things to the person inside."

"I assume you're referring to you and Melvin."

"I'm referring to all sorts of people who find things like loyalty and honesty more arousing than a beefcake photo."

His face reflected his surprise, then his annoyance. "Hey, I did that calendar for charity," he said. "It helps the kids' hospital in Detroit."

Casey just looked at him, shaking her head slowly. "I wasn't even thinking of that," she assured him. She'd done it again—opened her mouth without giving her words any thought. "Honest I wasn't."

"Sure. Look, can you just get your cats so we can go back to sleep? I've got to go to work in the morning."

She should just do as he said. Dig out Midnight, grab Snowflake, and go back to her own room before she made more of a fool of herself. But her feet refused to move. "No," she said. "You think I deliberately said that and I didn't. I'm sorry if I hurt your feelings."

He made a face. "My feelings are not that easily accessed," he said. "Now could you—"

"I don't believe that," she said. "I think your feelings are just as likely to be hurt as mine. I think you want to play tough and pretend like you're unfeeling, but you aren't."

"Fascinating analysis," he said. "All wrong, but fascinating."

"If I'm so wrong, why is your heart racing?" she asked. "Who says it is?"

She was beyond her initial awareness of his masculinity, she told herself. She was only concerned now that he understand that she didn't mean to hurt him.

"I can tell it's racing," she said, and placed her hand on his chest, over his heart. The world suddenly stopped.

His skin was warm and slightly damp beneath the light matting of fine blond hair, but all she could feel was his racing heart—pounding, throbbing, vibrating like the sudden electricity in the air. Her own heart responded, calling to Mike as if they were soul mates, matching his beat for beat. She could not move her hand; it would take a strength beyond what she possessed. She bit at her lip nervously and let her eyes stray up to his.

"This is not a good idea." His voice was slightly raw as he reached for her hand. She thought he was going to move it, but he must not have had the strength, either. He just covered it with his own.

"This is definitely not a good idea," he said again, but this time his voice was more than raw. It was ragged and hoarse.

"No, it's not," she whispered back. She wondered if

he'd heard her; her voice seemed weak and wispy all of a sudden. "I should go."

"You should."

Her feet didn't move. But how could they when his eyes would not let her go? When his touch held her prisoner?

Ever so slowly, his lips came down on hers, bringing a promise of heaven with them. His touch was gentle at first. Like the first snowflakes of winter kissing the pine boughs, his mouth barely brushed hers. She hardly felt any pressure at all, yet at the same time she felt such a jolt to her heart that she wondered if it was still beating.

The pressure of his lips grew slowly, like a rose unfolding in the morning sun. She kissed him back, hungrily, with a need for his touch so strong that she couldn't help but move closer to him. No kiss had ever taken hold of her like this; no touch of a man's hand on hers had ever so hypnotized her.

He let go of her hand, only to encircle her with his embrace. She moved in closer still, her hand slipping from his heart so that her arms could hold him. His hands felt like fire on her back, even through the fuzzy robe and flannel nightgown, leaving a trail of longing so deep that her knees went wobbly.

"I never knew fuzzy red robes could be so sexy," he said, his voice a sharp whisper that cut away at her defenses even more.

"I thought you said it wasn't."

"I was lying."

His mouth took hers again—hot, hungry and demanding more than just a kiss. It was asking for possession of her soul, for a refuge from life's storms, for a dance beneath the stars. It spoke to her in words of magic that only her heart could understand. It sang to her lips, whispered to her desires and awakened some long-lost dream of wonder.

Then it was over.

As if some hidden hand had pulled a string, they moved apart. Really apart, not letting a hand, a sleeve, a bit of robe connect them. Mike looked as shaken as Casey felt. For a long moment, his unguarded eyes met hers, and she could read the shock and astonishment in them. During that eternity, anything could have happened.

If she made the slightest move toward him...

If she gave him the merest of smiles...

But then she took a deep breath and the air seemed to clear somehow. The spell was broken, their hearts freed. Or were they now imprisoned?

"I'm sorry," he said stiffly. "I shouldn't have kissed you."

"I started it." She looked away and found the strength to shut the doors to her soul and lock them tight.

"You're a guest in my house," he said.

"Who barged into your room in the middle of the night," she noted, braving a glance in his direction. "Look, I'm the one who should be apologizing. I don't know what came over me, but I promise it won't happen again."

"It was late," he said. "And we were both caught off guard."

She nodded. "We weren't thinking straight."

"We just have to be more careful."

"And give each other space."

"No problem."

"It'll be easy."

"Now that we know the rules."

"And each other's routine."

"Right."

"Absolutely." She gathered up her cats and sped back to her room in record time.

"No more walks at night to look for Simon," she told her cats.

And no more stray touches, she told herself. She was keeping her distance from Mike. She would be done with her research in a few weeks and could do her writing elsewhere, if she needed to. She was here to write a family history and that was all she was going to do.

* * *

Casey stopped in the kitchen doorway. The bright morning sunlight streaming in the far window blinded her for a moment. Or was it the sight of Mike in his blue state-police uniform? He and the handyman were deep in conversation, and Casey was able to gaze her fill of Mike. For a sweet second or two, she let herself remember the taste of his lips, the feel of her hand on his chest, the way their hearts had raced in unison.

Then she pushed the memory aside. Last night had been a mistake. One huge, gigantic, colossal mistake, and she was never repeating it.

Mike looked up, frowning when he saw her. "I thought you slept later," he said.

"I thought you'd left already." She would never have come down if she'd known he hadn't.

"I had to get together with Barry," Mike replied. "We need to get the doors fixed."

"They should have been fixed long ago," she agreed.

"Fun as it is to jaw with you folks," the handyman said, "I gotta be getting home to take the missus to church." He pulled a notebook and a pencil stub out of his coat pocket. "Which doors is it you want fixed?"

"All of them," she said.

He looked at Mike.

"Every damn last one of them," Mike agreed.

The handyman looked from Mike to Casey, then back to his notebook, a half smile on his face. "So we got doors popping open at odd times, have we?" he muttered, then looked up. "You sure it ain't Simon? I heard tell he likes these kinds of tricks."

"No, it's not Simon," Mike snapped.

"Even a ghost can't open a well-closed door," Casey stated.

"Huh," was all the older man said as he made more notes.

It left time for Casey to glance Mike's way, but finding

he was glancing her way at the same time, she turned to gaze out the window. Everything looked as if a Pause button had been pushed somewhere. The landscape was waiting for snow to make it feel like Christmas. The trees and bushes were waiting for spring to make them feel alive.

And Casey—what was she waiting for? For someone she could trust forever, someone who would never ever leave her, she suddenly realized. Then wondered just where that thought had come from. That wasn't what she was waiting for at all.

"So how soon can you get the doors done?" Mike asked.

Casey turned, almost relieved at the interruption. Mr. Slocum was closing up his notebook and pocketing the pencil stub.

"The doors've been bad for years," he said. "What difference is another week or two gonna make?" He chuckled as he pulled open the back door. "Course, if'n it's Simon opening them, I could spend from now until doomsday fixing them, and they ain't gonna stay closed."

The handyman left, leaving Mike and Casey standing in the kitchen. For a moment, just a fraction of one, she considered inviting him to have breakfast with her, but then resolutely kept her mouth shut. They were going to give each other space; that was the agreement.

"I've got to go to work," Mike said, and left before she could change her mind.

Casey spent the morning working on the family history—or trying to work on it—but Mike kept haunting her. His gorgeous body. His earth-shattering kisses. His careful, distant silence this morning. She finally took a stroll downtown in the afternoon, needing to escape the house.

She'd missed the pickle festival's bratwurst-and-pickle lunch at the fire station, but various choirs were performing at the elementary-school gym and the craft fair was still on over at the junior high. Neither was really within walking distance, though, so she walked over to the historical society instead and meandered through the gift shop. Her family needed a pickle ornament to hang on their tree, and how could she not buy a few boxes of chocolate-covered pickles?

"Aren't you staying with Mike Burnette?" someone asked her.

Casey looked up—right into Darcy's eyes. "Yes, yes, I am," Casey said slowly. Darcy looked to be about Casey's own age, and like someone she'd pick for a friend. It was disconcerting. "I'm Casey Crawford."

"I'm Darcy Middleton. Mike and I..." She stopped and then grinned slightly, her blue eyes lighting up. "Well, knowing this town, you know about Mike and me."

"Yes," Casey admitted.

Darcy looked around the gift shop. A few curious shoppers were watching them. "Can we take a walk?" she asked.

Casey had a sudden sense that this was a rerun. "Uh, you aren't a Tae Kwon Do champ, by any chance, are you?"

"Tae Kwon Do?" Darcy looked totally confused. "Gracious, no. Why do you ask?"

"Just curious."

Casey paid for her purchases, then they strolled outside. Darcy led the way around back, where a cell block of the old county jail had been restored. Law and order, cops and robbers. She couldn't get away from them, Casey thought with a sigh. Darcy sat on a bench facing the row of cells. Sun was filtering through the bare branches of the trees and lending a faint warmth to the air.

"How is he?" she asked Casey. "I mean, how is he really?"

Casey sat down also. "Mike?" she said. That was a strange question. "Okay, I guess. I've only known him for a few days now."

"A few days?" Darcy looked surprised. "But I thought...everybody said..." She sighed. "You're not his new girlfriend, are you?"

Casey shook her head. "His aunt hired me to write a family history," she said. "I only met him on Thursday."

"Thursday? Bummer," Darcy said, and kicked at a little patch of ice by her feet. "I was really hoping he was dating again."

Casey wished she had walked to the arts-and-crafts fair rather than come here. This wasn't a discussion she ought to be having, or one that she wanted to have. Darcy was too nice, and that made Mike too vulnerable. And what that really made Mike was too dangerous.

"He says he has hundreds of girlfriends," Casey said.

"Did I really hurt him that badly that he won't try again?" Darcy asked.

Casey truly wished she was someplace else. She didn't want to get pulled into Mike's life. "I don't know," she said lamely. "I really don't know."

Darcy forced a smile. "I know you don't. I wouldn't have dragged you into this except that I thought that you and Mike were dating." Her smile became slightly more natural. "He is a great guy, you know. Maybe you should—"

"No, I shouldn't," Casey said quickly. "We do not get along at all." She ignored that little video screen in her head that was playing back scenes when they'd gotten along just fine. "We fight all the time. We can't agree on anything."

"Oh." Darcy looked disappointed as she got to her feet. "I was just hoping he'd found somebody."

"I'm sure he will. It just won't be me. We're barely speaking to each other." She got to her feet. "I really should be getting back."

She hadn't lied when she said she and Mike were barely speaking. It was true and continued to be so as the week progressed. Silence took up permanent residence in the house, seeping out from the woodwork and filling the rooms. She knew Mike was around; they passed in the halls occasionally, but he always seemed to be on the verge of leaving, and they rarely spoke.

Casey missed him. Well, she missed having someone to talk to; she didn't miss the sudden emotions that would flare up between them. Though if that was true, why did her stomach get tied in knots whenever he was around? It was all too confusing, and she took to exercising Gus just to escape such confusion.

"You don't have to play with him," Mike said one evening late in the week when he found Casey throwing a ball for Gus. "He is my dog."

She was getting tired of this life of exile. It wasn't what she'd intended at all when she said they'd give each other space. "Fine." She handed him the tennis ball. "Far be it from me to come between a man and his dog."

"I meant it's my responsibility."

"I don't see any reason to leave a dog sitting in the house when I'm here all day and both of us can use the exercise."

Casey waited for a reply, but Mike just threw the ball toward the back fence, much farther than she ever could. The hell with him, she thought, as she stomped back to the house. Mike could hide from any and all emotions his whole life for all she cared.

He apologized the next morning. "I'm sorry I snapped at you last night," he said as she was heading toward the bathroom and he was heading down the stairs. "You don't have to take care of Gus, but I appreciate you doing so."

He was gone when she came down, leaving no trace of having had any breakfast. But then he hadn't been eating at home for days now. All he used the house for was sleeping and bathing. Everything else, even playing with Gus, was done outside or off the property. She was going to have to show him that they could coexist here without going to such extremes of avoidance.

"There's some stew warming on the stove," Casey told him that evening. "You're welcome to it."

He'd been jogging with Gus. It was starting to snow outside and both of them had little snowflake sparkles flickering in their hair.

"I told you not to fix anything for me," he said.

"I didn't make any specifically for you," she lied. "I just ended up with more than I'd planned on."

He wiped his brow, avoiding direct eye contact with her. "Thank you, but I have to shower and get back to the station," he said. "I'll grab something along the way."

"Fast food?"

"Cop food," he said.

By the weekend they'd begun writing notes to each other—short, clipped and to-the-point missives tacked with magnets to the refrigerator door.

"Faucet on kitchen sink leaking. Mr. Slocum coming to fix it." She didn't bother signing it.

"Thank you." Mike didn't sign his note, either. In fact, he just wrote on the bottom of hers.

"There's some blueberry muffins in the bread box."

"Thanks anyway."

"Gus was limping this morning. I think he got ice between his toes."

"I'll keep an eye on it."

"Why are there cop cars driving by so often? Do you think I'm going to steal something?"

"How do you know how often they drive by? Aren't you supposed to be writing this family history?"

To be truthful, this had been the most unproductive week Casey could ever remember. With Dubber's help, she'd gotten more boxes of letters and diaries and photo albums from the attic, but she'd barely made sense of a tenth of it. She just couldn't concentrate. And Simon didn't help. After all the trouble he'd caused, there hadn't been a trace of him all week.

Mike must really have been hurt by Darcy to avoid even casual relationships. He reminded her of Midnight, who'd been so leery of everybody right after Casey had found the cat. But then she thought of Mike—broad shoulders, the most tempting lips and hands that promised to keep her safe. Maybe the comparison of him to her cat had been a little off, but he was still carrying scars from his hurts. She knew that much was true.

It started snowing while Mike was patrolling I-94, just a few flakes blowing across the highway, but by the time he got home in the late afternoon, there were a couple of inches covering the driveway.

In normal times, he would have just left it to shovel tomorrow—if then. The Randalls had a new riding lawn-mower-snowplow that Dubber was anxious to break in. In normal times Mike would've used his free time to take a walk with Gus.

But these were not normal times. And since Casey was in the house Mike was out here shoveling his drive, with Gus lying at the edge of the yard relaxing and watching winter come in.

His neighbors must be figuring he'd lost it, since Dubber had already made the rounds announcing their new machine and his increased capacity to keep drives and sidewalks clean. But Mike didn't care, not one bit.

"The whole neighborhood should learn to mind their own damn business," he muttered to Gus.

Gus showed how well he could mind his own business by totally ignoring Mike and his words.

"Hell," Mike said. "No one's talking to me anymore."

He paused a moment to straighten up and glare down the driveway. The damn thing was made of some strange, space-age material. Once a little snow fell on it, the whole thing tripled in size. If he had any brains he'd quit right now and leave the whole thing for Dubber tomorrow.

But if he'd had any brains, he wouldn't be in the pickle he was in. He wouldn't have let Casey stay the way he had. Or he wouldn't let her get to him the way she did.

There was no reason to make it personal. She'd needed

a safe harbor and Myrna had wanted a family history. If he'd had any brains, he would have just done what Myrna wanted—kept an eye on Casey while she burrowed through boxes and trunks, gathering her data. Watch over her but keep a professional distance, like any good cop would.

Sure, he might be affected physically by her. And he had been—slightly. Maybe a little more than slightly. But that was no reason to let her under his skin. That had been totally unprofessional.

If he'd had any brains, Mike would just put everything back to normal. Do all the things that two adults living in the same house would do. Eat together, if it worked out. Say a few words about the weather. Be polite. Be civil.

"Yo, Mike!"

Mike turned and saw Ed Kramer's police cruiser stop at the foot of the drive. Mike sauntered down.

"Been keeping an eye on the place like you asked," Ed said. "No sign of anything."

"It's been quiet while I've been around, too." Maybe because he was careful to avoid being in the same room with Casey. He shook his head to put his mind back on the right road. "Maybe Myrna was overreacting."

"Better to be safe than sorry," Ed said. "It ain't no trouble to take a few extra passes down the street."

"I appreciate it."

Ed put the car in gear. "No problem. Don't want nothing to happen to your little lady."

"Hey!" Mike cried. "She's not my—"

But Ed had already pulled away. What was with everyone in this town? Couldn't they accept the fact that there might be some single, unattached people around who were happy that way? And Mike was one of them.

He turned and walked back up the drive. "I don't suppose you'd want to go for a walk?" he asked Gus.

His dog gave him a dirty look and let out a few low growls.

"Just a walk, big guy. A short and slow one."

Along with a growl, Gus showed him some teeth. Damn, the dog had never been such a grump before. Maybe there was a Christmas ghost in the house; everybody sure was on edge.

Nothing had happened last year, but then he and Gus had only been in the house a few weeks before the Christmas season hit. Maybe the ghost—assuming he existed—was shy. Or else he wanted to let them settle in before he came around, whining and moaning about what a hard life he'd had.

Mike wished the thing would come out in the open, someplace where he could have a few words with him. Mike would explain how life was hard and then you died, so he should quit his bitching. Of course, Casey would leap to the ghost's defense if he did that, saying the thing was grumpy because he'd had a true love but lost her.

"It'd take a woman to come up with some cockamamie nonsense like that," Mike murmured.

Gus just grunted.

Hell, it might not be male, anyway. Did ghosts have genders? How did anyone know, if they couldn't be seen? Or did people assume that since a ghost was the spirit of someone who'd lived before, it had to be the same sex it had been when alive? And if it had a specific gender, did it get the hots for a ghost of the opposite sex? Did ghosts make love? Could they if they wanted to?

Mike shook his head and threw the snow shovel up by the side of the house. "I need to get something to eat," he said to Gus. "My empty stomach is making me so light-headed, I'm starting to think all weird. You want to come along?"

The dog stood up and made his way toward the back door.

"Hey," Mike protested. "I thought you liked french fries."

Gus climbed the steps and began scratching at the door.

"All right, cool it." Mike hurried over to the back door and opened it.

Gus took a couple of steps in, then stopped to look back, his long body straddling the threshold.

"Nah." Mike shook his head. "It wouldn't be a good idea. I don't think anyone would be comfortable if I ate at home."

Mike closed the door behind him and started to trudge down the drive. It was snowing harder. He had to admit it would have been nice to go into a nice warm kitchen and help Casey whip up some dinner.

But Mike knew that would not have been a good idea. There was too much warmth in that big old kitchen with the linoleum floor and yellow cabinets. The only thing that would happen if he went in there was someone would get burned—most likely him.

Pulling his collar up against the cold, Mike shuffled toward downtown. He sure hoped the special at the diner wasn't the same as yesterday's and the day before. Damn, but he hated meat loaf.

Chapter Seven

"No, that's silly, Dad," Casey said, sitting on the bottom step as she spoke into the portable phone. "I'll be home next week for Christmas. We can celebrate my birthday then."

"You hate celebrating it at the same time as Christmas. It's almost lunchtime. If we leave now, Val and I can be there by dinnertime to take you out."

"I really appreciate the offer, but it's not necessary," Casey repeated. She wasn't sure how she felt about her birthday anymore, anyway, not since she'd found that newspaper article. Her feelings were all jumbled up and she hadn't found a way to untangle them.

She heard her stepmother's voice in the background, then her father came back on the line. "Val says you probably have a hot date and I should stop trying to horn in on your time."

Casey laughed. "You never horn in on my time," she assured him. "I love being with you and Val, but I don't want you to come up. It's been snowing here since yesterday afternoon and the driving is terrible.''

"So you don't have a hot date." She could feel his frown over the telephone lines. "How come someone as pretty and nice as you are hasn't found the right guy?"

"Dad, I don't need a guy in my life to be happy."

"You aren't serious about that Melvin guy, are you?"

Why was everyone picking on poor Melvin? "Dad! There's nothing wrong with Melvin." She was glad Mike was outside shoveling the drive again, though maybe the mention of Melvin would get him speaking to her once more. "He's very nice."

"He's not the type of guy you need."

She just closed her eyes and sighed. They'd had this conversation more times than she could remember. Not just about Melvin, but about every guy she'd ever been friends with.

"You need somebody strong who'll take care of you," her father continued. "Not somebody you need to take care of."

She heard the back door open and the sound of Mike stomping the snow from his boots. Gus dashed over to her, shaking the snow from his body so that she could experience a snowfall herself.

She just smiled at the pooch and scratched his head. "I need to get back to work, Dad. I'll talk to you later."

"You promise you'll do something fun tonight?"

"I promise." She stood up, releasing the connection as she did so.

"Casey?"

She nearly jumped at the sound of Mike's voice, but turned slowly as if she hadn't. He was in the doorway between the dining room and kitchen.

"I'm sorry," he said. "I didn't know you were on the phone."

"Not anymore," she said. "I just got off."

"You have some mail," he said, and brought a few envelopes over to the table.

She made a face at them. "Birthday cards, most likely," she said.

"Is it today?" he asked. "Happy birthday."

"Thanks."

"You look too young to be avoiding them," he said.

She didn't want to get into her feelings about her birthday. If she hadn't shared them with her family, she wasn't going to share them with a relative stranger.

"It's hard having a birthday so close to Christmas," she said.

He just looked at her for a long moment. "I was going to make myself a cup of tea. Want some?"

She was more than surprised by his offer; she was stunned. But she just nodded. "Sure. It's time for a break."

"Regular tea okay? I don't think I have anything herbal."

"Regular is great," she replied.

While he put the water on the stove, she got two mugs out of the cabinet, then they stood in silence and watched the years pass until the teakettle began to whistle. It had been so long since they'd talked, she didn't seem to know how to start. Finally, the water was boiling and they took their mugs to the table. Casey sat down with hers and started opening her birthday cards.

"Birthdays start you thinking about your birth parents, don't they?" Mike said.

Casey took her time reading a humorous card from her grandmother—time she used to compose an answer. She put the card down with what she hoped was a believable smile. "Yeah, it does. Guess it's only normal."

"Even more so if you feel you have questions unanswered," he said.

"Do you?"

He shook his head. "Not really. Stephen answered most of them for me. I was lucky."

"Yeah."

Not knowing what else to say, she opened another card. It was from her twin brothers, who claimed they were on such a tight budget that they could only afford one card. She had to smile at that, knowing their budget included such big-ticket items as dates every night, car expenses and the right clothes. Her dad liked to laugh and say they were just like he'd been at that age. Casey put down the card.

"You ever wonder who you got certain traits from?" she asked.

Mike just shrugged. "Can't say that I have, not having very many unusual traits, if any."

"Oh, come on."

"I'm serious." He sipped at his tea, then stared off in space. "I can't sing. My artistic endeavors would be graded as mediocre. I was a reasonable athlete—along with about half of my high-school class. Nope, nothing remarkable about me."

"You're brave," she said.

He frowned at her.

"Dubber told me about you saving those kids. That's pretty remarkable."

"No, that was a stroke of good luck. I just happened to be passing when the car crashed."

"But you risked you life for them. Not everybody else would have."

"Lots of people would have. I was just the one on the scene."

"Was their mother there?" Casey asked.

He nodded. "She was thrown from the wreck, but was trying to get back into the car when it started on fire, of course."

"Of course." Casey kept the bitterness from her voice. "What kind of mother wouldn't want to save her children?"

Mike gave her a strange look that said she hadn't been

quite as successful as she'd thought. "There's more to this birthday business than normal reflecting, isn't there?"

"No," she said. "You're reading much more into it than is there."

He watched her for a long silent moment, skepticism in his eyes. "So where do you want to go for lunch?" he asked.

"Lunch?" She'd reached for another card, but stopped. "I thought we were giving each other space."

"We are, but birthdays are the exception," he said. "Today's supposed to be my day off, but with heavy snow like we're getting, we usually all get called in. So I can't promise you dinner, but we can do lunch."

"But it's awful out," she protested, even as her heart told her to accept. "Why don't I just make something?"

"Oh no, you don't," he said, and pulled her to her feet. "Get your boots on, young lady. We're walking downtown to the Daybreak Café for a birthday lunch."

She ignored the rush of wonder that his hands on hers caused, or the giddy light-headedness that came from his smile. "You don't have to do this, you know."

"Would you just get your boots on? I'm hungry!"

She laughed and went into the mudroom to slip into her boots. All right, so they were talking again. And doing things together. All it meant was that they were both lonely and wanted some companionship. The basic rules hadn't changed.

And wouldn't.

They turned out to be the only customers at the Daybreak Café and were ushered in like royalty. Mike led Casey over to a corner booth. The walk had brought a rosy glow to her cheeks and seemed to have chased the shadow from her eyes.

He was glad; she'd looked so troubled earlier. Even though he'd vowed to keep away from her, he couldn't just pretend he hadn't seen that pain in her eyes. He had no idea what she needed, but he was sure it wasn't to be left alone. Stan, the café's owner, brought out cups of steaming hot chocolate and promised big bowls of the chef's special chili.

"And figure out something great for dessert," Mike told him. "It's Casey's birthday."

"Her birthday?" Stan's eyes grew round. "I know just the thing." And he hurried off.

"You shouldn't have told him that," Casey protested. "I don't want a fuss made."

"Sure you do," Mike said. "Everyone wants to be fussed over on their birthdays."

"Oh?" she said. "And when is yours?"

That wasn't what he'd intended. He didn't care for birthdays or holidays. "Doesn't matter," he said quickly. "You'll be long gone by that time."

The sudden dose of his own reality set him back on his heels slightly. It was true; she was only here temporarily. But somehow reminding himself of it took the warmth from their outing. He stared out the window, watching the snow fall and thinking how different the street looked from little over a week ago, when it had been filled with laughing people and a lively little parade. Now it was snowy and deserted. It was like his life—filled with laughter and nonsense one minute, lonely the next. Mike shook his head and took a big drink of his hot chocolate. What was wrong with him?

"So when are you putting up your Christmas tree?" Casey asked. "You've got to be the last person in town without one."

Mike made a face. How did she always know just what he didn't want to discuss? "I don't put one up."

"You have to," she said. "An old house like Myrna's, one with so much history, just calls for a big tree."

"It's crazy to do it just for me," he said.

"It's not just for you. It's for Gus, too."

"Single people living alone don't have Christmas trees."

"I do."

He just looked at her, then sighed. She was like Gus with a bone, worrying it to death. "Does Melvin?" he asked. "No, don't tell me. Of course he does."

"Actually, he doesn't," she said. "But he has an excuse. He has allergies."

Allergies? What a crock! And she was letting him get away with that? "What's he allergic to—green?" Mike snapped. "He can get a fake tree if he's allergic to real, and real if he's allergic to plastic."

"It's not that simple."

"No? He's allergic to ornaments? How about lights? Or maybe the music?"

She gave him a pointed look. "We were talking about you and how you've put your good times on hold just because you aren't sharing them with a partner."

"We were talking about Melvin's lies," he corrected.

"Don't try to change the subject."

But then the chili came, and he chose instead to dig into the big, steaming, aromatic bowl of liquid fire. She just didn't want to talk about Melvin because she knew she'd lose that battle, so she was trying to attack him and his way of life. It wasn't going to work, though.

But as he ate the chili and let the spicy meal warm every inch of him and then some, Casey's words played over and over again through his head. He hadn't put his life on hold, had he? He'd decided after Darcy not to ever marry, so there was no tomorrow to save things for. But was he doing it anyway, subconsciously waiting for an event that would never happen? He was living in a rented house, but that was no big deal. He hadn't had a serious relationship since Darcy, but that was no big deal, either. Neither was not having a Christmas tree. Or matched dishes or towels. None of it meant a thing.

This all just boiled down to the fact that Casey wanted a Christmas tree. Something Melvin apparently couldn't give her, but something Mike certainly could. Chalk one up for Mr. March.

"If you want a tree, we could have one. You will still be here then, won't you?" He suddenly realized he had no idea what her plans were. She seemed so much a part of the household so quickly, he couldn't imagine her not there.

"Well, I was going home for Christmas," she said. "But only for a few days. Then I'll be back."

"So is it worth getting a tree?" he asked. "You should've said something sooner."

"Maybe if you hadn't stopped talking to me, I would have."

"I didn't stop talking to you. I just rationed the number of words I said."

"Rationed?" She laughed. "How many was I allowed a day? Ten? Fifteen?"

He stiffened slightly. It wasn't like that at all. Hadn't she felt the fire between them? Hadn't she realized the danger? "You don't understand."

She just shook her head and reached across the table for his hand. "You're right, I don't," she admitted, giving his fingers a squeeze, then letting them go. "I have no idea why we struck sparks those few times. It took me by surprise, too, and for a while I didn't know how to react."

Her hand had left warmth on his, a slow fire that continued to burn. "And you do now?"

"Sure. I act as if it didn't happen."

His eyes seemed caught on her lips, as he remembered their taste and softness. He forced his gaze down, carefully watching his food as he ate. "I'm not sure I can."

"Then you act as if it did," she said. "It's not like it has to happen again."

"No, I guess it doesn't," he said slowly. Cautiously.

"We can eat together. Share chores. Watch TV together," she said. "And just be careful. We are adults, after all. It's not like something's going to take over our minds and have us do something we don't want to do."

It wasn't his mind he was worried about. "You and Melvin have that much control over everything you do?"

She sighed and visibly counted to ten. "Melvin is off-limits," she said carefully. "I am tired of talking about him."

So dump the jerk, Mike thought, but didn't say the words. "Fine," he snapped.

"Are you ready for dessert?" Stan asked, appearing at their table to pick up the empty chili bowls.

What Mike wasn't ready for was the end of his Melvin discussion with Casey, but he just nodded at Stan, who in turn waved to someone in the kitchen, who brought out a huge ice-cream sundae. Chocolate, cherries and whipped cream covered what had to be a small mountain of ice cream.

"I'm not supposed to eat all this, am I?" Casey groaned, as the concoction was put on the table between them.

"Of course not," the man assured her, whipping out two spoons. "The Matterhorn's a two-person sundae. It's to share. You can depend on Mike here to help you."

"Thank goodness," Casey said, and took her spoon. She grinned across the table at Mike. "It's good to have a man I can depend on."

He wanted to ask if Melvin would have been able to eat his share, but he didn't. He was learning that Casey didn't want to hear the truth about the wonderful Melvin. "I'm here as long as you need me," Mike told her.

"Or as long as the ice cream lasts."

But that could still be a hell of a lot longer than someone else.

"So where's Casey and Gus? They go for a walk?" Mike asked the cats. They were sitting on a kitchen stool, staring at him as he finished the peanut butter sandwich that was supposed to fill all the empty spots the last twenty-four hours' sporadic meals had left.

He'd been called in yesterday afternoon, just as he'd expected, and had worked until after lunch today. Snow always made a mess of traffic on the highways and state roads, yet half the drivers seemed not to realize they had to drive with extra caution.

"I wrote out so many accident reports I could do it in my sleep, which was what I was just about doing at the end," he told them, then grimaced. "Man, I don't know what's the matter with me lately. If somebody had ever told me I'd be talking to a pair of cats, I would have arrested them for being drunk and disorderly."

The white cat yawned, while the dark one checked out the kitchen window. Mike had gotten in about half an hour ago, changed into jeans and a sweater and made himself something to eat. Even though he was exhausted, he couldn't seem to relax. He probably needed to know Casey was okay before his eyes would close.

"You know, it wouldn't hurt you guys to smile a little. Maybe even wag your tail a couple or three times."

They jumped down onto the floor and ambled out of the kitchen without even a tail flick as the back door opened. Casey came in, stamping the snow off her boots. Her cheeks were rosy; her smile brought new life, new energy, to his weary bones. She took off her stocking cap and shook her glorious red hair free. He wasn't nearly as tired as he'd thought.

"You just get in?" she asked as she took off her coat. "You look beat."

Gus gave him a quick sniff, then hurried into the living room. "I'm fine," Mike said stiffly, and looked out the kitchen window. Why was she always harping on how bad he looked? It was enough to give a guy a complex. "Where's Dubber? If he's not going to shovel the drive, I'd better get out there and do it."

"He ran home to get a ticket for me," Casey said. "His class is putting on *A Christmas Carol* tonight and he has a part in it."

Mike grunted. He was getting a little tired of the smile

in her voice every time she talked about Dubber, and the scolding in her voice when she talked to him. Shouldn't it be the other way around?

Dubber came rushing into the kitchen. "Here's your ticket, Casey."

"How much do I owe you?" she asked.

"Nothing. It's my treat."

"You got another ticket on you?" Mike asked.

"Sure." Dubber pulled a stub out of his pocket and held it out to him. "They're two dollars."

"Okay." Mike counted four dollars out of his billfold. "Here you go."

Dubber returned two dollars to him. "I said they were two bucks apiece."

"That's okay," Mike replied. "I was paying for Casey's and mine."

"You can't pay for Casey's," Dubber said. "Hers is my treat."

Mike noticed the boy's voice had risen and he suddenly seemed a bit pink in the face. Boy, talk about being wound tight. Mike took back the two dollars Dubber was holding out.

"What part do you have in the play?" Casey asked.

"I'm the Ghost of Christmas Past." Dubber's mood changed as quickly as his voice. "Scrooge learns a lot about himself from the different ghosts."

"Christmas Past is one of my favorites," Casey said.

Mike turned away. Whoever heard of a favorite ghost?

"My grandma says Mike could learn a lot from the ghost that lives in this house," Dubber said.

Mike spun around to glare at the boy. "There's no ghost here."

"She says the ghost that lives here denied himself a pure love, so that's why he has to spend eternity in pain."

Damn. Women, kids...nobody listened these days. "Dubber, go out and clean the drive."

"All right." The kid gave Casey a big smile. "See you at the play."

"I wouldn't miss it," Casey replied. "Thank you for asking me."

Mike considered reminding Dubber that he was going, too, but it was more than obvious that the kid didn't care. Mike took the time to glare out the window above the sink while the boy bounced out the back door.

Casey moved next to him, putting an arm around his. "Looks like you need to get to bed."

Her touch shot jolts of electricity through him; her words awoke all sorts of images that his electrified body wanted to pursue. His hands running over her smooth skin, his lips trailing down that tempting hollow that that droplet had followed weeks ago…

"I'm fine," he said, holding himself stiffly. "I'm used to late hours and double shifts."

"You don't sound fine."

Did she really want him to list the reasons why he didn't? The touch of her hand. Her clean, womanly scent. The sparkle in her eyes… "I don't like sitting around the house," he said.

"You've been gone for almost twenty-four hours," she argued. "What in the world do you want to do?"

He forced his gaze away from her smile, from her lips and from those tempting, wonderful curves. That was not a question she really wanted an answer to.

"I've been sitting in a car for forever," he said. "I need to work the stiffness out of my joints before I sleep, and Gus is tired of walks."

"I saw some sleds in the garage. Is there a sledding hill near here?"

"Butcher's Hill," he replied, nodding.

"So are you game?" she asked, her voice light with hope and laughter.

He made the mistake of turning to look at her, of looking into those green eyes that had been trying for days to capture his soul. He was lost. In a split second, three quarters of the oxygen disappeared from the room and the temperature went up to about 3,000 degrees Fahrenheit. He couldn't breathe. He couldn't think. All he could do was marvel at the promises of glory that those eyes made.

"Come on." She stepped back, picking up her coat. "Don't be such an old poop. It'll be fun."

With distance between them, even just a few feet, the temperature returned to normal and he could breath again. "When are you going to learn not to annoy someone bigger than you?" he asked.

"Maybe after I'm done sledding," she said, laughing.

He went to get his coat—only to discover his gloves were gone. "Your cat's been thieving again," he said. "Have you considered therapy for her?"

"Maybe you shouldn't leave them out," she said as she went into the hallway.

"Sure, blame the victim," he called after her. He could hear her footsteps on the stairs.

Gus came to the doorway to look at him. "It would be nice if you would remember you're my dog," Mike told him as he pulled on his coat. "You're supposed to be protecting my property, not letting those little buggers rip me off. If she stays around here much longer, I won't have anything left."

But what did he have now? He was constantly losing his breath around her. His sanity was questionable. And his dog had deserted him. Good thing his heart was locked up tight.

"Here they are," she said, producing his gloves. A little bit of red fuzz clung to one.

"You have a red glove thief now?" he asked.

She just laughed and plucked the fuzz off. "She hid them under my robe."

So the gloves had gone where he couldn't. Wouldn't. Shouldn't. He just pulled them on and tried not to think about anything else.

They went out to the garage, retrieved a pair of old plastic sleds, then walked down the street to the park. This was crazy, he told himself. He hadn't gone sledding in years. He ought to be home, taking a nap. But then he looked over at Casey next to him and wondered what it would be like to go down the hill on a sled together. To have her pressed up against him as they raced toward the bottom. To have his arms wrapped around her to keep her safe. Like a dream, he thought, and one that was best not lived in real life.

When they got to the sledding hill, Mike saw it was a good news–bad news situation. The recent snowfall had been a good one—heavy and wet in the beginning and powdery afterward, creating a great surface for sledding. The bad news was that the hill was filled with kids.

"Keep your eyes open when you're on the hill," he warned Casey. "You blink and one of these kamikaze sledders will wipe you out."

"Yes, sir."

Mike sighed. Casey was back to her womanly tricks again—pert, smart alecky and totally uninterested in what he had to say.

"Fine," he said. "Don't listen to me. But if you get knocked down, don't lay there whining and crying, expecting me to run up and rescue you."

"I'm not the crying-and-whining type," she said, and walked over to the top of the hill.

"No, I can see that."

"I also don't believe in waiting around for rescue," she said.

"Makes it tough for your knight in shining armor," he said.

"Don't believe in them, either." She set her sled in place.

"You believe in ghosts but not knights in shining armor?"

She stooped down with one knee in her sled, but squinted

up at him. "Sure. I may be impressionable, but I'm not stupid." She pushed off with her free foot and went careening down the hill.

Mike just stood there, watching her. What was that supposed to mean—she was impressionable but not stupid? He got into his sled and followed her down. Some kids got in the way and he had to veer off the icy path, stopping far short of where she had.

She picked up her sled and came over by him. "Not much of a run," she said. "I beat you."

"You want me to run over some kids?" He picked up his sled and they started the trek back up the hill. "So how come you don't believe in knights in shining armor?"

"I don't like the whole concept of rescue," she said. "It's so...so...so beholding. If I'm in trouble, I'll get myself out."

Maybe Aunt Myrna was right in keeping it a secret that she'd sent Casey here for her own protection. "That's not always possible."

"Then you leave it to the professionals," she said. "You don't mix it up with emotions. Who'd want to be loved because of gratitude?"

They'd reached the top again, and she took advantage of a lull in the sledding to push herself off. Who would want to be loved because of gratitude? Not him, but then he wasn't looking for love, attached to other emotions or otherwise.

They must have sledded for the better part of an hour, racing down and leaving their worries at the top of the hill. It had been a long time since Mike'd had so much fun. Casey was a great companion—lively, athletic and full of laughter.

"We should be heading home," she said as they ended a run. "It's going to get dark soon and I'm sure our babies are wondering where we are."

It was getting dark, but Mike didn't want to go home. "Let's do one more."

"And then we'll go home?"

"One more run, but on one sled," he said.

She gave him a wary look, but tossed her sled off to the side. "But just one more."

Up at the top of the hill, she got onto his sled and he pushed them off, jumping on at the last minute. For one glorious, all-too-short moment, they raced down the hill with her leaning into him, wisps of her hair flying about him and his arms holding her as tightly as he wanted.

It was crazy. It was stupid. It was playing with fire, just to see if he could touch her and not get burned. He let his lips brush the top of her hat. He let her scent surround him. He felt a fire start to smolder in him, and for that moment he let it burn. There was a sudden wildness about him, an urge to fly into the face of the wind and let his hungers take them where they would.

But then they reached the base of the hill and coasted to a stop. The ride was over and so was his reckless abandon. She was pulling away from him, the same smile on her lips that was always there. To her, it had just been another sled ride. Which was fine with Mike. Just the way he wanted it.

While she got her sled, he picked up his, feeling unbelievably weary in body and soul.

"You still awake?" Casey leaned closer to Mike in the dark auditorium and whispered, "Dubber'll be coming on in a minute."

"I'm awake," Mike assured her, though his voice said he wouldn't be for long.

He should have skipped the play, Casey thought. Or the sledding. He'd been exhausted when they'd gotten back to the house, but he'd insisted on helping make dinner, then cleaning up, and then taking Gus out to play ball for a while. Maybe he feared he'd fall asleep if he stopped for long.

Dubber came on the stage then, rattling chains and shouting his lines. Casey nudged Mike.

"I'm awake," he said.

"Stay that way long enough to remember something to comment on," she whispered back.

The play was a rather abridged version, short enough not to let the youngsters in the audience get bored, but long enough to tell the story. The main interest most people had in it, though, was seeing their own child. Every time a new character came on stage, there would be applause and the flash of cameras going off. Dubber's entrance was no exception.

As the play went on, Mike sighed softly, and Casey could feel his weariness. She should have insisted that he go to bed, even if she had to put him there herself. The very thought caused her cheeks to turn hot, and she was grateful for the darkness of the auditorium. She had thought that, knowing how they reacted to each other's touch, they could avoid trouble just by avoiding touches. What a fool she'd been.

All her heart needed to start racing was the sound of his voice. All her mind needed to dream of caresses was to see his hands. She had gotten a lot of work done on the family history in the past few days, but she wasn't sure how. It seemed that all she ever thought about was Mike.

Suddenly, loud applause broke out and the auditorium lights went on. Casey joined in the clapping as the actors came out for bows, then in a few minutes, she and Mike joined the crowd trooping out into the hallway, where refreshment tables were set up.

"Tiffany certainly put an interesting spin on her role," Casey said. "Whoever saw the Ghost of Christmas Future in a karate outfit?"

"How many sober people have seen a ghost of any kind?"

Dubber came out into the hall, still wearing his ghostly chains. "Hi, Casey," he said. "How'd you like it?"

"It was just great," she said, and gave him a hug. "You were the best Ghost of Christmas Past I've ever seen."

He turned beet red before moving on to greet his family.

"Well, you made his day," Mike said. "Maybe his year."

"Nothing wrong with that," Casey said.

Mike was exhausted, and she was ready to call it a day, too, so they turned toward the exit. Down the hall and then to their right. They were almost to the door when they heard a voice behind them.

"Miss Crawford." Tiffany was bearing down on them, still wearing her white karate outfit. "I thought we had an understanding."

"Tiffany, I'm sorry I—"

"Didn't I tell you to keep your hands off my man?"

"It was just a quick hug," Casey said.

"Did you or did you not accept a ticket for tonight's performance from him?" Tiffany demanded.

"He was just being friendly."

"Ha! I bet that's what Mrs. Robinson said."

"Who is Mrs. Robinson?" Mike asked.

"Don't play the innocent, Mr. Burnette." Tiffany turned her attention to Mike. "This is as much your fault as anybody's. If you'd occupy her time like a real man, she wouldn't be out cruising."

"Casey is out cruising?" Mike asked.

"All right, people. Listen up." The barefoot little thug commanded their attention. "This is the second time I've had to talk to you, Miss Crawford. Once more will be your third strike and you'll be out."

The girl turned to Mike. "And as for you, Mr. Burnette, I'm making this woman your responsibility. She obviously has too much time on her hands. I want you to fill that void in her life."

"What?"

"Old people should play their games with other old people," Tiffany said. "And leave us kids alone."

With that, she turned on her bare heel and stomped off down the corridor. They stared after her until she disappeared around a far bend, then they turned to each and started to laugh.

"Why didn't you do something?" Casey asked.

"Hey, I don't want to tangle with that kid. She's tough."

"You could have at least pointed out that we aren't old."

"I don't think that was what she wanted to hear," Mike said, moving toward the door. "Maybe I should talk to her father."

They went out into the night, meeting a blast of wintery wind head-on. Mike slipped his arm around Casey's shoulders and she moved closer to him. It was warmer there—safer, too. A place to run to when the storms were coming and the wind was blowing. It was a strange sense, a strange feeling for her, the great rescuer, to feel as if she was being rescued.

They got to his car, but neither made a move to get inside. Or even to step apart. They just turned, moving closer if anything, and the world around them disappeared. There was no snow, no howling winds, no school parking lot. It was just the two of them with a growing warmth surrounding them.

Mike leaned down, touching her lips with a electricity that shot through her. Reaching up, standing on her tiptoes, she kissed him back, meeting his fever with one of her own. His hunger with hers. There was nothing but their lips joined in wonder and magic. Then his mouth covered hers, his tongue slid between her lips and touched hers. Darting and dancing, teasing and tempting. Her knees went wobbly and she had to hold on tighter, had to let her arms encircle his neck, had to cling to him as if she was lost and only he knew the way back home.

They parted after an eternity had passed and found that they were still in the parking lot. Still by Mike's car. Casey took a deep, steadying breath and leaned back against the door. This was so unlike her. She'd been kissed before, but the earth had never moved. Winter had never been traded for summer for those moments of bliss. She felt worried, vulnerable and as if she ought to look for a place to hide.

"Well, let's hope Tiffany was watching," she said, not meeting Mike's eyes. She stared at the car tracks and footprints in the snow. The frost from her own breath. The little fuzzy pills on her mittens. "Maybe she'll believe I'm not after Dubber."

"Maybe she'll think I'm filling that void in your life." Mike's voice was none too steady, either.

She brought her eyes up to his. Slowly. Uncertainly. Then found her gaze caught in the trap of his blue blue eyes. For one blessed moment, his soul spoke to hers, their hearts danced in unison. Then a shade seemed to come down, and he blinked away the intimacy.

Casey felt as if she'd been suddenly set loose, a kite whose string was cut. She was glad. It was what she wanted. But she felt a bit unsteady, too, as if the wind was just carrying her along in any old direction.

"Anything to keep Tiffany nonviolent," she joked.

"Anything?" he asked.

There was a tremor in his voice that set her heartstrings playing a soft melody. She was being swept away and didn't care a bit.

"Anything," she repeated softly, not sure any longer that she was talking about Tiffany.

Chapter Eight

Mike gripped the wheel tightly and concentrated on his driving, trying to outrun the gloom that was close on his heels. The roads were pretty good, but there still were slick spots that he needed to watch for. Sort of like living with Casey. It was pretty relaxed and comfortable, but every once in a while they'd hit an icy patch and have the complacency skid out from under them.

"You know, I could have gotten the tree by myself," Casey said.

"No problem. Gus needed the exercise." Like last night, for instance, at Dubber's play. Or earlier yesterday afternoon when they'd been sledding. But Melvin wouldn't give Casey a Christmas tree, so Mike would. Even if he'd woken up in a foul mood.

"I could have brought Gus along," Casey said, turning to wave at the dog sitting in the back seat. "He and I are buds."

Mike looked in the rearview mirror at Gus with his big

stupid grin. Casey's words were certainly true. In fact, his dog seemed to like her better than him lately.

Mike forced his eyes back to the road, squinting into the afternoon sun. "Cutting down a Christmas tree is hard work."

"I'm not afraid of hard work," she said. "It's better than making somebody do something they don't want to do."

"Who said I didn't want to do this?" he asked. "It was my idea, wasn't it?"

"You wanted to buy a tree from the lot by the hardware store."

"And we're cutting our own. No big deal."

She leaned back in her seat and turned to stare out the window. Dare he hope that she was taken by the beauty of the winter scene?

"Where'd you grow up?" she asked. "Around here?"

One hope dashed to the ground. "Chicago," he said.

"I'm from Fort Wayne. City but close to country. We always bought our tree from our church, but I always thought it would be the most wonderful thing to go cut our own."

Silence climbed into the car with them, riding along like a stowaway. It started nudging him once he turned off the highway, and really began nagging at him when he passed a sign advertising the tree farm.

"We used to cut our own tree every year," Mike said slowly, concentrating on his driving. "The three of us would drive out to this tree farm just north of Rockford. Even with the expressways it was a three-hour trip, so we'd make a day of it. Leave early in the morning, stop for lunch and then go cut the Christmas tree."

Why was he telling her this? It made no sense; this wasn't something he talked about. But he went on. "On the way home, we'd always play this silly alphabet Christmas-wish game. I'd say I want angels for Christmas, and my mom would say she wanted angels and bananas, then my dad would say he wanted angels and bananas and a cable car.''

Mike stopped a long moment, unable to go on, but unable not to. "My dad died the spring after my tenth birthday and then we stopped going. We moved into an apartment and got a little fake tree.''

"And that's why you didn't want to go get a tree,'' Casey said softly. "You should have just told me.''

He didn't look her way. He couldn't. "It's not that I didn't want to get a tree,'' he said. "It just felt strange.''

"I didn't want to horn in on precious memories.''

"You didn't,'' he said gruffly.

That wasn't it at all. It wasn't the past that was troubling him, but the future. Cutting your own Christmas tree was something special, a ritual that meant something because it was part of a whole. And the whole was important because it was made up of people who had committed to each other forever. Something he would never do with someone. It wasn't his memories of the past that saddened him, but the fact that he wouldn't be making any more of them.

"Take a left at the road up ahead.'' Casey's voice was soft, as if she could read his thoughts.

He didn't want her sympathy. He'd rather have her annoyance than pity. "Hope the trees aren't full of bugs,'' he said.

"They'd be frozen. It's winter.''

He just shook his head as he turned at a gate. "Until they get into the house where it's warm. A guy in Baroda once got a tree and set it up in his house and the next day he thought he heard it clicking. When he looked, it seemed to be moving. Then—''

"It blew up and his house was filled with bugs,'' she said, and laughed. "Urban legend number 4,572. Only I heard it with a cactus and scorpions. It really was much more effective that way. What kind of killer bugs can be hiding in a Christmas tree, for goodness sakes?''

She was trying to make him smile, and it was working.

No matter how he tried to hold on to his grumps, they were slipping through his fingers like sand at the surf's edge. He parked the car in front of a small pole barn and they went inside.

A tall, husky woman in boots, jeans and a flannel shirt sat in the office watching a television game show. "Axes and crosscut saws are behind you," the woman said as she took their money. "The trees are out back."

"Are there any restrictions on size?" Casey asked.

The woman laughed loudly. "No, honey. It's like picking out a man. If you can handle it, it's yours."

"Good," Casey said. "I like them big."

"Uh-huh." The woman was eyeballing Mike. "I can see that."

"I meant trees," Casey said, sounding flustered. "I like big trees."

"Sure," the woman replied, snorting.

Mike enjoyed the confusion on Casey's face and the embarrassment staining her cheeks. "Don't be shy, honey," Mike said, putting his arm around Casey's shoulder. "You know you dumped Melvin 'cause he was such a little wimpy guy."

Casey cast him a glance that said she was not amused, and shrugged his arm off her. "I'll have you know he was big in ways that count," she said, and started for the door.

Mike frowned. "What's that supposed to mean?" He grabbed up a saw and hurried after her.

The woman just chuckled. "Y'all have fun now," she sang out as the door shut behind them.

Casey moved on ahead of him with Gus, trudging through the calf-deep snow, and began to course the snow-covered tree lanes, obviously looking for that special one. There hadn't been much foot traffic here since the snow-storm of the last few days, and the pure, untrampled beauty of the hillside brought peace to Mike's heart. Gus took off, following some rabbit tracks, while Mike just trailed along after Casey, snow falling softly from the branches he brushed in passing.

Why had he told Casey about his childhood Christmases? There'd been no reason to except that the more he was around her, the more he seemed unable to hide parts of himself. It was like the past was a festering sore that would only be healed when exposed to her sunshine. Which was crazy. There was nothing wrong with his past. It was a little jumbled, a mixture of pain and happiness, just like everyone else's, but nothing that needed healing.

Up ahead, Casey stopped. "What do you think?" she called to him, waving her hand at two adjacent trees. "Which one do you like better?"

"They look the same to me," he replied.

He was more struck by the glow on her face, by the radiance that outshone even the sun glittering off the snow. Maybe she did possess some sort of magic healing rays. He did feel more alive in her presence, more anxious to explore life. Though what he'd really like to explore about now were those lips of hers, and those gentle curves under her coat and...

"They can't look the same," Casey said, and turned to the tree on her left. "Look, this one is taller."

Was he really supposed to be looking at trees, when he could be watching her? "They're still both big, cone-shaped, green things that smell all piney."

"You are no help," she exclaimed, and began to walk around the tree.

"It's not like this is a major commitment, you know. What are we talking about—two, three weeks tops that we have to live with it?"

"And you can't even make a short-term commitment. Pretty sad." She began to slowly circle the other tree, bits of snow falling from upper branches and glinting like crystals in the sun.

The beauty of everything around her caught him by surprise, and he fought its hypnotic effect. "The truth is you can't decide, either, and you're trying to get out of making the decision.''

She stopped walking to glare at him. "And that is intended to goad me into making a decision you're too wishy-washy to make?"

"Is that a challenge to my manhood?" he asked.

A slight smile crept onto her lips. "A real man would know which tree is right."

"Oh, really?" he said, and took a step closer to her.

"A real man would take one look at the trees and say, 'That's the one for my house.'" She lowered her voice, making it all gruff.

And making it do something extraordinary to his breathing. "Is that so?" he said, and came a bit closer.

She grinned at him, a hint of devilment in her eyes. "A real man wouldn't need a saw, either. He'd just rip it out with his bare hands and carry it home on his back."

"I think a real man would object to these slanderous accusations," he said.

She backed up a step, but her laugh was challenging him. Her smile was teasing. "What slander? I was only telling the truth."

"So was I," he said, and reached down for a handful of snow.

But she was too quick for him and darted around the other side of the tree.

"You can't hide from me." He followed her, only to be hit with a snowball from behind.

"Who's hiding?" she said with a laugh. "I was only searching for the best shot."

"Is that right?"

He took off after her, catching her by the arm only a few yards away. He wasn't sure what he'd been going to do, but somehow she tripped or he tripped or the earth moved, and suddenly they were lying in the snow side by side.

Her fiery red hair lay across the snow, so dazzling he should have been blinded. Her green eyes danced with laughter and a promise of much more. Something stirred within him—a hunger, a need, a desire to possess so much stronger than anything he'd ever felt before that it stunned him. He ought to push away, pull her to her feet and get busy cutting down the damn tree.

But her lips were so close and so very tempting. Just a little touch, that was all he needed. That would be enough to get him through the day. Or the night. Or whatever lay ahead.

Then she was kissing him. He was kissing her. He pulled her into his arms as if closeness was possible, as if their winter coats didn't block all contact. And it didn't, for somehow he could feel her softness, feel her racing heart and the raging pull of her femininity.

They'd hit that icy patch again, but it was wonderful, nothing to be feared. It took them higher than the clouds and spoke to the clamoring hunger in their hands and their hearts. He kissed her and kissed her again, letting his lips draw all the wonder and magic from her that she could give.

Then something changed. A wetness on his cheek slowed his fall into passion and he pulled slightly away. Gus was breathing down into their faces.

"Gus, old buddy," Casey said with a laugh.

Mike just rolled over onto his back with a groan, not caring that the snow had now become an unpleasant, chilly bed instead of the perfect frame for Casey's beauty. Gus came over and licked his face. "Thanks, pal."

Casey just laughed some more and sat up. "Go for it, Gus. He needs some cooling down."

Mike just gave her a sharp look, then frowned at his dog. "If you want to do something useful," he told Gus, "go over and pick a Christmas tree so we can go home."

Unbelievably, Gus walked over to the two trees, sniffing each carefully before raising his leg, giving one tree a golden shower. Casey just looked at Mike.

"The other one," they both said in unison.

* * *

Mike had wrestled the tree into the far corner of the living room, just to the left of the front windows. It lightly brushed the ceiling and filled the room—the house—with the wonderful scent of Christmas.

"Is it straight?" he asked from somewhere behind the tree.

"A little to the right."

"That enough?"

"Too much."

A grumbling could be heard from behind the branches, but Casey just laughed. There was no way anything could spoil today. Going for the tree had been perfect, everything she'd always thought cutting your own tree should be.

"Want to hold it steady while I tighten the base?" he asked.

She reached in to hold the trunk. "Your wish is my command, sir."

"Do I dare test that statement?"

There was a note in his voice that sent a shiver down her back and curled her toes. "Maybe," she said softly. "Just maybe."

She turned to see Snowflake and Midnight skulk across the living-room floor, moving slowly and cautiously toward the tree as if it might attack them. She smiled at them, then stared down at the pine needles brushing her arm.

Why had it been so perfect? she wondered. She hadn't gone with family, not even someone who might be family someday. The tree wasn't for her house, where she'd decorate it with her ornaments. And she wouldn't even be here on Christmas to enjoy it—she'd be back home with her family for the holiday.

Mike crawled out from behind the tree and jiggled it. "Doesn't look too steady."

"We need to anchor it to the wall," Casey replied.

"Good idea. Otherwise these guys'll bring it down for sure."

Gus and the two cats were sitting at the base of the tree, gazing upward at its topmost branches.

"And we need to keep Gus—uh, how can I say it?—uninterested in the tree."

Mike smiled and patted his dog. "I've got some dog-away spray down in the basement. Once we're done decorating, I'll fix it up."

Once *we're* done decorating? So this wasn't going to be *woman's work?* Casey hid a smile as she went to the attic to get the boxes of old decorations down while Mike went to the basement to get the dog-away spray and cords to anchor the tree to the wall. It took her several trips to get everything, and by the time she had it all down, the tree was secured.

"Do you think it'll stand up to the cats climbing it?" she asked.

"Sure," he replied. "They're already testing it."

She looked where he was pointing, about two thirds of the way up, and gazed into a pair of dark, shining eyes. And off to the right and above was the tip of a white tail. "You guys aren't going to bother the ornaments, are you?" she asked.

"They wouldn't do that."

Casey laughed as Mike's arm slid around her shoulder. Hers went around his waist. There was something about the innocence of children and animals that gave holidays like Christmas a special meaning. A spirit that soothed the fiercest of beasts. Maybe even a tough cop like Mike Burnette.

"Are you a top-down person?" she asked. "Or bottoms-up?"

"Am I what?" he asked. "I'm not sure that's a question I should be answering to a sweet young thing like you."

She punched him playfully. "Do you start decorating at the bottom of the tree and work up? Or do you start from the tip and come down?"

He took a long moment to examine the tree, his arm tightening slightly around her. "I haven't done this kind of

thing for ages," he finally said, in a voice so soft she almos
didn't hear him. "Why don't you lead the way?"

She wanted to hold him, to soothe away the hints of pas
hurts, but knew this wasn't the time and that wasn't the
way. "I do bottoms-up," she said. "But I also do it the
long way."

"The long way?"

She pulled reluctantly away from him. "I take all the
ornaments and lay them out first. That'll take a while with
this stuff. I don't have any idea what we have."

"I'm not going anywhere, are you?"

She shook her head.

"Well, since neither of us has a date, it's no big deal
We'll go the long way."

It might have been shadows created by the headlights of
cars passing in front of the house. It might have been the
winter winds sneaking through hidden cracks in the house.
But Casey was sure it was more than that. She was sure
that all the spirits of Christmas were creeping into the
house, knocking on the door to Mike's soul and looking to
soften his hard edges. Feeling them so filled her heart with
joy that she could hardly breathe.

"The first thing we need are the lights," she said. "Why
don't you run down to the hardware store and get some
while I make us a quick dinner?"

He turned to look thoughtfully at the tree. "How many
do we need?"

"Enough to make it look magical," she said. "Sand-
wiches okay?"

"Sure. Anything's fine."

By the time he got back from the store, she'd fed the
animals, heated up the leftovers of some soup she'd made
earlier in the week, and had made a plate of ham sand-
wiches. She heard him at the door, but when she turned
she was amazed at the size of the bag he was carrying.

"How many packages of lights did you get?" she asked

"I'm not sure. I told Chuck the tree touched the ceiling

so he picked out the boxes.'' Mike put the bag on the kitchen table and began to unload it. ''Then I added a couple more.''

Lights, lights and more lights. She couldn't believe it and went over to his side to peer into the bag. Much as she loved her dad, he never put enough lights on their Christmas tree. Neither did her uncles or her grandfather. She'd thought it was a guy thing, but obviously not an every-guy thing.

''This is wonderful,'' she said, squeezing his arm. ''Lights make the tree.''

''It gets better,'' he said, picking up one of the packages. ''Look, they play Christmas carols and blink in ten different patterns.''

''Ten?'' She groaned, envisioning a nightmare of dueling light shows occurring on the tree each night. She counted up the number of boxes. Ten. That would mean ten different strings playing ten different songs and blinking in ten different patterns.

''One pattern per evening,'' she said. ''The same one on all strings.''

''That'll be no fun.''

''It'll be all the fun you need.''

''And what about all the fun you need?'' he said.

He was right behind her, closer than her silly senses had warned her, and able to tickle the back of her neck with his breath. She wanted to lean back, to turn into his embrace and let his fire melt all her resistance. But she wasn't sure all of a sudden. It was one thing to be swept away by passion. It was quite another to willingly step into its path.

''We'd better eat before the soup gets too cold,'' she said, and moved the boxes of lights to the end of the table.

They ate in silence, a nervous silence filled with awareness, it seemed to Casey. She was conscious of every move of his hands, every time his gaze brushed her. And of the uncertainty nagging at her heart. She did manage to eat, though she remembered none of it.

Somehow it felt safer in the living room, where the sense of the spirits was still strong. She thought of telling Mike about them, but knew that would break the mood. And though she wasn't sure she wanted to act upon it, she knew she didn't want to send it packing, either. Instead, she studied the big tree before her, from the broad bottom to the tip almost touching the ten-foot ceiling, and let its peace and serenity touch her.

Just a few lights were on in the living room. Enough to see what you needed to—the old furniture, the colors in the oriental rug covering the floor, the cove molding on the high ceiling—but not enough to see the fading paint and random cracks. The whole thing created an atmosphere where one could feel both the spirit and the spirits of Christmas. Casey took a deep breath and let her worries go.

"Isn't this room beautiful?" she murmured. "The tree adds so much to the house. A holiday spirit. Contentment. Joyous memories."

"Ten different Christmas carols playing at once would add even more Christmas spirit," he said.

She just laughed, completing her escape from concerns. Why was she suddenly so wimpy and worried? There was nothing here to fear.

Together she and Mike put the lights on the tree, changing it from an ordinary tree to one that had been kissed by the stars. It was wonderful, glittering as if diamonds had been sprinkled all over it. Best of all, Mike just left them as lights. No blinking by color or position. No Christmas carols.

"It looks beautiful," she exclaimed.

He slipped his arms around her. "It looks like a big tree with lights on it."

"You and that ghost that lives here," Casey said. "You're both members of the Christmas grouch clan."

"No way, lady." Mike's grasp tightened around her. "First of all there ain't no such thing as ghosts. And if there were, we'd have nothing in common. He's dead and I'm not." He bent down slightly to brush his lips against her neck. "And I can prove it if you want."

Did she? Maybe. "I think we've got more work to do on the tree."

She slid out of his embrace and sat on the floor, slowly unpacking the ornaments. There were boxes and boxes of wonderful old ones. Fragile little vases and trumpets and drums. Globes with indented sides and ones with flowers painted on them. Little shepherds and kings and camels. Whose were these? she wondered, and wished she knew more about ornaments. Had some belonged to Simon? Or to the nephew who lived in the house after him?

"Thought you might like a sip," Mike said, and put a glass of wine on the low table next to her.

"Thanks." She looked up from her spot on the rug and took a sip, then another. "Very nice."

He sat down next to her and picked up a box from the floor. "Where'd this one come from?" he asked.

"It was upstairs."

"In the attic?"

His voice sounded different, strained, and she frowned up at him. "No, it was in the bedroom I'm using. Why? Shouldn't I have brought it down?"

"No," he said slowly. "It's all right. They're just ornaments. Might as well use them."

Obviously they weren't *just* ornaments. "Whose were they?"

"My parents," he said. "So I guess they're mine now."

"We don't have to hang them," she said, and sipped again at her wine. "We have enough."

He stared down at the box in his hands for what seemed like two eternities, then gave a shrug. "Hey, they were made for hanging on a tree, right? Seems sort of wrong to leave them in a box all the time."

"Probably makes them question their self-worth," she said.

He just looked at her.

"You know, then they'll have to go into therapy, to a support group for unhung ornaments. They'll all gather around and talk about how you deprived them of the chance to reach their full potential as ornaments." She shook her head. "Not a burden I'd want to carry around my whole life."

A smile started to form on his lips. "This is really serious," he said. "I had no idea the trouble I was causing."

"Perhaps there's still time to save them."

"We can always hope," he said, and opened the box as he walked over to the tree.

The first one he hung up was a tiny spaceman, then a little sailboat made of wood shavings. "We went sailing on our vacation one year," he said. "Boy, was my dad seasick. He vowed he was never having anything to do with sailing again, and I was so upset because I had loved it. He got me this ornament to say he was sorry."

"That's such a sweet story," Casey said, and touched the ornament gently as he hung another. A tiny teddy bear. "What's the story behind this one?"

"That one was my very first ornament," he said quietly. "My mother bought it for me."

"The first of many, eh?"

"No." He shook his head. "My mom bought me other ornaments. My mother bought me just that one. She sent it through the agency for my first Christmas."

"Oh." Casey suddenly realized that when he talked of his biological parents it was always mother and father; his adoptive parents were mom and dad. "That was nice of her. It must be comforting to know she was still thinking of you even after you were gone from her life."

"I guess." He took another ornament from the box. "I never thought about it that way."

No, why would he? Did he have any reason to doubt that he had been surrounded by love from the very moment he'd been born?

But tonight was not a night for gloom and sad thoughts, so Casey just ignored any depression that might come close. She pulled out a little holly ornament.

"So tell me about this holly," she said. "Do we find some ivy to hang near it and then sing 'The Holly and the Ivy'?"

He shook his head. 'That's mistletoe," he said. "Not holly."

"Oh." She looked at it more closely and saw that he was right. A daring thought came over her then, a wildness that she knew was part an attempt to distract her silly heart and part boldness from the wine. She held the mistletoe over her head. "Maybe I should wear it in my hair then."

"I'm not sure you should," he said, his voice carefully controlled.

"Why not?" she said. This wasn't what she wanted, some philosophical discussion. She wanted to laugh and play and forget. "Are you going to buck tradition?"

"I was hoping to hang some ornaments."

"And you can. Once you satisfy the mistletoe gods."

"The mistletoe gods?"

"Sure. They're easily satisfied, but get really nasty if you don't."

He made a face, one that said he was sorely put upon. "Far be it from me to rile the gods," he said, and leaned over.

She knew he was going to brush her cheek with his lips. It would be a quick kiss, not unlike the one you'd give a maiden aunt or your mother when the guys were around. So she turned her head at the last second and his lips met hers.

It was as if a bolt of lightning had come down to earth and shot through her. Her lips, her tongue, her whole self seemed to quiver and tremble as a strange, strong yearning took hold. Mike's lips were so gentle, yet so demanding. His mouth was pulling all sorts of secrets from her soul and she was admitting to them all.

She wanted to feel his hands all over her, to touch him in hidden, magic places that would start a fire in him to match her own. She wanted to know all his fears and shoot them down one by one. She wanted to sing and dance and spin out of control in his arms while he kept her safe and secure.

As earth-shattering as their other kisses had been, this one outranked them on the Richter scale by ten to one. Her heart, her soul, her mind shuddered and stood dumbfounded as the potent power of his lips was made known. She could scarcely breathe and certainly couldn't think. And when Mike slowly pulled away, she found her knees ridiculously wobbly.

"So did that satisfy those mistletoe gods?" he asked in a voice that was as rough as sandpaper.

"Yeah," she gasped, surprised she could talk at all. "Now maybe we'd better work on the Christmas-tree gods."

"And what do they want?"

"Just that we hang our ornaments," she said. "Just that we hang our ornaments."

So they hung ornaments and sipped at their wine, but all the while Casey was ever so conscious of Mike's hands, of his nearness, of the way his breath would tickle the back of her neck when he leaned close to her. She really tried to concentrate on the ornaments, but he was hanging his on the very same tree. How could she not notice him?

She reached over to hang a candy cane on an empty branch and found he was hanging a little Santa on it also. Their hands brushed and their eyes met. Suddenly both Santa and the candy cane were forgotten as she moved into his arms once again.

His lips spoke of hungers that their souls echoed. It was all the magic of Christmas and all the sparkle of the Fourth of July. She'd felt such promises in the air, in his touch, in the steel strength of his body pressed against hers. She moved against him, hearing a distant melody that sang to her soul.

Then suddenly they pulled apart, both gasping for breath, both trembling with a fever that had only one cure. She took a deep breath and tried to laugh. It came out shaky.

"You take that side of the tree and I'll take this side," she said. "And no fair coming on my half."

"You drawing a line in the sand?"

"I just want the tree done," she told him.

She was much more sensible than this, she told herself as she worked on hanging ornaments. She was never swept away. Every time she had made love in the past, and there hadn't been many, it was in a long-standing relationship. One where she'd known her lover for a long time before he became her lover. One where she thought there would be a future—until that future got too close and too scary.

Nothing could happen here between her and Mike. They didn't have all the prerequisites she insisted on. They hadn't known each other long. They weren't in a relationship that had developed slowly over the years, and it sure wasn't one with a future.

This was all just some fluke. It was the phase of the moon or the position of the stars or Simon's weird sense of humor. Her common sense helped her finish hanging her share of the ornaments, then while Mike hung gold tinsel garlands, she sat back on the sofa to admire the tree.

"Very nice," she said, finishing her wine. "We should do this professionally."

But then he came to sit next to her, in the only spot left by her cats and Gus, and he was very, very close once more. Her lips were dry, but licking them only seemed to increase the fever that was causing the problem. And her well-thought-out excuses were fading as fast as dew in the summer sun.

"I think it's getting late," she said, gathering the last bit of sanity she had left.

"It's been a long day."

They got up slowly, moving as if it was necessary to stay as far apart as possible. Mike turned off the lights as Casey started up the stairs. He was right behind her, but she stopped to stare through the darkness at their tree. All sorts of other feelings seemed to hover in the air, making the tree seem miles away.

Love and longing and belonging. Hurts. Disappointments. Love lost and found again in unexpected places. Tender touches. Little moments of joy. The house had a history of love, no matter what the stories, and that love was still in the air here. It was all around them, pulsating, throbbing, beating with the memory of all the Christmases that had ever been celebrated here.

Casey turned and slowly climbed the rest of the stairs. "You know," she said to Mike, "there wasn't a pickle ornament."

"I think the festival's a recent thing."

"But there should have been one," she said.

"Why? Those ornaments looked to be forty, fifty, sixty years old and more. Maybe they didn't make pickle ornaments back then. Or maybe Simon hated pickles."

She slowly shook her head, unable to explain it as she stopped at the top of the stairs and leaned against the wall next to Mike's door. "There was a pickle ornament. I know there was, but it's not there."

"Guess I won't get my most favorite wish then," he said with a laugh.

"And what would that be?"

"Suppose you found it," he said, answering her question with one of his own. "What would your wish be?"

"I don't know," she said, and found herself moving into his arms again. "For everyone to be happy."

"Why not just you?" He brushed the top of her hair with his lips; she could feel the gentle touch.

"Because I couldn't be happy unless everyone else was, too."

"Maybe you're too generous." His lips moved to lightly touch her forehead, then her nose, then finally her lips.

Raising up slightly on her tiptoes, she pressed her lips harder to his and let the feelings of the evening blossom again. She felt safe and secure, at home in his arms. But oh so very much more. As if in this one place only, happiness could be found. As if in his arms was home.

His arms pulled her closer, steely bonds that held her tight and tighter still as she moved against him, crushing her breasts into his chest. She could feel his heart racing, or was it her own? It was suddenly impossible to tell. Her arms tightened her hold on him as her hands played across the solid muscles of his back. Then they pulled apart slightly, enough to breathe.

"This is not a good place to be playing with fire," he whispered into her hair.

His words teased at her; his breath tickled. She lay against him, her eyes closed and her heart racing. She needed him with all sorts of yearnings that she'd never felt before, never dreamed of feeling. She tried to think, tried to be rational, but it was impossible. How had this yearning sneaked up on her?

Ever so slowly, her hand crept up to his shirt and unbuttoned a button so that her fingers could slip inside. His chest was warm and slightly damp under the thin matting of hair. She wondered...

His hand closed over hers, stopping her movement. "Casey," he moaned.

She freed her hand and undid another button. There was enough room for her fingers to slide in. She'd never felt so driven, so possessed by a need to touch and feel and explore another's body.

"Is this what you really want?" he groaned, pulling her so tightly against him that she could feel his hardness.

"Yes," she breathed into his lips, into the night and into the thousand explosions of light that hid behind her closed eyes.

She felt him move then, and he swung her up into his arms, carrying her into his room. After placing her on his bed, he lay down beside her. The room was lit only by the pale lights of night coming through the window, but she could see the fire in his eyes, feel his desire in his touch.

She wrapped her arms lightly around him, running her fingers through his short hair, then reaching up to place tiny kisses around his mouth. He groaned in deep, wrenching hunger and caught her lips with his. His passion was untamed, wild and raw and more needful than her heart could take.

His lips brought her fire higher, hotter, and then his hands were under her sweater, hot and demanding against her skin. They unhooked her bra, freeing her breasts for his trembling touch. Every caress, every brush of skin on skin drove her higher into the stars, craving him with an urgency that defied understanding.

She needed to touch him, to feel with her fingertips the fever overtaking them both. She slipped her hands under his shirt, ran them over his chest and felt his heartbeat echoing her own. A tightness reigned in her stomach, a delicious twisting that begged for release.

He helped her pull her sweater over her head, then she helped him get his shirt off. Then it was jeans and underwear amid the touching and holding and tasting. She was hot and hungry and ravenous in her desires. For these few moments she was everything to him and he to her. They needed no other, nothing else.

"Uh, wait a minute," he said, and pulled away to fumble in his nightstand.

"What are you doing?" she asked.

She heard the rustle of paper, though, and knew he was getting a condom. She hadn't even thought about it! Then he moved, coming back to enter her gently, slowly, as if she was fragile. She was too needy to be patient, however, and moved to take him in. Her body surrounded him, clasped him completely.

For a glorious moment in time, they moved as one. Were as one. Their breath, their pulse, their very beings were in total unison. Then, wrapped in each other's arms, they felt their love explode. They raced upward into the heavens, then with slow meandering, came gently back to earth. Casey just sighed, and smiling a tiny smile, cuddled into Mike's arms to fall asleep.

Chapter Nine

Mike moved softly through the mists between sleep and waking, feeling the soft warmth of Casey stretched out beside him. It felt so right and good that he just snuggled deeper into his covers and pushed against her, against her soft, strong body.

Then Gus barked—fierce, angry sounds coming from downstairs that said something was wrong. Somebody was after Casey!

Gus's barking came again—loud rapid-fire yelps that drew Mike into the real world as abruptly as if he'd stepped into a puddle of ice water.

In the pale light of the room, Mike could see Casey stir slightly in her sleep, and he vowed she would be safe. Nothing was going to disturb her or those cats cuddled around her on his bed.

He hurried out from under the covers, grabbing up a pair of jeans as he glanced at the clock—five-thirty—but almost fell over when he tried to shove his foot into them. "Oh, hell,'' he muttered as he threw the jeans across the dark room. They weren't his.

He found another pair—ones that went on a lot easier—and pulled them up as he fumbled in his nightstand for his gun. Then he was out in the hall and down the stairs. Gus was in the living room, by the Christmas tree.

"You'd better not just be barking at the tree," Mike muttered, and carefully checked out the room. No sign of anything, but the faint smell of peppermint was in the air. A burglar with a fresh-breath fetish?

He went over to the front doors, but they were still securely closed. So were all the windows in the dining room, and the kitchen and the kitchen door. There wasn't a single thing that looked amiss.

"This was fun," he told Gus. "What was it—a mouse? A peppermint-stealing mouse?"

But Gus showed no guilt and trotted over to the back door to be let out. "Probably should check around outside, too," Mike agreed, and he slipped into his boots and coat. His gloves were nowhere to be found.

"Surprise, surprise," he muttered. He should just buy the cat a pair of her own.

Once outside, Gus ambled over toward the garage, sniffing along the snow. The sun wasn't due to come up for another couple of hours, but the snow made it bright enough to see easily. Mike stuffed his hands in his jacket pockets, hunched his shoulders and walked slowly around the house. No sign of anything wrong. Another false alarm.

He walked back along the driveway, the snow crunching and squeaking beneath his booted feet. It was cold, damn cold. Probably down close to zero.

Normally Mike enjoyed this predawn time of day, especially in the winter, when everything was so white and quiet you could hear a sparrow sneeze in the park three miles down the road. The air had a pleasant crinkle to it, like Christmas wrapping paper.

Mike stopped and shook his head. A pleasant crinkle?

Like Christmas wrapping paper? Another few days and Casey would have him singing carols at that big shopping mall over in St. Joseph's.

"Oh, man," he muttered. Things had been wonderful last night. Unfortunately, they'd gone too far. Now what was he going to do? "Gus." The first thing he needed to do was get in out of this cold. "Come on, boy. Let's get back in."

But his dog ignored him. Gus had been doing a lot of that lately. Maybe Mike should wake Casey up so she could get the damn dog to come in. He seemed to do whatever she wanted. "Come on, Gus," he snapped.

His dog continued to ignore him. Just what he needed. Mike jammed his fists still farther into his pockets.

No, he wasn't going to wake Casey up. Hell, he'd let himself freeze to death before he did that. She'd wake up soon enough the way it was, and he still hadn't put things together in his mind.

Events had gone astray and he needed to make sense out of them. Figure out a way to make their life as normal as possible for as long as Casey was going to be here. It would be best for all if she didn't stay, but she was in danger. And Mike couldn't exactly go to his great-aunt and say that he'd had sex with her biographer and could she please find the woman someplace else safe to live.

"Gus!" Mike stamped his feet, trying to get some feeling back into them. Damn, it was cold. He stepped off the drive into the deeper snow alongside the garage.

The feeling quickly returned to his feet—the feeling of cold, powdery snow melting on the inside of his boots. "Gus, come on," he called, as he tramped farther into the backyard. "Get in the house."

This time Gus listened and hurried in once the door was open. Mike shed his boots and jacket, then lingered indecisively in the kitchen. He didn't need to get up for work for another hour. Should he go back to bed, spend one more hour lying in Casey's warmth, or just stay down here and not run the risk of waking her up?

Even before he made a decision, his feet were taking him up the stairs. Gus was sprawled out on the bed in Mike's spot. He thought of telling his dog to move, but only for a moment. There was no way he could sleep anymore, and it didn't seem right to lie in Casey's warmth when he still had no idea what he was going to do. After showering and getting dressed for work, he sank into the easy chair in the corner.

Mike didn't know how long he sat there, staring over at Casey sleeping. Long enough for it to get light outside, but not long enough to have put things in order in his mind. And certainly not long enough to figure out what he was going to say to her.

Suddenly he was aware that her eyes were open and she was watching him.

"Hi," she said softly. "What are you doing way over there?"

He shrugged and fought against the invitation in her voice. "I've been up for a while. Gus needed to go out."

She looked over her shoulder at the dog, still sprawled out on the bed. "Looks like he came back." The unasked question hung in the air: *why didn't you?*

"I figured I'd get ready for work."

"Oh. " She glanced at the clock on his nightstand. "What time do you have to leave?"

"In about forty-five minutes." Damn. Why hadn't he lied, said he needed to leave now?

"Great. Enough time for me to take a quick bath and make us some breakfast."

She climbed out of bed, bending down quickly to get her flannel shirt and slip it around her. He caught only fleeting glimpses of her smooth, soft skin. Enough to tantalize him with memories of last night and tease him with promises of tomorrow. His mouth went dry and he couldn't have spoken to save his life.

"I seem to have scattered my stuff all over," she said. "Sorry."

"No problem." Mike swallowed hard and turned his attention to the winter scene outside his bedroom window. He knew it was cold outside, but his heart felt even colder. The starkness of the black-and-white picture couldn't even begin to match the melancholy in his heart.

"Are you sure?" she asked, sounding more and more uncertain with each and every word.

"Sure. Positive." But he kept looking outside.

In a moment, he heard the bath water running and Gus whining at the bathroom door as he tried to get in. Fifteen minutes. That's what it would take her to bathe and get dressed. He had fifteen minutes to figure out what to say.

"Boy," Dubber exclaimed. "What's with Mike? He sure was grumpy."

"I think Gus got him up too early," Casey said, as she put their breakfast dishes into the dishwasher. "And he said he's not a morning person."

"Since when?" Dubber asked. "He's never been grumpy like this except when Darcy dumped him."

Casey didn't want to pursue that line of thinking. There were too many roadblocks that would get her into trouble. Though there really could be only one reason Mike had been so grumpy this morning. And that one reason was last night.

Was Mike regretting their lovemaking? Had he found her lacking in some way? Was he finding that his love for Darcy was still strong?

Whatever the reason, breakfast had been so deadly that Casey'd felt like hugging Dubber when he'd walked through the back door. Instead, she'd just made extra pancakes and fed the lad as Mike left for work.

"Got anything you need help with?" Dubber asked.

A million things, none of which she could discuss with

an eleven-year-old boy. Casey straightened and closed the dishwasher door. "Don't you have school?"

He shook his head. "Christmas vacation," he said. "You're still writing that book, huh?"

"Yes. And it's a whole lot of work," Casey said.

"Oh," Dubber replied, nodding.

"Work that a writer has to do by herself."

"Oh, I gotcha." He nodded again. "I gotta go, anyway. Tiffany wants me to go Christmas shopping with her."

"That could be fun," Casey said.

"Yeah, right." Dubber's expression vacillated between disbelieving and thoughtful as he slipped on his coat and stocking cap. "I'll drop by later and see how Mike is."

"That would be nice," Casey replied.

Once Dubber was gone, she went into the dining room to work, but couldn't seem to concentrate. Her cats followed her, jumping onto the table and lying on her papers, so at least she had an excuse why she couldn't do anything. But the real excuse was that blond, six-foot-something lug that was driving Michigan State Police car number 9348.

How did he feel about last night? How did she feel?

It had been great. Wonderful. Not what she had planned. Did she regret it? No. It had been perfect. Mike had been perfect. She hadn't been looking for involvement—and still wasn't—but she wouldn't change a second of it.

But Mike obviously didn't share her opinion, and they needed to clear the air when he got home. She still had at least a month's work here before the book was done. They couldn't have a month's worth of breakfasts like this morning's.

The cats moved off her papers suddenly, streaking after something only they saw, and she got down to work. In spite of her impending talk with Mike, she got a lot done on the history. She found a whole stack of letters from Stella's younger brother, Robert, the one she and Simon raised, which he must have written while he'd been away at school. From the neat penmanship of a teen commiserating on Stella's miscarriage, to the more mature hand of a college student anxious to come home for Christmas, the letters proved to be a wealth of family information. That must have been Stella's third miscarriage. How terrible for her, to be married to a man who loved another and unable to have a child of her own.

Casey was surprised when she heard Mike at the kitchen door. Surprised and suddenly a little panicky. It was almost five. Where had the day gone? She hurried into the other room before he had a chance to take his coat off or take Gus out.

"I thought we could go for a walk," she told him.

"We?" he said.

"Yeah." Casey smiled. "Gus, you and me. The three of us."

He looked as though he wanted to refuse, but didn't. She got her coat and followed him outside. Without a word, they started down the street. Mike had a leash for Gus, but didn't put it on as the dog stayed close to them, romping in the snow and picking up a white layer of it on the top of his nose.

Casey walked silently by Mike's side, not holding his hand though she desperately wanted to. Maybe it was a need to know that he hadn't found her lacking. Or maybe it was just her racing heart needing his touch. When he hadn't spoken after the first few blocks, she decided she'd better make the first move.

"We need to talk about last night," she said.

"I know." His voice was stiff, as if he'd placed a wall around himself. "Look, I'm sorry. Thing's just happened and—"

She nodded. "I hadn't planned it."

He didn't look her way. "No, it didn't 'just happen,'" he said, as if she hadn't spoken. "That makes it sound like we had no responsibility for it. I knew what we were doing and—"

"Mike, we're both adults." She touched his arm lightly,

trying to force his eyes to meet hers. This was harder than she'd expected. "We both knew what we were doing."

"And about those condoms," he continued as they crossed a street. "They'd been in the drawer for a while now. I didn't just get them...." He looked at her a moment before his gaze skittered off again. "I mean I wasn't planning on—"

"Mike," she said softly. "It's okay."

He looked at her then. "I'm not the type of guy who's always looking to get laid. I don't want you to think that's all it was."

"I think I had too much wine," she said, and dragged a mittened hand through the snow on the top rail of a fence. "And I know I acted goofy about the mistletoe...."

"No, it was nice," he said. She could almost hear a smile in his voice. "Cute. And you made me look at those ornaments for the first time in years. I'd been almost afraid to before."

They reached the end of the fence and she brushed her mitten off on her coat. "I can understand that. There are a lot of memories attached to them."

"But memories can be good things," he said. "Things to cherish, not run from."

She took a deep breath, then jumped in headfirst. "Did last night make you think about Darcy?" she asked. "It's okay if it did. It'd be only normal, I suppose. I just wondered."

He stopped walking to stare at her. "Darcy? Why would it remind me of Darcy?"

Casey could feel her cheeks grow red—the curse of being a redhead. "Well, you know. You loved her and then we were making love." Were they? "Or having sex."

He just shook his head slowly. "I can honestly say Darcy never came into my mind last night."

"I just thought maybe you were comparing..." No, that was coming out badly. "That you were wishing it was her."

He took Casey's hands in his, and even through her mittens, she felt warm. "I never wished it was anybody but you," he said. "It was wonderful."

Her cheeks got redder, if possible. "I thought so, too."

"I'm sorry it happened," he said. "But in another way, I'm not."

"I'm not sorry at all," she said. "And I don't want us to stop being friends."

"I don't want to stop, either," he replied.

"Deal then?"

"Sure."

They sealed it with a kiss. Not a passionate one that would send steam out from under their coats to melt the nearby snow, but one that lasted long enough to leave them glassy-eyed and gasping not for air but for sanity. They pulled apart when Gus started pawing at them.

"I guess he wants to go home," Mike said.

"That's okay by me," she replied. "It's pretty cold out here."

They turned around and went back to the house, holding hands. Yeah, maybe the weather was cold, but she sure wasn't. Not when her heart was singing the way it was.

After dinner Mike sought refuge in the garage. He needed time to think and sort things out. They'd made love, and Casey was all right about it. She wasn't mad or regretful or looking to tie him down. How did he really feel about it, though?

Casey found him there before he'd had time to answer any of his questions. "Boy, you're getting this place put back together," she said, her arms crossed and her hands tucked under her armpits from the cold. "Wouldn't it be smarter to wait until summer to do this, though?"

"It's not so bad out here." Certainly not when she was here to steam up the room. His eyes wanted to watch her, to count the number of times she smiled at him, but he forced his attention back to soldering the new section of water pipe running along the garage ceiling.

She came closer, leaning against the ladder. Not directly filling his line of sight, but he could see her even if he closed his eyes.

"Where's Gus?" she asked.

"The heat's on up in the apartment," he replied, indicating the room above them with his head. "He's sacked out where it's warm."

"Smart dog."

"More like lazy," Mike muttered. She wasn't affecting him much at all. He could—

"Boy." She brushed off the dust and dirt that had fallen from the ceiling onto his leg. "You're really mean to him."

A fire exploded inside him. So much for not being affected. "I knew you'd take his side." His voice sounded as strangled as his heart felt.

"Why not?" Casey replied. "Gus is a big sweetie pie."

"And what am I?" Mike reached up to wipe off the pipe. It was a stupid question, a childish one, but it came out, anyway.

"You're big, too."

"Thanks."

She leaned back against the ladder—and him—and laughed. It was suddenly steamy in here. Even in the cold of the unheated garage, he felt sweat on his brow.

"You know, it's a little hard to work with you hanging on to me."

Casey stepped back, leaning against the wall. "What are you doing, anyway?"

He hadn't really wanted her to move, but took advantage of her distance to breathe. "Replacing the section of water pipe that had frozen and burst."

"Won't that happen again?"

"No, not after I'm done with it." He held up the thick cable that was lying on top of the ladder. "This is a heater cable. It puts out a low-grade heat. Enough to keep the pipe from freezing, especially since I'm going to insulate it next."

She waited in silence while he climbed down and put his soldering equipment away. "Why are you doing all this?" she asked in a little voice of worry. "Are you going to kick me out of the house?"

He looked at her in surprise. Was she serious? Her green eyes weren't dancing. "Of course not," he said. "But there are a lot of students from the college that want a place off campus. If I fix the place up and clean it, I shouldn't have any trouble renting it."

"Have you talked to Myrna about this?"

Mike put the last of the equipment away. "She said to do what I wanted. She doesn't care."

"About the house or about renting the apartment?"

He went back up the ladder to wrap the heating cable around the pipe. Casey came over to hold the end as he wrapped. "She doesn't care if I rent the apartment, but she's hyper about the house. She's got a thing about how her family built it and nobody outside of the family has ever owned it."

Casey didn't reply to that as he climbed back down the ladder. He didn't know whether it was his memory or just the force of her body, but he could see her womanly shape even in the bulky down coat she was wearing. Or maybe it was just those green eyes. More woman than a man deserved.

He definitely needed to get his mind onto something else. A garage in the winter was definitely not a place for love and romance. "By next week, I should be able to start cleaning up upstairs."

"I can help."

He moved the ladder about eight feet and climbed back up. "You don't have to. Mostly I'll just be hauling trash at first."

"I can do that."

"You're not here to clean. You're here to write Aunt Myrna's history."

"I could do both."

"Doesn't sound like efficient use of your time," he said, and came down to move the ladder again. "I'm sure you have better things to do than clean an old apartment."

He moved it under the last section of pipe, then climbed back up to wrap the end of the cable around the end of the pipe. When he glanced down at her, her wonderful green eyes looked all uncertain and worried. Damn. She was leaving soon. He couldn't forget that, and neither should she. But when she looked at him that way...

"You know what I'm thinking about?" he asked as he climbed down the ladder.

She was just watching him, her soft, full lips partially open. It seemed so natural to kiss her. So he did. And again. Then still again.

"Umm," she murmured, and lay against his chest. "I like the way you think."

"Actually, I was thinking how great a hot cup of chocolate would taste about now."

She sighed.

"Hey," he said. "Us guys like chocolate."

"In the house or out here?"

"I think it would be much more comfortable in the house."

"Umm." She looked around the garage. "Are you done in here?"

"There's always tomorrow," he replied, kissing her.

And then he kissed her again before she slipped out of his embrace and hurried out the door.

"I'll clean up out here and then come in," he called after her.

"Don't be too long."

He stared after her as she walked across the yard. Even wearing jeans, a bulky jacket and boots, she could raise his temperature to the boiling point. Maybe he needed to roll around in a snowbank before he went inside.

A soft clicking on the bare wooden stairs told him that Gus was awake and coming down.

"Good thing she's not going to be here too much longer," Mike told his dog. "A woman like that can get to be a habit."

"Everything's been digitized," the librarian said. "And you can do a search by name or date."

"Wow!" Casey said, and meant it. The library at Andrews University here in town was far better than she'd expected.

"Isn't it great? We got a grant a few years back for some computer-science students to enter all the back issues of the *Herald Palladium.* We are really lucky."

"I'll say," Casey said. "This is going to make my job a whole lot easier."

"And you can make copies of anything you find," the librarian said. "Just put a dime in the slot here."

In the past Casey had spent days going through microfilm copies of old newspapers and had expected to do so here, also. Of course, all this progress had a downside, too. The faster she was done with her research, the sooner the job would be over and the sooner she'd be gone.

She tried telling herself that it would be good to get home, but her heart didn't seem to believe it. Things had been going so well with Mike for the last few days; it was hard to imagine just walking away from it all.

Best not to think about it then, she told herself, and got down to work. She searched the back issues of the newspaper for the name Van Horne and was overwhelmed with data. Articles and articles in which they were mentioned, giving her a unique sense of what life was like back in the early part of the century. Photos of Simon and his brother at all different kinds of community events; each of them separately at family affairs. She discovered that Simon had loved peppermint and that Stella had founded the local garden club. Casey followed through with searches for

Simon's brother's children and then for Stella, her brother and her brother's children.

Casey spent hours poring over the computer screen, delving even further into the lives of the family. There were just too many articles and too much information to figure out what was important and what wasn't. She began making copies of everything, slipping dimes into the slot until she had a thick stack of printouts. When she went to get change from yet another dollar bill, a slip of paper fell from her wallet. It was her clipping from the *South Bend Tribune* about her abandonment. She frowned at it for a long time, then thought, *Why not?* She'd found lots of articles about Benton Harbor in this paper. Grabbing up her change, she went back to the computer.

She told it to search for abandoned babies, in Benton Harbor and in the year after her birth. It would find one similar to the one in her wallet, she told herself. And maybe a follow-up one when she'd been placed in foster care. Why was she even doing this?

That was a good question, she thought as she watched the machine whir through its search. Why *was* she doing this? Was she looking for pain? No, she didn't think so. Maybe she was feeling strong and ready to handle whatever came up.

What came up was a slew of articles. Maybe there'd been more abandoned babies at that time beside her, she thought as she flipped through the articles. Then stopped. The headline screamed out at her: Mother Charged with Child Endangerment.

It was her mother, Casey realized as she read, dumbfounded. They had found her. Two weeks after she'd abandoned Casey in that church basement, they'd found her, when she'd had to seek medical attention. Rosemarie Widdington. She'd been sixteen and looked about fourteen in the photo.

Casey tried to read Rosemarie's eyes, tried to see something in them that said she was scared or sorry or anything, but what could you see in a lousy newspaper photo that had been digitized and further blurred? She just looked sullen and slightly defiant.

Casey sat back with a sigh. She stared at the screen for one more moment, then hit the button to kill the search. She didn't need to read any more. But the image of her mother's face didn't disappear when the screen cleared. It continued to dance in Casey's mind.

Her mother. She had a face now and a name. Did it make it easier or harder?

It made it time to leave, Casey decided, and she gathered up her stuff. She wanted to be home all of a sudden, then stopped with a quick laugh. No, it wasn't home. It was Mike's house—silly mistake to make. But that was where she wanted to be, someplace she felt safe and able to think.

It was later than she'd thought, she realized as she hurried out to the car, and she hadn't even thought about dinner. Well, she'd see what was in the fridge and whip something up. If she hurried, she'd have time to bake some quick bread in the bread machine.

The animals were all waiting for her when she got in. She let Gus out and refilled the cats' dry food before checking out the refrigerator. There were lots of ingredients, but no ideas popped into her head. She flicked on the kitchen TV as she let Gus back in, then pulled a cookbook off the shelf.

"There's got to be an idea in here someplace," she said, as voices from some talk show or other filled the kitchen. "Do we have flank steak? Do we have chicken tenderloins? I don't think so. It looks like I'm going to have to go to the store if I want something edible."

She picked up the remote control, but before she could turn off the set, the regular program was interrupted by a news flash—images of men milling about, smashed up cars and a police car upside down on a snowy country road. Her breath caught.

The announcer's voice seemed to fill the room, but made

little sense. "High speed chase...police from various departments...a serious accident off the interstate...state police..."

The words were a blur as Casey stared at the TV. It showed a dark blue police car lying in the road. A Michigan State Police cruiser. Fear clutched at her stomach, stealing her breath away.

Don't let it be Mike. Don't let it be Mike.

The camera panned back to the disabled car again. Number 9348. Her heart stopped. Mike's car.

Chapter Ten

"Oh, Gus, it can't be him," Casey said, hugging the dog to her and trying to keep back the tears. "Mike will be fine. He has to be."

But her assurances couldn't stem the flow from her eyes. She looked around for a tissue, settling for a paper towel.

"Don't you worry none," she said, after blowing her nose. "That big lug of a guy will come through that door in a couple of hours. And the first thing he'll say is what's for dinner? You just wait and see."

She went into the living room, though, turning on the larger television, as if the bigger screen would contain more information, then sat on the floor with Gus on one side and her cats climbing into her lap. The Christmas tree was a silent reminder of the joy they'd shared, and she tried hard not to let it into her line of vision, but it didn't matter. The smell of pine was enough to bring Mike into the room.

On the TV screen, images of ambulances and emergency crews now danced. No one said anything about Mike being hurt, but then they didn't immediately give names in situations like this, did they? Didn't they wait until the next of kin had been notified?

And who would that be? His father? Mrs. Jamison? Certainly not herself. Casey wouldn't learn anything until they announced it to the public.

She could feel the fear build up in her body, coming out not as a shiver but as a good old-fashioned case of the shakes.

Oh, God. Please don't let Mike be hurt.

Gus woofed sharply and ran from her to the back door. For a moment Casey danced with hope, but then quickly came back to earth and followed Gus out to the kitchen. It wouldn't be Mike. Gus never barked when Mike came home.

Casey took a deep breath and opened the door. It was an older woman she'd met at the Pickle Festival.

"I'm Dorothea Kinder," she said, putting a plate of Christmas cookies into Casey's hand. "I just heard the news."

Casey stared down at the little green Christmas-tree cookies and then back up at Mrs. Kinder, who was coming into the house. "Thank you—"

"I don't supposed there's been any further word," she said. "All I saw was Mike's car on the news."

Casey just shook her head. "That's all I saw, too."

"You have the TV on?" She peered around the room, then nodded. "Good, we'll know as soon as there's something to know. Oh, what pretty little pussycats." She petted the cats, then frowned at Casey. "Tea. That's what we need, a nice cup of tea. You just sit down and I'll make us some."

"You don't have to—"

There was another knock at the door, but Mrs. Kinder just shooed Casey over to the kitchen table as the cats fled for upstairs. "Sit. Sit. Sit," the older woman said. "We'll take care of everything."

Casey was about to ask who the "we" was, but soon
found out. Mrs. Kinder opened the back door to two other
ladies, both carrying casseroles—which Mrs. Kinder put in
the refrigerator—and offering pats on the back and hugs to
Casey.

"He'll be all right, you'll see."

"He's such a strong young man. Takes more than a car
wreck to stop him."

An elderly man came in with a basket of apples. "Have
you eaten?" he asked. "You need to keep up your
strength."

"She's having tea first," Mrs. Kinder said, pushing a
steaming mug into Casey's hands before peering at the old
man's apples. "These look delicious, Theo. Perhaps we'll
slice some up for nibbling."

"Good idea." He nodded, then looked at Casey. "Where
are the knives? No, don't you bother. I'll find them."

Gus came over to sit half under Casey's chair as people
streamed into the house. Stan from the Daybreak Café came
over with a pot of chili. Chuck from the hardware store
brought a coffee urn and paper cups. Mrs. Randall was
there with a ham and someone else brought a gelatin salad.

The news was rerolling the footage from before, showing
the accident scene, and everyone stopped talking for a long
horrible minute. The cameras seemed frozen on the over-
turned police car.

"My Margie's cousin's brother walked away from a
wreck way worse than that," someone said.

"And Mike, he'd be wearing his seat belt."

"Sure, seat belts stop everything."

"Along with air bags."

"Right, those cop cars got air bags."

But the assurances just rolled right off her like rain off
a slicker. Now that fear had taken hold of her heart, it
wasn't letting go. Casey had seen his police car. How could
he be all right? There was no way he could be. Everyone
was fooling her, fooling themselves.

Someone else came in. Casey heard Mrs. Kinder fussing about a casserole, but Casey's eyes were glued to the TV set. How long did it take for them to name names?

"Casey?"

She turned. Darcy had pulled a chair up next to her. The other woman's eyes were shadowed, as if she knew some terrible secret.

"Have you heard something?" Casey asked.

Darcy just shook her head. "About the accident? No. But how are you?"

What kind of a question was that? Casey wasn't the one in the accident. "I'm fine," she said. "Why wouldn't I be?"

The phone rang and Casey started, clutching her hands together. But she couldn't move to answer it. What if it was bad news?

"Shall I get it, dear?" Mrs. Kinder asked, and picked up the receiver. It must have been another neighbor, for the old woman just repeated the little bit of news they all had.

"You see what it's like," Darcy said softly. "You know now, don't you? The waiting, the awful waiting."

Casey just turned slowly toward the other woman, taking in her pale skin, the worried eyes, the unsteady breath, and knew it was all a reflection of herself.

"You love him," Darcy continued, almost too quietly to be heard. "I can see it in every terrified inch of you."

"That's crazy," Casey said. "I'm worried, yes, but we all are."

"Your worry is different."

"No, it's not. He's just a friend," Casey insisted.

"Sure." Darcy got to her feet, then reached over for Casey's hand. "Just remember the fear never ends. It'll be there every time he goes out the door."

"As it is for every friend," Casey said.

Darcy just gave her a searching look, then went over to the coffee urn Chuck had brought in and began passing around filled cups. Casey watched her for a moment, then turned her gaze back to the television. No matter wha Darcy thought, she was wrong. Casey cared about Mike sure. But she wasn't in love with him. He was a friend. confidant. A buddy.

A hand fell on her shoulder. "Casey?" It was Dubbe "There ain't no need to worry, Casey."

Casey just hugged him. "I'm fine, honey. I really am.'

Dubber's face turned bright red, but he stood his ground "We're gonna find out what's going on."

"I'm sure one of the stations will report something new soon."

"Nah, reporters don't know nothing," Dubber said dis missively. "We're getting a scanner. A police scanner. Ti fany's pulling the one out of her father's car."

Even as he spoke there was a sharp, insistent banging o the back door, as if someone was kicking it. Dubber opene it and Tiffany strode in, carrying an electronic-lookin black box with wires hanging out of it.

"What took you so long?" Dubber scolded as he fol lowed along.

"It was a built-in kind," Tiffany replied. "So I had t get a battery. It's sitting on the sled outside."

Dubber hurried outside while Tiffany put the box on th counter, then began emptying her coat pockets of wires an electrical clips.

Dubber staggered in, carrying a black box that looke like—

"Tiffany," Casey said. "Did you take the battery out o your father's car?"

"Uh-huh." The girl helped Dubber place the battery on the countertop next to the scanner. "This thing only work on DC power."

"Isn't he going to be mad when he finds out what yo did?"

"Yeah, I guess." Tiffany slipped off her boots and bus ied herself with attaching the scanner to the car battery "But a woman's gotta do what a woman's gotta do."

She fiddled for a few tense moments, then stepped back. "There. It's all hooked up."

Some people had drifted in from the other rooms, and now all waited for information to come spewing out of the scanner. But all the unit did was squawk, putting out an uninterrupted stream of static.

"It needs an aerial," Dubber said. "Casey, got some coat hangers?"

"Upstairs."

Tiffany smiled after Dubber, then turned to Casey. "That's the thing I really like best about my guy," the girl said. "He's not just a pretty face. He's smart, too."

Dubber was back quickly, and after a few minutes of fiddling, he and Tiffany were able to reduce the static to intermittent bursts. Casey didn't find the words any more intelligible than the static had been. Most of the talk consisted of numbers, almost all preceded by a ten, and other code words.

"What's going on?" she finally asked.

Tiffany began translating. "Bank robbery in Dowagiac," she said.

"Policeman shot there," Dubber added.

"Three robbers escaped in a pickup."

"Going west."

"Heading for the interstate to Detroit."

"Local police joined in the chase."

"Perps tried to run a police blockade."

"Got caught."

"Three perps injured."

"And some cops." Dubber just looked up at Casey. "No names released yet."

"Man, oh, man," Mike exclaimed, shaking his head. "Those mutts sure made a mess of my cruiser."

"Just be glad you got out before they hit you," his sergeant replied.

The cops had been chasing the perps all over the back

roads of Berrien County, but they'd been so familiar with the roads it had been impossible to set up any effective roadblocks.

Mike had been afraid that the jerks would take out a school bus or a civilian, so, when they got close to the Christmas-tree farm, he'd cut across it, using the farm's series of private roads. Luck had been with him, and he'd popped out on the county road less than a minute before the perps'd come roaring down in their monster truck. Mike had heard the truck before he saw it and had parked his cruiser across the little, two-lane blacktop before diving into the ditch. The driver of the getaway vehicle hadn't seen the cruiser until he came around the curve, and by then it'd been too late. They'd slammed into his car, sending it rolling while they did an end over end. The capture hadn't been a problem then.

In a matter of minutes, the area had been filled with police officers, emergency crews and a zillion reporters. The crash had been spectacular, and lots of pictures—still and video—were being taken of his vehicle and the getaway truck. Mike was only too happy to deal with the perps, getting them under restraint and arranging for their secured transport to a local hospital, while others dealt with the media. He'd had enough of that last year after he'd rescued the kids.

"How'd we do?" Mike asked.

His sergeant shrugged. "Could've been worse. Garvey from Dowagiac should be released tonight. Bullet just grazed his arm. Manning'll be out a little longer. He spun out on some ice on a curve and wrapped himself around a big tree."

Mike winced. "How bad?"

"Stable," the sergeant answered. "He's in surgery now."

Mike shook his head. "Damn. Him and Colleen just had a baby last month. This is going to be really hard on her."

"Comes with the territory," the sergeant growled.

Mike knew that, but during times like this he was happy he was single. He could handle his own hurts, but he sure as hell didn't want to dump them on anyone else.

"You got a ride home?"

"Yeah," Mike replied. "Ed's taking me."

"Good." The sergeant grunted. "Guess you're back on vacation for a few days. We'll try and get you a new cruiser by early next week."

"That's fine."

After a quick wave, the officer stomped off toward his own car, shoulders slumping. Mike was glad to stay behind. All he had to do was get the mess cleared off the road. Just broken cars, not wrecked bodies or wrecked lives.

At times like this he knew it'd been right to let things between him and Darcy wither and die. Poor kid had been a basket case by the time she'd been delivered to the hospital that was patching him up after he'd pulled those kids from a burning car. Mike hadn't even been hurt all that much—a little bit of ointment, some bandages, some rest and he'd been as good as new.

Hell, if he'd been really hurt who knew what might have happened. She could have gone off the deep end, and he knew he wouldn't have been able to live with that. Going the trail alone was a bit lonely at times, but loneliness was better than carrying a basketful of guilt.

"All set to roll?"

Mike started slightly at Ed Kramer's words. "Yeah, I'm ready."

"Want to go say goodbye to your cruiser?" Ed asked.

"Sure."

They walked through the packed snow over to the scene, where several news cameramen were still milling about, but the two of them stayed back out of the cameras' range. Mike's cruiser had already been flipped back on its wheels and was getting readied for hauling to the police impoundment lot.

"Wow," Ed exclaimed.

Mike just shook his head. Totaled didn't even come close to describing the condition of his car. The whole left side was so pushed in that the car looked like a slice of toast, and rolling over in the ice and mud a few times hadn't improved its appearance any. It didn't look like the wrecker would even be able to scavenge parts out of it.

"Boy," Ed said with a laugh. "And you don't have a scratch on you."

"Helps not to have been in the thing when it got hit."

"Yeah, better to be lucky than smart."

"Amen," Mike replied.

They stood watching as the pile of metal was loaded on a wrecker van, then Ed tapped him on the arm. "Come on, sport. Time to go home."

Neither spoke much on the ride back to Berrien Springs. For Mike, it was a time to unwind and catch his breath. The day had been wild, hectic, and he was looking forward to a quiet evening.

He'd tell Casey about the chase over dinner. She'd get a kick out it, especially when he admitted that going to get the Christmas tree at that tree farm had made the difference. If he hadn't driven around their private roads that day, he would never have known how to cut those perps off. Of course, by telling her, he was running the risk of never hearing the end of it, but he thought it would be worth it.

"Looks like you have company," Ed said as he turned onto Mike's street. Cars were spilling out of his drive and down the street on either side of his house.

"Who the..." Mike stopped. Chuck Freeman's van was there and so was Stan Kovac's car. It was neighbors and folks from town. "What are they all doing here?"

Ed shrugged. "They were probably worried about Casey."

"Why?"

"Your car was totaled and you're asking why? Probably half the town is planning your funeral."

"But I wasn't interviewed. Nobody mentioned my name.

Why'd they all assume I was involved? It could've been any state cop."

"Maybe the cameras caught your car number."

"Yeah, but..." Hell, this shouldn't have happened. There was no reason for it to. He'd been doing his job and had been in no more danger than a bunch of other cops, less than some. Now Casey was probably a basket case with worry.

Ed pulled into the driveway and people started spilling out of the house, lining the driveway and filling the yard.

"You should've left your gumballs off," Mike growled. The car's mars lights were splashing the snow-covered ground with spots of red and blue. "Everybody's probably thinking you've come to announce the bad news."

"Just bringing the hero home."

"I was doing my job," Mike snapped. "Like any other cop would have."

"Sure."

Mike stepped out of the car and into a chorus of cheers from his neighbors. He shook the hands extended toward him and murmured thanks, while all the time his eyes searched the crowd. Where was Casey?

"Daddy." Tiffany jumped into Ed's arms, then slipped back to the ground. "I can put the scanner back real easy, but I'll need your help with the battery. It's really, really heavy."

Mike looked questioningly at Ed, but the big burly cop just shook his head. "I never ask," he said. "It's a lot easier on my nerves if I don't know."

Mike just smiled, then went on searching the crowd for Casey. Where was she? She wouldn't have left, would she? A cold hand of fear clutched at his stomach. That wouldn't make any sense. She wouldn't just up and go without telling him. Unless, of course, everybody coming over here had made her so worried that she couldn't take it.

He continued to smile and receive well wishes from his neighbors, but his heart felt frozen.

* * *

From the living-room window, Casey watched Mike get out of Ed Kramer's car, trying to keep tears of relief from her eyes. That would be a great way to welcome Mike home—rush to his arms in tears. Boy, if there was anything destined to end this relationship in a split second it would be that. And the last thing Casey wanted to do was end the relationship.

It was a disheartening realization. Casey knew it as clear as day the minute Mike had stepped out of the police car: she was in love with him. She hadn't planned it, didn't want it, but facts were facts. She was in love.

She wanted to run out and make sure he was fine. She wanted to get him in the house and ask him what the hell had happened to his car. She wanted to scold him, to hold him, to shake some sense into his macho body. She wanted lots of things, but knew that she couldn't get any of them. Not if she showed the slightest hint of having been worried.

She steadied her heart and took a deep breath as she put Gus's leash on. "What do you say, Gus? Ready to go out?"

Gus had been ready for ages. It was Casey who had been dragging her heels, but he politely refrained from pointing that out. She tugged open the front door and was waiting when Mike got to the front steps. He looked so good, so unaffected that she wanted to cry again. But then his gaze stopped on her and she saw the light of gladness in his eyes. She forced herself to be bright and cheery.

"Hi," she said. "Heard you had an exciting day."

"I guess." He grinned before bending down to pet Gus. He scratched the dog's head for a moment, then looked back up at Casey. "I thought maybe you'd be gone."

"Gone? Gone where?"

"Home."

There'd been a tremor in his voice, some emotion she couldn't quite name, but it touched a spot deep in her soul. She just shook her head and fought against the tears again. She could do it. She had to do it.

"And leave Gus here with this mob?" She smiled at Mike as she waved to the people watching them. "They would have smothered him with their worrying."

His lips smiled at her, but his eyes took on a shadow. "How are you?" he asked.

"Gracious, I'm fine," she assured him.

Her arms ached to touch him, her lips begged to brush his, but she just kept her smile bright and her voice cheery.

"Got lots done at the library today," she added.

Suddenly she thought of her last discovery—her mother's name—and wondered just when in the afternoon it had become so unimportant. She'd forgotten all about it. And it could stay forgotten, she realized.

"And how are you?" she asked.

"Fine," he said. "Car's not so good, but I'm fine."

"When you gonna kiss her?" someone called out.

"Yeah, let's see a real welcome."

Casey managed to smile at everyone. Her definition of heaven would be to be in Mike's arms right now, but not as a joke. Her emotions had walked a tightrope all afternoon and were starting to wobble pretty badly. She wasn't sure what even his slightest touch would do.

"Come on, everybody," she said. "Give Mike a break. He's tired."

"Too tired to kiss a pretty girl?"

"No man's ever that tired."

"No real man."

Mike's eyes took on a dangerous twinkle. "They're getting unruly," he said, moving a step closer. "This could get ugly."

She tried to play along. "We must do whatever's necessary to preserve the peace."

"That's my sworn duty."

He reached out for her and she came into his arms. She couldn't help herself. All the worry that had been piling up all evening came rushing out in her kiss. She clung to him, afraid to let him go. She needed to tell him she was so glad he was safe. That she never wanted him to be in danger again. That she couldn't have borne it if something had happened to him.

But she couldn't say any of it in words—he wouldn't let her—so it all came out in her kiss. In the demands of her lips and the hunger of her touch. Her arms held him close; her heart pulled him closer still. She wanted to hold him completely, to keep him safe within her so that she never stared that fear in the face again.

But then a noise reached her, a movement off to her side stirred the realization that they weren't alone. She pulled back from him slowly, trying hard not to gasp for breath or let her knees give out. After a moment, she was able to turn to the crowd around them and smile.

"Well, are you all satisfied?"

"I bet Mike ain't," someone called out.

"Takes more'n that to satisfy a man."

"A real man, that is."

Casey felt her cheeks begin to flush, but she held her smile firmly in place. She absolutely refused to look at Mike.

"Let's get inside before we freeze to death," she said. "We can make a start on all the food."

"Oh, not me," someone said.

"I've got to see to the family."

"It's my bowling night."

One by one, they trickled off to their cars or walked down the street to their houses.

"Boy, I sure know how to clear a room, don't I?" Casey said.

Mike just watched her, almost holding his breath for her real thoughts to come out now that everyone was gone. She just went on into the kitchen. He followed slowly.

"You know, it's almost funny," she said. "I was just sitting here, trying to figure out what to have for dinner, when Mrs. Kinder came over, and then half the town, I think. And they all brought food. We have enough casseroles and salads to last through New Year's.''

"How'd they all know?" he asked, sitting on the edge of the kitchen table.

She shrugged and pulled open the refrigerator. "It was all over the TV. What do you have a taste for—chicken or tuna casserole?"

"I don't care. Chicken's fine."

"Sounds good." She put the casserole on the counter. "I'm sure it's still on the news, if you want to see it."

"Not really."

She made a face. "Me, neither. Been there, done that," she added with a laugh.

"Was my name mentioned?"

"Nope. They showed your car." She put the casserole into the microwave and fiddled with the settings. "I guess your car number showed up—3984?"

"Nope—9348."

"Whatever."

She seemed a touch hyper, he thought, but it didn't have to mean anything. It certainly didn't have to mean she'd been worried. Maybe she got hyper around crowds. Or over chicken casserole.

"Want me to set the table?" He got up and walked over to the silverware drawer.

"You don't—" She turned and bumped right into him. "Oops."

But then she looked up at him and he looked down into those green eyes and she was in his arms. His lips came down on hers and spring burst out all around them. The tensions of his day disappeared. The fears, the hecticness, the surges of adrenaline—they all vanished in the blink of an eye. In the touch of her lips.

He could feel her peace flow over him, washing away the hard edge from his job even as a slow fire began to spark inside him. He pulled her closer to him. Closer and closer and closer still as his mouth drew hungry breaths from hers.

She kissed him back with a fervor that surprised him, but just for a moment. That fire grew, engulfing all rational thought, all power to think. Her lips were all he knew. The softness of her pressed against him was all he felt. The sound of her heart pounding in time with his was all he wanted.

Then the microwave buzzed.

They pulled apart slowly, reluctantly. The air was charged with their passion. The slightest movement, the merest touch would ignite it.

The stupid buzzer kept ringing.

"I guess it's time to eat," Casey said with a trembling laugh.

"I'd better get the table set."

While she took the casserole from the microwave, he pulled silverware from the drawer, dropping the forks like a klutzy junior-high kid on his first date.

"You okay?" she asked him.

No, he was burning with a fever that was of her making. "I'm fine," he said. "Just coming off my adrenaline high. Makes me a little light-headed." He thought that sounded pretty good. Better than that he was horny.

She looked concerned, though. "Maybe you should sit down. I can set the table."

"I'm fine. Honest." He got clean forks out without dropping them and carefully set the table. "See? No need to trade me in yet."

"I wasn't going to."

She must have bought his explanation, for she just busied herself getting the casserole and some salad on the table. She even let him make tea for the two of them and carry the mugs over. Then they sat down to eat.

"I really had a great day," she told him over dinner. "I've got some pictures of the family from old newspapers. Not the greatest quality, of course, but really interesting."

"Oh yeah?"

He kept waiting for her to really relax, to talk about her fears, but she didn't. She did talk practically nonstop, but all about Simon and Stella and the garden club she'd started and his fondness for peppermint.

After dinner she showed him all the new pictures and articles and pages of notes that she'd gathered from the newspaper. Stella. Robert. Joseph. The names meant little or nothing to him, but the sound of her voice was hypnotic. And her hands, touching the papers, awoke that slow flame again. He could imagine them on him, touching him and—

"I think Gus needs to go out," Mike said.

Casey looked startled, then looked over at Gus sprawled out on the sofa asleep. "He does?"

"Yeah," Mike said, and backed away from her a step. "We always go out at this time." He glanced at the clock. "At 7:48."

"Since when?"

"Since always. Gus, time to go out."

Gus responded with enthusiasm and Mike fled outside. He needed space to breathe, cold air to cool his ardor and something to occupy his hands if not his head. They could only play ball so long, but there was always that garage apartment, and Monday was garbage day.

So while Gus slept in the garage apartment, Mike spent the next few hours hauling trash out to the curb. Through the dining-room window when he passed, he could see Casey working on her laptop computer. Each time he saw her hand run slowly through her hair, saw her bite her lips as she worked, his own breath caught and the fever returned. And more trash got hauled.

Boxes of junk, old lamps, bags of garbage. An old stuffed chair that looked as though it had been a home for mice. Old curtains. Surely, she had to quit working soon. It was getting late.

A stack of yellowed newspapers. Some water-stained old books. Rusty paint cans. Dried paintbrushes. A ladder missing half its rungs. Finally the dining-room light went out.

At last. He carried out an old bed frame, just to be sure,

then roused Gus and crept back into the house. The first floor was silent and he could hear the faint creaks of some-one moving around on the second floor.

"Guess we can call it a night," he told Gus, and went up the stairs.

A light shone out from under Casey's bedroom door, but he was sure she was settling down for the night. He breathed a sigh of relief as he went into his own room.

This was crazy, almost unbelievable. He'd been so wor-ried about Casey's reaction to his day, but he was the one who ended up with the problem. She'd been fine. He'd been the one craving the soothing and solace.

He sat on the bed and took off one shoe, tossing it toward the closet. His aim was off. Rather than fall on the rug with a soft thud, it took a crazy turn and hit the closet door, making enough racket to wake up Dubber's household.

A few seconds later, his bedroom door burst open and slammed against the wall. "Mike?" Casey asked. "Are you okay? I heard a noise."

She was in her flannel nightgown and her thick socks, and looked so sexy it took his breath away. She'd spoken, he knew she had, but for the life of him he couldn't figure out what the words had been.

"Are you okay?" she repeated.

"Uh, yeah." He forced a coherency into his head. "It was just my shoe. Though I may need a new wall. You always enter rooms that way?"

"It kind of flew open," she said with a grin.

His heart reacted to her smile like it had been shocked into double time. "Kind of?" He would just sit here and the reaction would pass. Or he could go haul more trash, though he might have to borrow some. That apartment was pretty well cleaned out.

"I think Simon helped." She came farther into the room.

"Simon was worried, too?"

"Well, you said you got light-headed after being in a chase. I was afraid you'd keeled over."

"I'm fine." Except that she was too close and coming closer. If she would just leave...

"Are you sure?" She stopped in front of him. "You look kind of funny."

He had to get her to go. "Melvin keel over a lot?" he asked, knowing this would work. "I'm a bit tougher than he is."

But she just laughed. "You sure are," she said. "Melvin gets nauseous at high speeds."

"Like thirty?"

"Make that twenty-five."

Why wasn't she getting mad? She'd always leaped to Melvin's defense. "He probably wouldn't have liked diving in a ditch to avoid the crash, either."

"Is that how you escaped getting hurt? I wondered."

She sat down on the bed next to him. His body cried out for her, his hands ached to slide under that silly nightgown with its little teddy bears and run along the cool length of her skin.

"You should have asked," he said. His voice sounded half-strangled.

"I wasn't sure you'd want to talk about it."

She touched his hand lightly, running her fingers over the back of it and causing shock waves to race up his arm. He could scarcely breathe. He wanted to grab his hand away, but couldn't move.

"I don't know how you guys feel about those things," she continued as her fingers moved slowly up his arm, still with that featherlight touch that packed a wallop even through his shirt. "You know, whether you'd want to talk about it or not."

"I'm not sure you ought to do that," he said, his voice trembling.

"I'm willing to risk the consequences."

She reached over and began to unbutton his shirt. One button, then another, then another until his mouth was so dry he couldn't breathe. Couldn't speak or think or do anything but feel his heart beat.

No, there were a few things left he could do. His hands could reach out to touch Casey's face, to slide over the softness of her cheek and brush ever so lightly those lips that drove him crazy. They were warm and moist and oh, so very kissable. So that was what he had to do—kiss them and kiss them again and kiss them once more.

His hands slid over her back. The flannel nightgown might as well not have been there. He could have sworn he felt her skin right through it, felt the fire that was consuming him spreading over her. He let his hands pull at the fabric until he could get them underneath it, to feel if her skin was really afire or if it would cool him, cool his ardor.

But she was pushing his shirt off even as her lips were taking everything he had to give. Pressing against him, harder, stronger, more insistently. He could feel her tremble as if a mixture of fear and hunger and wonder were racing through her, each burning in her heart. Her hands slid over his shoulders, caressing his scar and wiping all memories of pain away forever. He fell back against the bed, taking her down with him.

"I thought we weren't going to do this again," he whispered into her hair. The scent of it drove him wild, made it impossible to think.

"When did we say that?" she answered.

Her voice teased him, turned his desire into a need so raging and strong that he was sure he would explode. He pulled her nightgown off over her head, then let his lips touch the tips of her breasts. One at a time, he took them into his mouth, tasting their sweet fullness as his blood surged.

"This isn't fair," she said softly, as her hands tried to unbuckle his belt. "You have more clothes on."

"That can be fixed."

His lips could not stray from the wonder of her softness, but his hands unbuckled his belt and undid his pants. Together they pushed the rest of his clothes to the floor, so that they lay naked side by side, heart to heart, lips to lips.

He got his condom from the drawer and slipped it on, then pulled her closer once more.

They kissed, they touched, they awoke new passions that they had never known existed, and then at the last moment, he entered her. They held still for one sweet, delicious, explosive moment, then their passions burst forth and they moved as one. Clung together as if they were one, and then slowly lay back in each other's arms, still one in peace and love.

"Thank you," he whispered, kissing her forehead softly.

"What for?"

"For you," he said, and closed his eyes.

Casey climbed carefully from Mike's bed. He was sound asleep, but Gus opened one eye. She shook her head at him and he closed his eyes as she slipped from the room. Casey crept carefully down the stairs with Snowflake following her.

So much had happened today. There was no way she could sleep. Mike's accident. Her realization that she was in love with him. Making love. She went into the living room, leaving the lights off as she and Snowflake settled on the sofa. She could see the dark shape of the Christmas tree in the corner and took a long, deep breath. It had indeed been quite a day.

A faint scent of peppermint seemed to fill the room, but Casey didn't stir. Snowflake sat up slightly, as if watching something only she could see. Casey didn't need to see Simon, though; she could feel his presence.

"Hi, Simon," she said softly. "How's it going? We've had quite a day, haven't we?"

She didn't sense the tension in the room she'd felt around him before. It was almost as if he was just a friend over for a visit.

"I was so scared today," she told him. "I was sure something had happened to Mike, but I couldn't let him know."

A tiny shiver went through her, a trace of the day's ter-

rors, as she laid her head back on the sofa and closed he
eyes. Saying the words aloud seemed to help. Saying them
aloud to Mike would help the most, she suspected. Bu
would hurt the most, too.

"If I tell him I was worried, he'll know I love him. And
if I tell him I love him, he'll know I'll worry. Either way
I lose. So I guess I have to keep my mouth shut."

For a split second, the grief and longing and regret ir
the room were so thick she could almost touch them. Bu
then the sense of Simon's presence and the peppermin
faded and she was alone in the darkness with Snowflake
Alone and on her own. The cat curled up in her lap, ready
to go to sleep.

"Those aren't the only things that happened," Casey
said softly. "I keep forgetting one big one."

Only was it so big if she kept forgetting it? No, i
couldn't be. She had finally put the past in its place. Her
worry over Mike had showed her that it was now and tomorrow that counted the most. Not yesterday, or some day
long past. Or people long distant from her life.

Casey picked up Snowflake and tiptoed up to her owr
room. There she took her wallet from her purse and that
horrible, stupid clipping from her wallet.

"This has haunted me for too long," she told her cat.
"It doesn't matter what my mother thought of me."

She crumbled the paper up into a ball and tossed it toward the wastebasket. Snowflake caught it in a rare momen
of agility and batted it across the floor. Casey just laughed
softly. That's all it was good for—a cat toy. The words
printed there had no power over her anymore.

"Come on, Snowflake," she said as she picked up the
cat. "We've got a better place to be. Let's get back to
bed."

Chapter Eleven

"Okay." Casey stopped just inside the entrance to the mall and stomped the snow from her boots. Shoppers streamed all around them, so she pulled Mike off to the side. "Do you have a list with you or do you just wing it?"

He looked confused. "How do you 'wing' Christmas shopping?" he asked. "I'd end up with no gifts."

"Or the perfect ones," she said. "I like to just look and wait for something to call out to me."

"You really should see someone about all these voices you hear," he said, and pulled a paper from his coat pocket. "I need a toy store, a department store and a hardware store."

"And some imagination. Now, who are you shopping for?"

"Stephen's family. Joy gave me a list, complete with sizes and colors."

Casey took the list from his hand and frowned at it.

"Don't you know Christmas is supposed to be full of surprises?"

"I don't do surprises," he said.

She put the list in her pocket and took his hand. "We'll start down at this end."

"I suppose Melvin's a creative shopper," he said.

"As a matter of fact, he is."

"Maybe you should have asked him to go shopping with you then."

She frowned at him, then pulled him into a store specializing in blue jeans. "I bet there'd be something here Kate would love."

Mike just looked around the store, as if the clothing displays were some sort of foreign symbols. "Joy said to get her a case to store her CDs."

"Just look, will you?" Casey said.

He took a step toward a rack of denim blouses. "She won't like whatever I pick. It'll be the wrong color or size or style."

"I'll help you figure out sizes."

He looked through the blouses carefully, looking at each one as if he was hoping for a sign that said Kate Would Love Me. He stopped at one. "I've seen a lot of the college girls wearing this kind of thing."

"There's nothing a sixteen-year-old wants more than to look like a college girl," Casey said, and peered at the size tag. "I say take it."

"Are you sure?"

"Why are you so afraid to take a risk?" she asked. "If someone isn't crazy about a gift, it's not a rejection of you."

He frowned at her. "I'm not worried about rejection," he said. "I just don't trust my reading of people."

"But as a cop, you read people all the time."

"That's different. It's not personal."

Casey just took the blouse off the rack, grasped him by

the arm and went toward the cashier. "Believe me, sixteen-year-old girls are just what they seem."

"What about twenty-six-year-old girls?"

He was looking into her eyes, asking her some question only her heart could hear. But it wasn't translating for her. Her mouth went dry, her breath got ragged and her hands itched to hold him.

"We aren't girls," she murmured. "We're women."

"Hey, Casey! Hey, Mike."

The spell broken, Casey turned. Dubber and Tiffany were next to them, their arms loaded with packages, but smiles on their faces.

"Hi," Casey said. "I thought you guys did your Christmas shopping already."

"Only part of it," Tiffany said.

"Want to do mine for me?" Mike asked. "I got a list and I'll pay you."

Casey playfully punched him in the ribs and he responded by slipping his arm around her shoulders. Her stomach tightened deliciously, but she just smiled at the kids.

"You sure got a lot of garbage out by the curb," Dubber said. "My mom says you must've been cleaning all night."

"Just for a few hours," Mike said.

"What were you cleaning last night for, anyway?" Tiffany asked. "My dad told my mom that you'd be ringing bells."

Casey felt her cheeks go red even as Mike's arm tightened a fraction around her. She could feel his slight shaking; he, too, was trying not to laugh.

"Ringing what bells?" Dubber was asking with a confused frown. "Mike ain't got no bells in his house, unless you mean doorbells."

"I don't know," Tiffany snapped. "What about dumbbells? Doesn't he have a weight-lifting set?"

"Yeah, but how do you ring dumbbells?" Dubber waved his arms in emphasis and almost hit Mike. "I think you're the dumbbell. Your dad never said nothing so weird as that.''

"Who you calling a dumbbell?''

It was time to step in, but Mike beat her to it. "Kids, kids," he said. "Let's cool it.''

They quieted, but flashed glares in the other's direction.

"I think Tiffany's dad wasn't talking about real bells,'' Casey said. "I think he meant that Mike would be celebrating because he was okay.''

"And when you celebrate you sometimes ring bells," he added. "You know. Like on New Year's Eve.''

"Oh.''

"I get it,'' Tiffany said, then looked at her watch. "We got to get going. We're meeting my mom in half an hour and we ain't done yet.''

"It was nice seeing you,'' Casey said.

"Yeah. Later,'' Dubber said, as he and Tiffany hurried out of the store.

"Ringing bells?'' Mike said. "Where did that come from?''

Casey just laughed as she tucked her arm into his. "I don't know about you, but I distinctly heard bells last night.''

"Maybe Simon was ringing to get in.''

"No,'' she whispered softly, leaning close enough to touch his ear with her lips. "It definitely was not Simon ringing them.''

She got Mike to blush, then blush some more when she laughed.

Mike paid for the blouse for Kate, then they moved on, finding a set of books for Monica in one store and some skates for Brad in another, and a clock radio for college-age Rob. Casey got sweaters for her twin brothers and a desk organizer for her stepmother, who always complained she couldn't find anything. She found a wonderful sculpture of a father and child in a local artist's display for her dad, while Mike got a crystal decanter set for Stephen and Joy.

"Why don't I run these out to the car?" Mike suggested. "It'll make it easier to shop for more."

"I'm not sure I'm up for more," Casey said. "But go ahead. I still have a couple of things to get. I'll meet you down by the drugstore."

So while Mike went out to the car, Casey strolled toward the drug store. She found a sweatshirt-printing store that had a shirt with a dog on it that looked just like Gus, and couldn't help buying it for Mike.

In another day or two, her heart might actually be back to its regular pace and she could think about yesterday without tasting panic in her mouth. Somehow, though, she'd managed to keep her fears a secret from Mike. She had no idea how; she would have thought half the town could have written an article about it for the newspaper. But somehow Mike didn't seem to know.

"Casey?" Mrs. Kinder was coming out of the tie shop. "How are you feeling today?"

"I'm fine."

The woman patted her hand. "Did you get any sleep last night at all?" she asked.

Casey stared for a long moment. Just what was the woman suggesting might have kept her up all night? Worry, it had to be worry. "Uh, yes, I did," Casey finally managed to reply.

"Well, you tell that young man of yours not to be so crazy in the future," the older woman said.

"He's not really—"

"And to call to let you know he's okay," the woman added.

It was easier to agree than to explain the real situation. And besides, what was the real situation now? "Yes, I will," Casey said.

The other woman headed off, letting her finish her walk to the drugstore. What *was* the situation now? Casey asked herself. Things had changed so she no longer knew where they stood, but how did you ask your friend-lover-roommate to define your relationship?

Mike was waiting outside the drugstore. His eyes grew darker when he saw her approaching, and Casey suddenly didn't care how they defined their relationship, just so long as they had one.

"Sorry, I ran into Mrs. Kinder."

"Not literally, I hope. I'm pretty sure my homeowner's policy wouldn't cover it."

Casey just laughed and took his arm. "Only a few more small gifts to go," she said.

"And one major one," he said.

"One major one?" she repeated. "I got my dad's, my stepmother's and my brothers'. The family had a portrait taken at Thanksgiving to give my grandmother. Who's left?"

"Melvin."

"You are becoming more annoying than he is," she told him. "Melvin and I are friends. Do you have a problem with that?"

"Would he have a problem with me?"

"How could he have a problem with you?" Casey asked. "He's never met you and isn't likely to."

This was where he could tell her she was wrong, that he and Melvin would meet when he came to Ann Arbor to visit her. Or when they—

"There's the perfect gift for old Melvin," Mike said, pulling her to a stop outside the bookstore.

The window housed a display of calendars, and right in the middle was the Kops for Kids Kalendar.

"That's it?" Casey cried. "Oh, come on. I have to get one. A couple. Dozens. I can think of hordes of people to give them to."

"Hordes?"

"Hordes."

She dragged him into the store and found the calendar display inside. The Kops for Kids Kalendar was prominently in the middle. She took one from the pile and turned to March. Mike was standing by his police car, his short-sleeved uniform shirt open to show the rippling muscles of his chest as he gazed off into the distance.

"I was looking for speeders," he said.

"Sure." They certainly wouldn't have been female ones. Any woman under ninety-five would've slowed down for a better look at a hunk like this.

"I think I might just make it March all year round," Casey said. "I can't believe any other month could be so picturesque."

Mike looked decidedly embarrassed. "It's for a good cause."

"I'll say," she said as she flipped through the rest of the months. "Warming up my apartment with that pose is definitely a good cause."

"I meant the children's charity."

"Ooh, now he's kind of cute, too," she said, stopping at May as she peered at the tiny caption. "Tony Manning. State Police Post 25." She looked up at Mike. "There are two hunks in your unit?"

"He's married," Mike said. "And in the hospital. He was injured in the chase yesterday."

Casey's whole world started spinning. "Injured?" she said, her voice suddenly a whisper. "I didn't know anybody was injured."

Of course she did. The news report had said so. But after Mike had come home safely, she had refused to learn any more about the chase or the accident. She swallowed hard. "How bad?"

"His car skidded on the ice. Broken arm and a couple of ribs, plus some bruising. Enough to make it hard to hold his kid for a few weeks."

"He has a kid?" Mike's face blurred for a minute, then blurred even more. She was crying, she realized, but didn't know how to wipe the tears away.

"A baby," Mike said. "Hey, what's wrong?"

What was wrong? Good, decent family men were getting hurt. Lives were being smashed and broken. It wasn't Mike this time, but it could have been. Just as it could be him next time.

"Nothing," she managed to say, but the tears were coming down even harder, racking her body until she sobbed aloud.

And it wasn't just the bad guys she had to worry about. It was the ice, the speed, the cars that might break down at a crucial moment. It was the sun getting in his eyes. A deer running across the road. A truck jackknifing near him. It was a blowout. Someone else's blowout that left debris on the road. An oil spill. A kid on a bike. Vacationers trying to cross one more county before stopping for the night. Party goers having had that one last drink before hitting the road.

"Casey?"

She just shook her head, still trying to convince him it was nothing. But she felt his arms fold softly around her, pulling her to his chest, and she gave up the pretense and just let herself cry.

It wasn't as if she had a choice. The fears had finally gotten the upper hand.

"Oh, man," Mike muttered. He watched Gus dash off into the underbrush, then leaned against the tree to stare at the river. He was sinking and sinking fast. This was going to be one of his blackest moods yet. He'd thought getting out of the house, taking Gus for a walk, would help, but it wasn't doing a damn bit of good.

Actually, the whole thing made sense in a female kind of way—the whole damn emotion-laden, tear-soaked nine yards.

"I should have known better," he muttered. "With everything I went through with Darcy, I should have known better."

Well, now he did know better. Casey had been worried

about him, but had decided not to show it. So when Ed had brought him home yesterday, she'd pretended that everything was hunky-dory. And had continued to do so, until hearing about Tony's accident had brought her whole stupid facade crashing down.

Gus returned from his explorations and they began walking back toward the house. "A guy like me just can't let a woman in his life."

They came in sight of the house and Mike swallowed hard. He'd started the whole thing, so it was up to him to finish it. Bring the whole thing to a close with minimal pain to all concerned. Except him. He was a man and men were made to take pain.

"I'll tell her I'm moving," he said, then grimaced. "Yeah, right. That'll sure convince her we need to break it off. Moving ranks right up there with lying and cheating and stealing as a reason to dump somebody."

He waited a moment while Gus paused to inspect a bush. "So maybe it's got to be lying, cheating or stealing. How about, 'I lied to you, I'm already married'?" He shook his head. "She'd really believe that."

Gus finished and they moved on. "How about 'I've been cheating on you'? That might have a chance—if I didn't live in a town where everyone knew how often I breathed. They've been waiting for me to date ever since Darcy..."

Mike stopped. "That's it," he said. "Darcy."

It was perfect. Foolproof. No woman would question it. It was also a downright lie, but sometimes that couldn't be helped.

Mike turned onto his driveway, and his steps slowed even more. He wished he could live the past month all over again. He would do things differently. Oh, he surely would.

"Are you ever coming in, boy?" a voice called to him. "Or you going to lollygag out there the rest of your natural life?"

Mike stopped and stood there, staring at the older woman in the open front door. Thirty seconds ago he would have said his mood couldn't get any lower, but now he felt it sliding into the pits.

"Get your butt in here, boy. We got a load of talkin' to do and I don't want do it out here in the gosh-darned cold."

Mike took a deep breath. "Hello, Aunt Myrna."

His great-aunt hustled him and Gus inside and into the living room. No "How have you been? How's life treating you?" Nothing. Just a straight "Sit your ass down, I gotta talk to you." Gus, being the intelligent dog he was, hightailed it for the upstairs. Mike assumed Casey was still lying down, since she wasn't in sight.

"What did you do to Casey?" Aunt Myrna asked, settling herself on the easy chair. "She's mighty sad."

"I didn't do anything," Mike said. "One of the cops in my unit got hurt yesterday and she was upset when she heard about it."

His great-aunt's eyes narrowed. "She attached to this young man?"

"She never even met him."

"Then that don't make no sense."

It did if one thought about it, but Mike wasn't going to explain it all to Myrna. There were too many things she could misread if she wanted to, and she always wanted to. "I think Casey's very soft-hearted."

"Too soft-hearted," Myrna agreed, and leaned forward as if sharing a state secret. "Sometimes she needs to be protected from herself."

She what? Mike just stared at his aunt, warning lights starting to flash in his mind.

"Anyways, that's not why I'm here," his great-aunt said, leaning back once more. "I've been—"

"Wait a minute," Mike said quickly. "What do you mean, 'she needs to be protected from herself'?" A suspicion was starting to grow. A terrible suspicion.

His aunt just waved her hand at him, gaudy red-and-gold stones flashing from her fingers. "Oh, you know how some people are."

"Yes, I do," he said carefully. "I know how you are. You like to get your own way and aren't above lying to get it."

She looked horrified, putting that same ring-studded hand over her chest as if she was feeling faint, but Mike knew it was all an act. He'd seen it a few too many times. "I am only trying to do the best for everyone. Madame DeMarco will attest to that," she exclaimed.

"Your psychic doesn't know what's best for everyone any more than you do," Mike retorted. "Now, was Casey in real danger from someone who was looking to harm her physically?"

His aunt bit her lip and looked off at the Christmas tree before turning back to him. This time she was attempting the haughty Queen Victoria look. "Now, Michael, there are other types of danger, you know."

"Aunt Myrna."

"Well…"

"Melvin was not going to come here and assault her, was he?"

She just sighed and gave Mike a look intended to shrivel him up. It didn't. "If you'd ever met him, you'd see why I bent the truth a little," she snapped, abandoning her various poses. "He's such a weasel. Always leaning on her, always wanting help and acting like he can't do a thing on his own. Someone's always hurting his feelings, according to him."

"That's no excuse for making me think she was in actual danger," Mike said. "I had the cops here taking extra passes by the house."

"Really?" His great-aunt looked pleased. "That was so thoughtful of you." She turned serious again. "You see, she's always rescuing something. Always. And sooner or later, she would find she had rescued Melvin right into a permanent relationship with her."

"She said they were friends."

Myrna snorted. "She's too sweet for her own good. That's why I sent her here."

"Why? So she could rescue me?"

His aunt's look of surprise almost fooled him. Almost. "Why, Mike? Are you in need of rescue?"

"No, I'm not," he replied. "That's why it didn't work."

"You know what I think—"

They both stopped—froze, actually—as they heard the creaking of footsteps on the stairs. In another moment, Casey came round the bend in the stairs. She slowed her steps as she realized they were both staring at her.

"What's wrong?" she asked.

"Nothing," Mike said. She looked worn, beat, exhausted. As though she'd run a race about ten miles too long. "Aunt Myrna was telling me how she's looking forward to reading the family history."

"Actually, I have something exciting to tell Mike," his great-aunt said. "And I'm so glad that you're here in time to hear it."

Casey looked as bewildered as Mike felt as she came across the foyer and into the living room. She sat on the far end of the sofa from Mike, looking as small and defenseless as a child. He wanted to pull her closer to him, to let her rest in the shelter of his arm, but he hadn't forgotten about that little talk they had to have. He'd best keep his distance.

"You know this house has been in our family ever since it was built, don't you, Mike?" Myrna said.

Mike forced his eyes back to her, inclined to say *your* family, but he didn't. It wasn't Myrna's fault that he hadn't known anything about his birth family until he was an adult. He just nodded.

"I'd always loved this place, and Great-uncle Simon knew it, so when he died, he left it to me with the understanding I would pass it on through the family." Aunt Myrna paused and took a deep breath. "I was never blessed with any children of my own, but I think I've figured out the best solution.''

Mike went still. He didn't like where this conversation seemed to be heading.

"I'm going to give you the house, Mike." Her voice grew soft like a newborn kitten's. "I want you to marry, raise a family and grow old here."

"Oh, Mike, isn't that wonderful?" Casey cried.

Wonderful? Only if you liked being bought. He didn't want the responsibility of a house. Couldn't risk the luxury of a house. He'd get comfortable here, and the next thing he knew, he'd be thinking about filling the rooms. He'd forget the lesson he'd learned through Darcy's fear a year ago, and through Casey's tears today. A cop shouldn't marry.

He and Aunt Myrna had been over this route a million times, though, and every time she mentioned giving him the house, he'd said no, thank you. Did she think it would work if she did it in front of someone else? He didn't like being taken for a fool. She'd done it once by saying Casey needed protection. Now she was trying it again.

"Aunt Myrna—"

"We've got a lot to do before I leave again." She pulled her purse over and began delving into it. "I made an appointment with some lawyer in town. He's got the papers all ready for you to sign."

Just like that? He felt his lips go tight as anger started to build. "Aunt Myrna," he repeated, a little louder this time. "I don't want the house."

She stopped her search. "What?"

She meant well, he knew, and in spite of his annoyance over her lies about Casey, he just couldn't hurt her. "I can't afford it."

"I'm not selling it," she said. "I'm giving it to you."

"It doesn't matter."

"Maybe I should leave," Casey said quickly. "Why don't I fix us some tea?"

"There's no need to go," Mike said. "I'm not taking the house and that's all that needs to be said."

"Yes, stay," Myrna said to her. "Tell him what a pig-headed fool he is. He's going to need a house one of these days. Why can't it be this one?"

"I really would like some tea," Casey said, and got to her feet. "And cookies. We have lots of cookies. I'll make some tea and bring out some cookies, shall I?"

"Why am I going to need a house?" Mike was suddenly on his feet, too agitated to sit. "I was perfectly happy in an apartment before."

"Your wife and kids might not be."

"I have no wife and kids, and never will," he snapped.

"Then you're even more of a fool than I thought."

"I'm gone," Casey said, and hurried into the kitchen.

He was relieved to see her go. It gave him more freedom to speak. "I have a right to live my life as I see fit."

"No matter who you hurt?"

"If I do it right, I won't hurt anybody."

"I would bet you already have." Aunt Myrna's voice was smug, as if she knew she'd won.

He just stared at her for a long moment. "Believe me, it won't happen again," he said, and left the room.

"This is such a beautiful old house," Casey said. "I can't believe he doesn't want it."

"We don't know that he doesn't want it, dear," Mrs. Jamison said.

They were sitting at the kitchen table, sipping tea and munching on Mrs. Kinder's Christmas cookies. Snowflake and Midnight had joined them.

The older woman went on. "What we know for sure is that he doesn't want to accept responsibility for it right now."

"But it's been in your family for a hundred years."

Myrna smiled softly as she petted first one cat, then the other. "I'm sure Mike's more concerned with how long he's been in our family. I don't think he's come to terms with that yet.''

"Maybe if I talked to him..." Casey said.

"That boy's got a pack of stuff to work out," Aunt Myrna said. "Just leave him be. It'll be easier on your nerves that way."

"I'm sure you know best."

"Well." Myrna pushed herself to her feet, ignoring the little furry-faced scowls directed her way. "I'd best move my carcass. I got to meet with that lawyer even if Mike won't, then I'm going over to my niece's for a few days."

"Why are you so set on giving this place to Mike?" Casey asked. "You have lots of other relatives."

"But they're all settled in other places. Already made their homes. It would be hard for them to move and take up here in Berrien Springs." She shook her head with a smile. "That's why I'm giving it to Mike. Is Melvin coming to see that you go home for Christmas?"

Casey just shook her head at the abrupt change of topic. "I doubt it."

"Humph. Too bad."

Casey didn't ask why, but saw Myrna out to her car, then went in search of Mike. She found him up in the garage apartment, washing the tile floor with more dogged determination than the job called for. He was upset.

"Myrna's gone," she said. The room was almost empty, with just an old kitchen table and chairs left near the door. She sat in one of the chairs.

He wrung out the mop, and himself, if his sigh was any indication. "I heard the car."

"She was just trying to be nice."

"She was just trying to get her own way." He leaned the mop against the wall and pulled a chair away from the table a few feet, as if putting more distance between them before he sat down. "We've been over it all before."

"You could have at least listened to her arguments."

He leaned his forearms on his knees and stared down at

his hands. "I've heard them all. I don't want the damn house. It's too much responsibility."

He seemed so troubled, so torn. Casey wished she could help him. "It wouldn't be any more responsibility than you already have."

"Well, that's coming to an end." He looked up, staring her straight in the eye. "I've decided to move."

Casey stared back. He was what? "What's going to happen to the house?"

"I don't know. I just can't stay here anymore."

"Mike, that's crazy." She leaned on the table, wishing he hadn't put such a distance between them. "You and Myrna will work things out."

"Myrna has nothing to do with it," he snapped, then took a deep breath. "It's Darcy," he said slowly.

Casey went still, then sat back in her chair. "Darcy?"

He nodded. "I thought I was over her. I thought it didn't matter if she moved back here, but I was wrong."

He loved Darcy, not her. She loved him and he loved Darcy. Casey was stunned, frozen, paralyzed. No, then she wouldn't have this slow pain creeping around to clutch at her heart.

"You still love her?" she asked, begging for him to say she was wrong.

But he just shrugged and looked away. "I'm sorry," he said.

Sorry. As if that covered it. As if that made the pain and hurt diminish. As if it made her heart start beating again.

"Where will you go?" she asked. Amazingly, her voice still worked.

He shrugged. "I don't know. Maybe I'll transfer posts. There's some great apartments along the lake in Grand Haven. Or I could move east to Detroit."

"Detroit? Gus won't want to live in the city."

He turned away from her, his face set hard as stone. "I'll take care of it. I'll figure something out. Maybe I can find him a nice farm to live on."

"A nice farm?" she repeated. It hurt to hear he was still in love with Darcy, but this was ten thousand times worse. She had to be misunderstanding him. "You'd give Gus up?"

Mike looked straight at her. He had to have seen the horror on her face, the revulsion in her voice and the hope in her eyes that she'd gotten it wrong, but he just stood up. "Hey, he's just a dog."

"Just a dog!" she shrieked, leaping to her feet, too. "He's not just a dog. He's your friend. Your buddy. Your best pal."

"He's a dog," Mike insisted. His voice was careful and controlled. "I am his owner, not his daddy, not his friend, not his pal. If it doesn't work out to keep him, I won't." He turned away and picked up the mop.

In two quick steps, she was at his side. She grabbed his arm and swung him around to face her. "You can't mean that," she insisted. "You can't give him up. He loves you."

"He's an animal. He doesn't love." He plopped the mop down into the bucket of water with enough force that half the water splashed out. "He'll lavish his devotion on whoever feeds him."

Casey couldn't believe he was saying these things. How could she have been so wrong about him? He wasn't kind and loving and gentle. The man she'd thought she loved didn't exist. It should make it so much easier for her. But it didn't.

She just shook her head, her eyes filling with tears so that she could barely see or speak. "I hate people like you," she said in a hoarse whisper. "You deny your responsibilities because they're not convenient anymore. They don't fit your life-style. They're an embarrassment. Too much trouble. So you throw them away like they're empty cans of pop, not living, breathing creatures with feelings and fears and a lifetime of knowing how you didn't want them."

Mike's expression had gone from glaring to confused. Casey knew everything was getting jumbled in her head—Snowflake, Midnight, herself as a baby. But she didn't care.

"Snowflake was about seven when she was brought to the shelter where I volunteered. You know the reason presented for giving her up? 'No longer fits my life-style.'" Tears were streaming down her face and she wiped them away impatiently. "That's what the heartless no-accounts gave for a reason. Snowflake was devastated. She refused to eat. We had to take away her water dish because she kept putting her face into the water and we were afraid she'd drown. I hand fed her for weeks before she began eating on her own, and it was months before she began to trust that when I left in the morning, I would come back."

"She was lucky you were there," he said.

But the very gentleness of his voice only made Casey more angry. "And Midnight was 'set free' by some woman who'd gotten her as a plaything for her kids and then said she was too much trouble. So she dumped her in a parking lot. It was close to her house, though, and someone recognized her. But I wouldn't give Midnight back to her for a million dollars."

Casey took a breath, then rushed on before Mike could speak. "And then there's Zeke, who's living with my dad and stepmother. He was dumped at the shelter because he had an ear infection. An ear infection! It took a week's worth of medicine to clear it up, but his owners couldn't be bothered. The poor thing was so depressed and scared it was pitiful."

"This isn't exactly the same thing," Mike argued.

She was beyond listening to him anymore. "What about all the babies that are dumped someplace because nobody wants them? Just thrown away because they were a mistake. Who cares if they live or die? Babies. Cats. Dogs. We live in a society that throws everything away."

"I'm not throwing him away," Mike snapped. "You're blowing this all out of proportion."

"Oh, sure. It's all my fault. Blame me. Blame Gus. Blame everybody else." She wiped again at those stupid tears. "I don't know how I ever could have thought I loved you."

She turned and ran for the door.

"Casey!"

There was nothing he could say that would change anything. She raced down the stairs and back into the house.

Chapter Twelve

Mike stepped out of the shower and reached for a towel. He felt like hell, but that's what lying awake all night did to one. He'd known he had to talk to Casey—had to end it with her—but he had never imagined it would be as hard as it had been. It had worked—he had to admit that—but he hadn't meant a word of it. Not the stuff about Darcy, not the stuff about Gus.

But there was no doubt about it—Casey hated his guts now. He should be happy. And eventually, he'd probably be able to look at himself in the mirror in the morning. He was not at that point yet.

After dressing, he went down to the kitchen. He still didn't have a cruiser, which meant another day at home. Great.

Casey was in the kitchen, cleaning up the cat dishes while her pets sat on one of the kitchen chairs watching her. Gus was sitting at her feet, adoring her, which was what any sensible man would be doing. Seeing her slender body sent shivers down Mike's spine. The way her hair bounced when she moved made his breath catch.

Casey turned. And the disgust in her eyes reminded him of what a crud he was.

"Good morning," she said stiffly.

"Good morning," he answered.

"I've already had breakfast," she said. "Would you like me to leave the milk and stuff out?"

"No." He cleared his throat. "I'm not hungry."

"Okay."

"Thank you, anyway."

A walk in the winter air would do him good. Put a little cold oxygen in his lungs and clear the cobwebs out of his brain. He strode briskly into the mudroom and put on his boots and jacket. No gloves again. Damn cat. Well, he didn't need gloves, anyway. How cold could it be? This wasn't the North Pole, for goodness sakes.

Casey came to the mudroom door. "I would like to move into the garage apartment for the rest of the time I'm here," she said. "I think it would be best."

Great. Instead of imagining her every move here, he could imagine it there. "If that's what you want. I'll move some furniture over later this morning."

"There's enough over there," she said. Her voice was cold enough to give the snow freezer burn, but Gus didn't seem to notice as he sat at her side in the doorway.

"There's only a table and a few chairs over there," he replied.

"I have a sleeping bag."

She wouldn't even take furniture from him? He'd done too good of a job. "I'll move some stuff over when I get back. You can use it or not. Come on, Gus."

But the dog just sat there, looking from Mike to Casey.

"Damn it, Gus," Mike snapped. "You want to come for a walk or don't you?"

"There's no need for that." Her words came out even sharper than his.

"Fine." Mike stomped to the back door. "He can stay here. I don't care what he does."

"Gus, sweetie. Be a good boy. Go outside with Mike and keep him company."

Gus bounded forward and slipped outside as Mike opened the door. Damn it. He didn't need any company. He was a lone wolf. Someone who didn't need anybody or anything extra in his life.

"You'd do anything to show me up, wouldn't you?" Mike muttered to the dog as he closed the door behind them.

The walk to town was uneventful and breakfast was even worse. The scrambled eggs were hot, the ham was tender, the toast was warm and the orange juice was cold. And Mike couldn't eat a thing. He just kept seeing the hurt in Casey's eyes when she'd thought he was willing to give up Gus.

"Next time I'll just open a box of cereal," he said.

Casey was moving a dresser into the garage apartment—two drawers at a time—when they got home. She was halfway across the ice-covered driveway.

"Couldn't you have waited a half hour?" Mike asked, and tried to take a drawer from her.

"I can carry it," she snapped.

"Fine." It wasn't heavy, after all. "I'll get the rest of it."

"I can do it."

"So can I."

He found the shell of the dresser in the bedroom she'd been using and carried it down. This really would be for the best, he told himself. It didn't matter that he'd miss her like hell. It would be best for her. She'd forget about him and find someone who'd really make her happy.

She was coming down the garage steps when he reached the bottom.

"Want me to take the top?" she asked.

What, he was too weak to carry a dresser up some stairs? Maybe that was the real trouble all along—she'd always seen him as weak or sick or something other than himself. No, wait. He was the one who'd broken it off.

"I can do it."

He heaved the thing on his back and almost fell over, but he'd be damned if he'd let her know. With careful steps, he climbed to the top, proud that he hadn't bumped the sides of the stairs once. She'd see what a man he was. But when he put the dresser down at the top and turned around, she was gone.

"Just as well," he told Snowflake, who was frowning at him, at the room, at the world in general. "Hey, it wasn't my idea for you three to move in here."

Casey came back with a box that looked too heavy for her, but Mike knew better than to offer his help. He just went and got the roll-away bed. It was pretty damn heavy itself, but he could handle it. It weighed less than that frown she was aiming at him.

After an hour or so, all the furniture she would accept had been moved into the apartment. It shouldn't have looked cozy—the place badly needed painting and the furniture would have been rejected by most rummage sales—but it did. She and her cats added a life to it that defied description. Mike just stood in the doorway, feeling as useless as he had that first night when he'd brought her a blanket.

He wanted to beg her to let him into her warm circle. He wanted to tell her that everything he'd said last night had been a lie, that he'd only been trying to save her pain down the line.

"Thank you," she said. It was a dismissal.

"Anytime." He left.

His house had turned bleak and cold in that hour or so, and he had no need to loll about in its emptiness, so he picked up an old ice chipper lying around the garage and began hacking at the ice on his drive. He cleaned the drive thoroughly, until there wasn't an ice patch more than a half inch in diameter on the whole damn thing.

Then he noticed that the widow McLaren's drive could stand some cleaning. He thought Dubber normally took care of that, but obviously Tiffany had him tied up. Mike shook his head as he trotted down to Mrs. McLaren's house. Hopefully the boy would learn. And before it was too late. Mike started hacking away with his chipper.

"Land sakes, boy, what are you doing?" the widow called to him from her front porch.

"Just cleaning the drive, ma'am," he said. "Having a base of ice could cause you trouble."

"You got problems at home?" she asked him, loud enough for the whole county to hear.

"No, ma'am. Just being neighborly."

"You'd be better off putting that energy to fixing the troubles in your life and leave my driveway alone. It's just gonna ice up again." With that, she went back into her house.

It took him the rest of the morning to clear the drive, but after a quick lunch down at the diner, he went over to the Joneses' house to do their drive. Orville had problems with arthritis and Maybelle could hardly see.

Mike shook his head and laughed to himself. There were people who accused him of not having any Christmas spirit. Hell, he had more Christmas spirit than a hound dog had fleas. With his life in order, Mike started chipping away.

"That ain't going to get you out of the doghouse," Orville yelled to him from an upstairs window. "Get on home and say you're sorry."

"I haven't done nothing to be sorry for," Mike lied.

"There ain't a man alive who can say that and be telling the truth," Maybelle told him.

The anonymity of a big city sure looked appealing.

"Don't you worry none," Casey told Gus as she grabbed up a box of computer printouts. "I'm just moving over to the garage. I'll be back here to cook my meals. Mike is the biggest jerk that ever lived, but I won't let anything happen to you.''

Gus just wagged his tail. Casey had hoped he'd disagree with her estimation of Mike, tell her she was wrong, that all those horrible things last night hadn't been said. Or if they had, that they were all some sort of misunderstanding. But no, Gus just kept on wagging his tail as he followed her out of the house, across the driveway and up into the apartment. He obviously knew the truth, too.

Casey put her box down and sat on the bed. The place was a dump. Oh, it was clean and snug and quite cozy. But it was filled with castoffs, and she didn't just mean the furniture. Snowflake came over to be petted.

"It's all my own fault, you know," Casey told the cat. "I should have known better. All the signs were there. This was not a guy to get involved with. So why did I?"

It was as if she'd been possessed. That was it. Simon had done it.

Gus had been sniffing around the apartment, but stopped suddenly. Stopped and ambled over to the door. Sure enough, Casey heard footsteps on the stairs.

Her heart skipped a couple of beats. Mike? It had to be. He was the only one who'd think she was here. Maybe he was coming to tell her he'd been wrong. That it had all been a joke or a test or a fit of madness. She pulled open the door.

Tiffany was on the other side. "Hi, Casey." The girl came in and closed the door. "Whatcha doing up here?"

Becoming a basket case. "I have a lot of research to do for the work I'm doing for Mrs. Jamison," she said. "So I'm setting up in my own space here."

Tiffany looked thoughtfully at her, nodding. "Yeah, I heard you and Mike weren't getting along." She sat at the kitchen table.

"That's not it at all," Casey tried to protest, but her words lacked any backbone.

Great. The whole town was discussing them. Well, there was nothing she could do but ignore the whole thing and hope it would blow over. Although it didn't really matter, since she'd be leaving in two more days to go home for Christmas. And there really was no need for her to return. She'd have her research done by then and that was the only thing keeping her here. The absolutely, positively only thing in the whole world.

A burning in her eyes said she was on the verge of tears again. She needed a diversion and quick. "So what are you doing here, Tiffany?" she asked as she sat down.

"I was waiting for Dubber and Mrs. Randall, and I saw you moving stuff in here."

Great. By now the town's wireless telegraph had spread that piece of information and the word was being pushed out into the rest of the county. By this time tomorrow, the whole state would know she'd moved out of Mike's house and into the garage.

"Yes," Casey said, nodding. "I'm all moved in."

She glanced toward the window and could see the arrival of winter's early dusk. Along with the grayness came large snowflakes, floating and hanging in the air. By morning Mike's clean driveway would be all covered again. That should make him happy. It would give him a way to continue to avoid her.

The electric heater's fan took that moment to rumble into action, filling the room with gusts of warmth. She looked over at Gus, sleeping peacefully, and thought how nice it would be to just flop down herself. Casey slid farther down in her chair.

"Sometimes you have to smack them around a little. You know that, don't you?"

Casey forced her tired eyes to focus on Tiffany.

"I mean the guys," Tiffany explained. "Not so that you hurt them, but just enough to keep them in line."

"I'm not into hitting people, Tiffany."

The girl tried to hide her impatience. "I don't mean you should really hit them. Just smack them to get their attention."

Not being up on the nuances of physical force, Casey wasn't sure what the differences were, but she just smiled and nodded, hoping Tiffany would drop the subject.

"You don't want to make them bleed." Tiffany looked disgusted. "You do that and you get screaming and whining like you've never heard before. Momma always says if men had to give birth, there wouldn't be no human race."

Casey could almost follow the connection, and she found that a little frightening. "When you get older," she said, "you'll find that smacking people isn't always the best way to go."

"Yeah, that's what Momma keeps telling me."

For the first time since she'd met Tiffany, Casey thought she saw a chip in the girl's bravado. A shred of concern and doubt.

"Sometimes you have to let them go," Casey said. "A man who doesn't share your beliefs isn't going to change his mind because you threaten him."

"I guess not."

"You have to be yourself and hope that's enough."

Tiffany had found a scratch in the tabletop and was running her finger along it with precision. "Some of the girls in class are wearing makeup and—and..." She paused in her scratch inspection to look down at her own flat chest. "And other stuff."

"Men don't fall in love with makeup or a big chest," Casey said. "They might be tempted by it, but it's not why they fall in love. What you are inside is what keeps them with you."

Tiffany just sighed and went back to her scratch. "What if what I am inside isn't enough to keep Dubber?"

"Then you move on and look for the one who will love you."

Tiffany made a face. "But I don't want to."

"You'll have no choice. You can't hold on to a man who doesn't love you."

"Bummer."

"Exactly."

Casey stopped outside the diner. This was where Mike had taken her for her birthday and where he seemed to eat often. She had no idea where he was eating tonight, but did she want to take the chance?

Definitely not. She retraced her steps and went into the Beijing Palace. Chinese would be great.

The restaurant was dark and more crowded than she'd expected. She looked around but couldn't see any empty tables. It was three days before Christmas. Why wasn't everybody at Christmas parties?

"Just one?" an elderly Asian man asked her. "You mind sharing?"

"No, not all," she said, and followed him around to a table in the back. It might even be a good idea. She could meet someone new and impress him with her high spirits. Word would have to get out that she was fine. Not pining away at all. That—

The host had stopped at a table where a man was sitting. Mike.

"Here you go," the waiter was saying as he pulled out the chair for her and put a menu into her hands. "Specials are on the back. Enjoy."

She sat before her brain told her not to, but then she'd never been able to make any kind of scene. "I'll go," she told Mike. "I had no idea you were here."

"That's silly," he said. "There's no reason why we can't share a meal here. Besides, if you go now, it'll give the whole town something to talk about."

"Something more, you mean."

He nodded and went back to studying his menu. She tried to do the same, but her eyes kept straying. He looked tired. New lines seemed to have formed around his eyes since last night. Part of her wanted to smooth them away, to take him in her arms and hold him until the tensions faded. But then part of her wanted to kick his butt down to the state line and back. Giving up Gus, indeed! She buried her face in the menu.

But once they'd ordered, there were no menus to hide behind. They sipped at their tea, nibbled at their fried wontons and tried to avoid each other's gaze. In one of her idle glances around the restaurant, Casey realized almost every eye on the place was on them. This was ridiculous. She might as well make use of the time.

"I've been thinking about Gus," she said, leaning forward slightly. "I would love to have him if you don't want him anymore."

Annoyance flashed through Mike's eyes. "I never said I didn't want him."

"That wasn't you the other night talking about finding a farm for him to live on?"

"Well, yeah, but that wasn't because I didn't want him."

"No, it must have been because you wanted him so much." She tried to keep her voice low, though anger was pushing the volume switch up. She took a deep breath as Mike looked away for a moment.

"I thought he might be better off on a farm than cooped up in an apartment," he whispered harshly. "Assuming I can find one that allows pets."

"It's not impossible, you know."

"But it might not be the best for him."

"For him or for you?"

Their dinner came then, brought over by a smiling waitress who was too perky for words. Casey wanted to throw something at her. No, she wanted to throw something at Mike. This was the Christmas season. People were supposed to be cheery and happy; he was the one spoiling it for everyone. She dug into her Mongolian beef.

"Why are you trying to make me out as the villain?"

he asked once the waitress left. "I'm only trying to d
what'll make Gus happy."

"He'd be happiest with you rather than dumped some
place."

"I wasn't going to dump him," he whispered back.

"Sure, that's what you say now, but when the tim
comes and he's too much of a bother..." Damn. She wa
getting all teary. She blinked away the wetness, or tried to
as she bent over her food. She'd be damned if she wa
going to wipe her eyes for everyone to see.

His hand was suddenly on hers. "Aw, Casey," he said
"Don't get so upset."

She jerked her hand away. "I'm not upset," she said
her voice breaking slightly to prove her wrong. "But I sup
pose you don't think this is anything to be upset about
Have one dog, dump one dog. No big deal."

"Why are you blowing this all out of proportion?" he
hissed, angry again himself. "I'm trying to figure ou
what's best for my dog, and you keep making this int
some crime of the century."

"You don't understand." She pushed her plate away
unable to eat.

"You're right. I don't. Not at all."

"And that's the whole problem right there in a nutshell."
She looked around. "Where is our waitress? I need to go.'

"I'll take care of the bill," he said. "Go on home."

She wanted to refuse, wanted to tell him to take hi
money and... But she couldn't just sit here and cry. "Than
you," she said stiffly, and got to her feet. "I'll see yo
later."

He just nodded, and she hurried outside into the col
evening air. It was either stop crying or have little froze
tears on her cheeks. She stopped, but wasn't ready to g
home yet, so wandered toward the grocery store.

Two more days, that was all she had here. Forty-eigh
hours. She could be civil for that long. She could refrai

from crying that long. Then she'd go home and pretend that everything was absolutely, positively perfect. Simple.

The grocery store looked warm and inviting, and deserted, so Casey went inside. She could use some more cat treats, and Gus should have some doggie treats. She roamed down the pet aisle, mulling over whether Gus would prefer beef- or liver-flavored cookies.

"Cherry pie," someone said next to her.

Casey turned to find an elderly woman at her side. "I beg your pardon?"

"Cherry pie," she repeated. "Brings a man to his senses in nothing flat." The woman stuck her hand out. "I'm Moira McLaren, honey. I live across the street from you two."

You two? Casey and Mike weren't a twosome. They had been friends but had never been a twosome. "Nice to meet you," she replied.

"I'm talking about Mike, you know," the old woman said. "He's being such a ninny. Not sure if he deserves cherry pie, but it'd do the trick."

"I'll keep that in mind, ma'am."

"You do that, honey." The elderly woman patted her arm. "You be sure and do that."

Casey waited until she saw Mrs. McLaren leave the store, then hurried up to the checkout counter.

"Gus is getting a little treat, eh?" the woman there said.

"Oh, I'm sorry, Mrs. Randall," she said to Dubber's mother. "I didn't recognize you at first."

"Not being surrounded by five kids tends to be a disguise," she said with a laugh. "Sure this is all you want?"

Casey just stared at her few items.

"We got some new perfumes in aisle ten," the other woman said with a wink. "Some real sexy ones."

"That's all right," Casey said.

"Guaranteed to get Mike off his duff and toeing the line."

"Don't want him off his duff too much," Casey said, forcing a laugh. "I'm leaving in a few days."

The other woman frowned. "Yeah, but that's just for the holidays, right? Aren't you coming back?"

"No reason to," Casey said brightly. "My work here is just about done."

"Oh."

Casey nodded toward the few items on the counter. "So I'll just take those."

"Sure, honey."

Mrs. Randall rang the items up and Casey paid her, escaping outside with relief. Maybe if she was really lucky, she could walk the entire four blocks to Mike's house without meeting someone else with the solution to all her problems. Trouble was, she wasn't the one with the problem. Mike was.

She made it three blocks before a voice rang out. "Casey. Casey, honey."

Casey was tempted to ignore the voice and walk on, but that would have been rude. And she had this genetic defect that wouldn't allow her to even hint at rudeness.

"Hello, Mrs. Kinder. How are you?"

But her neighbor just enveloped her in a bear hug. "You poor dear." She released Casey and stepped back. "That's such a lovely old home. It's just made for a family. I don't understand that man, not at all."

It was obvious that the whole town knew that Mike had turned down his aunt's offer of the house. And the people probably knew to the penny how much money Mrs. Jamison had been going to give him to refurbish the place. It suddenly dawned on Casey that they probably also knew how many times she and Mike had made love. It definitely was time for her to leave.

"Mike has a lot of things to think about," Casey said. "He has to—"

"Oh, baloney. His problem is that he's just like Simon."

"Simon?"

"Yes," Mrs. Kinder snapped. "You straighten out Simon and Mike'll fall into place, too. You'll see."

Good heavens. Not only did the women in the town want her to bring Mike to his senses, now Casey was supposed to straighten out a ghost while she was at it. She really needed to leave soon. If she stayed around here much longer she'd become as nutty as everyone else.

Chapter Thirteen

Mike pitched the miniature basketball down the snowy driveway toward the garage. "Go ahead, boy. Go get it."

It was Gus's favorite toy, but the big dog remained sitting on the drive, gazing contemplatively toward the ball.

Mike squatted down and patted him on the head. "Getting a little tired of this game?"

The dog's tail wagged once.

"Yeah, I guess anything can get tiresome if you do it long enough." Suddenly unbidden images of Casey popped into Mike's consciousness. Vivid color pictures of the two of them making love. "Well," he murmured. "Almost everything."

They sat there, man and dog, staring at a stupid little brown ball, thinking about the rest of the day that stretched out before them.

"So," Mike said, his voice brimming with holiday cheer,

full of chocolate-covered pickles and red-nosed reindeer. "What do you want to do now, big fella?"

Gus didn't say a word in reply. He didn't even twitch an ear. Mike sighed. Every chance Gus got, he was off with Casey. On the rare occasions that Gus came around, he made Mike feel like a noncustodial divorced dad trying to come up with something new and exciting to keep his kid happy to see him. And failing.

"Casey's a mighty fine woman," Mike said. "Maybe I ought to let you go live with her. She's cheerful, likes animals and would never let you go hungry."

Gus thumped his tail once, then a second time.

"I'm going to have to get me an apartment someplace, big fella. And it's not going to be like here, where Dubber or his mother takes care of you when I'm gone. You'd be home all alone. A big dog like you would go out of his mind being cooped up in a little bitty place the whole damn day." Mike glanced away for a moment. "Besides, Casey needs someone to look after her and I can't think of anybody better for the job than you."

Gus lay down and dropped his head on his front paws.

"And I'll come visit."

Gus sighed. Yeah, Mike agreed. It might be the best solution, but it sure stank. But sometimes that was all you had to choose from—lousy and lousier.

"Hey, Mike."

Mike started at the sound of Dubber's voice and looked up. "Hey, Dubber."

The boy walked on over. "Sure is cold," he said.

"Sure is."

"Pop says that's what happens to weather in the winter."

"Your father's a smart man," Mike said. "You'll do good listening to him."

"Yeah."

Mike nodded and reflected on how nice it was to talk to another male. They'd acknowledged each other's existence,

brought up the subject of weather and covered it thoroughly
and now they were relaxing in each other's company.

Had Dubber been a woman things wouldn't be anywhere
near that comfortable for either of them. Right about now
the woman would have been asking him about his feelings
toward cold and what the weather really meant to him.
Asking him why he'd said a person should listen to his
father. Had he not listened to his own father at some point
in time and was now regretting it?

"Whatcha doing?" Dubber asked.

Mike stiffened up for a moment, but the boy's question
wasn't all that bad. It was actually something any young
fella might ask.

"Gus and I are playing ball," Mike replied.

From the corner of his eye, Mike could see Dubber look
toward the brown ball near the garage's double doors, then
back at him and his dog.

"Uh, what kind of a ball game are you guys playing?"

Nuts. Mike had been afraid that Dubber would want to
go deeper. "We're playing a mind game," he replied.
"You know what mind games are?"

"Uh, yeah." Dubber shifted from one foot to the other.
"I guess."

"Gus and I are using mind waves. We're each trying to
make the ball roll toward ourself and away from the other."

Dubber looked from them to the ball again. Mike knew
that he was being rotten, but he really didn't want any
company right now. He was hoping that poor Dubber
would get confused enough to go home and leave him and
Gus alone.

"How come the ball's not moving?" Dubber asked.

"It's because we're evenly matched," Mike said.
"We're at what you could call a standstill."

The boy grew silent again, just looking around the neighborhood. "Casey's got her apartment fixed up real nice."

"I guess." So much for hoping for solitude.

Dubber sat down next to him and Gus and picked up a

ANDREA EDWARDS
223

wad of snow, pounding it and shaping it into a ball. "Tiffany said you're supposed to go after Casey. That when Cinderella ran away, the prince went after her."

That remark, coming out of left field the way it did, set Mike's nerves on edge. But hell, none of this was the kid's fault. By now every woman in town was probably talking about how bad Mike had treated Casey, and there was little he could do about that, except maybe give Dubber a few of the facts. Set him straight so that he wouldn't go blundering through life with misconceptions about how things really were between men and women.

"That's a fairy tale, Dubber. If that happened in real life, the woman would be calling the police to say some nutcase was stalking her, and the prince would get put in jail or shot. In real life, you've got to let the woman run the show. Do things the way she wants to." When Mike looked up, he thought the boy looked worried. "Anything wrong?"

"I was gonna go over to Tiffany's house after dinner." He shrugged. "You know, just walk over without asking ahead of time, but maybe I'd better call first."

"Wouldn't hurt."

"I don't want to get shot."

With Tiffany, it was more likely to be a kick in the shins, but Mike said nothing. It was getting awfully cold. His knees were starting to stiffen up from squatting all this time, and Gus probably wanted to go in. Mike pushed himself to his feet, noting that Dubber was still looking worried. Life could seem pretty complex when you were eleven.

"Love is actually pretty simple," Mike said.

"It is?"

Mike couldn't help smiling while he put an arm around Dubber's shoulders. "Yeah, it is," he said softly. "First of all, it isn't just sex. That's selfishly using someone else for your own pleasure. And it isn't chasing the woman to the ends of the earth. That's just wanting to own her like she was some kind of prize palomino mare."

"You just gave me a bunch of ain'ts, Mike. Aren't there any is's?"

Mike stared at the garage for a long moment before nodding. "Just one, Dubber. Just one single thing." Mike paused a moment to swallow. "You have to be willing to do anything and everything to make the other person happy."

"Anything?"

"And everything. No ifs, ands or buts. No qualifications. No holding anything back. Just total, one-hundred-percent giving."

They stood there and watched some flurries whip in from the lake. Watched some cardinals flit among the evergreens in back. Listened to Gus sigh. And Mike pondered on how making the other person happy was darn near impossible in real life.

"Well, I gotta be gettin' on home," Dubber announced. "Mom wants me to clean my room."

"Best be gettin' then."

As Dubber was about to turn toward home, he hesitated, then put his hand out.

Mike looked at it a moment before reaching out himself. They silently shook, then Dubber turned and headed for home, leaving Mike to stare at the winter scene around him. Leaving him with a bitter realization.

It wasn't Darcy he loved at all, but Casey. And he loved her so much that he was making sure she was happy. She would never have a single night of worry, never have another day of fearing every time the phone rang. Myrna had sent her to Mike for protection and that's just what he was doing—protecting her from all that hurt that would come from loving him. Funny how these things worked out.

After sighing deeply and swallowing the lump in his throat, Mike took Gus to the garage and let him in. If Casey was watching, she'd be waiting at the top of the stairs; if she wasn't, Gus would scratch at the door. In either case, his dog would be let into a comfortable room filled with warmth and love.

Mike felt a sharp pinching in his eyes and rubbed at them. Damn. He couldn't believe how bad his life was turning out. It was worse than a country song. There a woman got the man's money and truck, but never his dog.

"Just what I needed," Casey muttered, and pushed the newspaper printout away. It was an article about Stella's death. Casey had known she had died in early December, 1907, of influenza, but when she'd first learned that it hadn't meant anything. But over the past few weeks these people had become real to her, and reading about her death hurt. Casey needed to be done with this project and gone from here.

She got to her feet and turned the light on. Dusk seemed to be arriving earlier and earlier these days. Or was it just that her heart was so heavy?

Gus suddenly raced to the door, but Casey knew who it was. She'd gotten good at reading footsteps. She opened the door. "Hi, Dubber."

"Hi, Casey." The boy remained outside, holding a large pot and a small one in his hands.

"Would you like to come in?" She stepped aside to let him into the room, then shut the door.

"I got some goulash for you and meat scraps for Gus."

"Mmm," Casey said, lifting the cover slightly. "It smells delicious. I'll have it for dinner tonight."

Dubber shifted his weight, a sign he was uncertain. "There's a whole lot there."

Casey laughed. "Then I'll probably have it tomorrow, also."

"Oh." Dubber made a face before looking away. "Uh, Mike likes goulash. In fact, it's one of his favorite things to eat."

"Well, if I see Mike, I'll send Gus over with some."

"Gus'd eat it all up himself."

Dubber looked so serious that Casey had a hard time not laughing, but she remembered her brothers at that age and

how desperately fragile their egos were. Still were, for tha
matter. She put both containers on her table.

"Would you like a cup of chocolate?" she asked. "
think the water's still hot."

"Yeah." Dubber nodded several times. "Sure."

After checking to make sure that the water was indeed
hot, Casey put some mix in a cup, poured in the hot water
and stirred. "I'm sorry, but I don't have any marshmal-
lows."

"That's okay."

They settled themselves at the table. "How are you and
Tiffany getting on?" Casey asked.

"Fine. Real fine."

"That's nice."

After that major attempt at conversation they lapsed into
silence. Casey hoped that Dubber would quickly finish his
chocolate and go home.

It wasn't that she disliked him. And it wasn't the boy's
fault that they weren't chatting. She was holding up her
end of any possible conversation about as well as the
Christmas tree she and Mike had decorated last week. The
lump that quickly came to her throat required several big
swallows of chocolate to eradicate.

"I was talking to Mike this morning." Dubber spat out
the words as if a sneeze had suddenly come on.

"I see," Casey replied softly. "And how is he?"

"Good." Dubber's head went bob-bob-bobbing again.
"Yeah. Real good."

"I'm glad to hear that.

"Yeah."

They both ducked back into their separate silences.
Casey's cup was less than half full, but she hadn't seen
Dubber drink anything. She did like the boy, but she hoped
again that he wouldn't stay too long. It would put her way
behind schedule.

"Although he could be better."

"I think you could say that about most people, Dubber."

"You know, he's a real good guy. Really nice and everything."

"Yes, Dubber. He's a fine man." Casey stood up. "Now if you'll excuse me, I have a lot of—"

"I bet if you two guys got together you could fix everything up between you."

Darn. That was the trouble with eleven-year-old boys. They didn't have the experience or patience to beat around the bush for a couple of hours and check out if you wanted to hear what they wanted to say. Boys Dubber's age couldn't even imagine you not wanting to hear what they had to say.

"You know," he continued hurriedly. "Go to dinner. A movie. Maybe both."

"Dubber, I—"

"I'll baby-sit Gus and your cats. Free. On the house."

Half the town had been poking at her and Mike, and Casey was getting fed up. But the look on Dubber's face was so full of eagerness to help that she couldn't even begin to get angry.

"We're past that point," she said softly.

"You could go to New Buffalo or Lakeview," he said. "There are some really nice places there."

"Dubber."

"My mom and dad went to Miller's last month. For their wedding anniversary, you know. It's really nice."

"Dubber," Casey said again, with a little bit more force.

"Yeah?"

"I appreciate your suggestions, but it won't work."

"Sure it will. You just have to try. Both of you. You gotta."

"Dubber, please."

"You're great neighbors. You guys are really neat to have for friends." Dubber shrugged. "Even as old as you are."

Casey wanted to laugh and cry all at the same time, but she gripped the edge of the table and kept herself from doing either.

"It wouldn't work," she said. "We're just not compatible."

"You don't like each other?"

"No. We like each other fine." She really wanted to end this discussion. "We just don't like the same things."

Dubber frowned. "Neither do my mom and dad, but they still got married."

The scene slowly blurred for Casey. She didn't want to talk to Dubber anymore. She didn't want to smile and be polite to her guest. She just wanted to put her head down and cry.

"Some people are made for each other," Casey said, feeling a weariness settle into her bones. "There's a certain magic." She shrugged. "Mike and I are just friends."

"Tiffany and I are friends, but we really like each other, too."

"Dubber, I have a lot of work to do."

"Okay." He stood up and drained his cup of what was probably lukewarm chocolate, then picked up his coat. "Remember," he said as he slipped into it. "I'm always ready to baby-sit the guys."

"Yes, I'll remember," she assured him, and shut the door.

Casey went back to work, refusing to let herself linger over Dubber's visit. So what if everyone in town wanted them back together? It wasn't up for a vote.

She pulled over a stack of printouts, copies of more-recent newspaper articles that she'd turned up in her search the other day. It was almost impossible to concentrate on anything, but she could make a pretense. The cats would be impressed, she knew.

Then suddenly it jumped out at her: a christening announcement from the 1950s. Rosemarie Schmidt Widdington—daughter of John Widdington and Sarah Schmidt, granddaughter of Robert Schmidt and Wilma Adamson, great-grandniece of Simon Van Horne and Stella Schmidt—had been baptized.

Casey started to laugh. It all made such sense now in

some horrible, fatalistic way. She and Michael were never meant to be. They were not destined for one another. She was a descendant of Stella, of the lonely, unloved wife. Simon was longing for his lost love Priscilla, just as Mike was longing for Darcy. It made such perfect sense now.

So why was Casey's laughter turning to tears?

Damn, but the wind was cold, Mike thought as he hurried up the back steps and into the kitchen. His hands were like ice. He either had to find the gloves that damn cat had stolen or buy some new ones. He gave Gus a pat on the head, then stopped short at the sight of Casey at the stove.

"Oh," he said, at his conversational best. Damn, but she looked beautiful. Her skin was glowing, her eyes were pink...actually. He hoped she wasn't still crying over him. He wasn't worth it.

"I thought you'd be going out for dinner," she said.

He took a step back toward the door. "I could if you want me to."

"No, don't be silly."

She turned back to the stove so he could admire another view of her. Soft curves, fiery hair that would feel as soft as silk in his hands... He swallowed hard.

"Dubber brought over some goulash and I was just heating it up," she said. "There's plenty for us both if you'd like."

"I'm not sure that's a good idea."

"No, really. I'm fine," she said. "And actually, I wanted to tell you something, anyway."

He wasn't sure if that was good or bad, but he just hung his coat up and set the table while Gus curled up in the corner to sleep. It was almost like old times, but not quite. Mike wouldn't let his heart forget that lots had happened since the last meal they'd had together here.

Casey didn't talk much as they ate, but when she finished, she looked up at him. Her eyes held a wealth of sadness and weariness, almost more than he could bear.

"I was finishing up my research this afternoon and discovered something interesting," she said. "I found out I'm related to Stella, Simon's wife."

"You're kidding."

"Nope." Casey smiled at him. "Isn't it a hoot? As soon as I read it, I laughed. No wonder things didn't work out between us. You and Simon are two of a kind."

"I'm not sure about any of that."

"That I'm related to Stella?" she said. "I'm pretty sure."

"No, that things didn't work because you are, or that I'm like Simon. I think we manage our own lives. What happens is because of who we are or what we've done, not who our ancestors were."

"I don't think it's that simple."

She got to her feet and began to clear her dishes. He wanted her to stay and talk some more. He couldn't bear to have her here with him for a such a few minutes and then lose her again.

"I'll be going in the morning," she said. "Have you made a decision about Gus?"

"No. Yes. I don't know."

"Promise me if you don't keep him you'll let me have him."

He nodded. "I can promise that."

She put her dishes in the sink and began to run water on them.

"You cooked. I'll do the dishes," he offered, though he knew it meant she would leave. And it did.

She went into the mudroom for her coat. Gus got up to watch her go, but stayed, for a change, at Mike's side. She turned at the door and smiled at them both, but didn't say anything. Then she closed the door behind her. Mike felt as though his life had just ended.

Casey stood at the window by her bed and watched the old house. It was two in the morning. All the lights had been out for hours now. Hers had been out, too, and she ought to have been asleep. There was no reason for her not to be, except that she just couldn't rest.

Maybe because she still had something to do. Slipping into her boots and pulling her fuzzy robe on over her nightgown, she hurried down the garage stairs and out into the yard. It was an awful night. A sleety rain was failing and by morning everything should be coated with ice. A terrible day to travel, but a worse day to stay.

She let herself in the back door and crept silently through the kitchen. At the living room door, she stopped. The smell of peppermint had never been so strong.

"Hello, Simon," she whispered. "I've come to say goodbye."

Emotions pulsated around her. Grief. Regret. Sorrow. Sadness. She let them engulf her as she walked over to the sofa and sat down. She would have liked to see all the lights on the Christmas tree one more time, but didn't turn them on. She didn't want to wake Mike. So she just gazed at the tree's shadow in the corner.

"I guess you understand," she said into the darkness. "You can't always choose who you love. And you sure can't choose if they love you."

She sat in silence for a long time, but she knew Simon was still there. Maybe wishing she was a descendant of Priscilla. "Maybe Darcy was," Casey said. "Maybe that's why Mike still loves her."

It was not a particularly comforting thought, though, and Casey rose to her feet. She walked over to the tree and closed her eyes, breathing deeply of the pine scent and the memories. They weren't just of her and Mike, though, but of Simon walking through the house, of bursting into rooms with bouquets of roses and sitting weeping before a roaring fire in the fireplace.

There were too many images, and she opened her eyes. She was alone in the room. The scent of peppermint was gone. And it was time she was, too. She hurried back through the kitchen to the yard and to the garage apartment.

Chapter Fourteen

Casey carried the box out to her car. It was just past breakfast and she was all packed, ready to go. All that was left for her to do was load the car. The freezing rain of last night had turned to snow, and it was miserable outside, but that was not going to stop her. She was miserable inside, too, so what was the difference? She had to get out of here.

She put the box down to open the car, but couldn't get her key in the lock. She tried again, but it still didn't work. Rats. The locks must be frozen. Now what?

She glared at the car and at the snow, and at the houses around the neighborhood for good measure. Why did this have to happen today, of all days? Why couldn't it have happened when she was safely at her parents' house in Fort Wayne? Why couldn't it happen next week, when she was back in Ann Arbor? She could live without a car there.

Well, standing around here wasn't going to solve anything. Maybe her hair dryer would help. She got a long extension cord from the garage, found her hair dryer and went to work blowing hot air at the lock. She knew she had company when Gus nudged her hand, but it took her a moment to find the strength to face Mike.

"What are you doing?" he asked.

He didn't look as though he'd slept much better than she had, but she was not going to feel sorry for him. She was on her way out of his life. "Trying to get my lock to work," she said, and went back to her task. "You know this house—every door that's even near it has troubles."

"Is that going to work?"

She shrugged, not liking to have him so close. He was making her forget how angry she was at him. "It has in the past, though it seems really frozen this time." She tried the key again. Not a smidgen of progress.

"Why don't I call Charlie down at the service station?" he suggested.

"Sure." At least Mike would have to go inside to do that, and she could relax again.

But he was gone for only a few minutes, then he was back, making suggestions, trying to help, and then finally advising that she come inside the house to wait for Charlie.

"You can't see the driveway from the garage apartment," he explained. "You'd better watch from the living room."

"This is fine." She walked a few steps down the drive to peer along the empty street.

"It's freezing out."

She glanced at him, bare hands stuck in his pockets and no hat on. "You can go inside," she said. "I'm not cold."

"Neither am I."

"Oh, for goodness sakes," she snapped, and started for the back porch. If she didn't give in, he was going to freeze to death out here or at least catch another cold. "Fine. I'll wait inside."

But just as she put her foot on the bottom step, a tow truck pulled into the drive. She was saved.

Charlie, giving a wave and a hi-de-ho to Mike, ambled

on over to her car. "Freezed up on you, huh?" he said
and jiggled all the handles. "Lot of that today."

"Can you unfreeze it?" she asked. "I need to get home
for Christmas."

"Oh sure." He ambled back to his truck.

"You shouldn't be going, anyway," Mike said. "The
roads are awful."

No matter how awful, the roads would be a lot safer than
being here with him. Her heart couldn't take that. "I'm a
careful driver."

"That's not always enough."

Charlie was back with a little blue can and sprayed about
half a gallon of deicer into the lock. "That'll do her," he
said. "Give her a try."

But the key still wouldn't turn. Damn. Casey felt ready
to cry with frustration.

"I got some heavy-duty stuff that's guaranteed to work."
He went back to his truck again, returning this time with a
red can, and sprayed enough into the lock so that it ran
back out and down the side of her car.

"You'd be better off waiting for the weather to clear
up," Mike muttered.

It didn't work. Not after Charlie sprayed some more. Not
after he heated the key. Not after he sprayed the heated key
and muttered some sort of magic spell on it. He tried the
other door, the back doors, even the trunk. Nothing would
open, no matter how much muttering, spraying or heating
he did.

"I could tow it to the garage and let her warm up inside," he suggested.

"It won't help," Casey said. "It's this house. It's put a
spell on it."

"It's just bad weather," Mike said. "Thanks anyway,
Charlie."

Charlie nodded and walked back to his tow truck. Casey
just watched him go, feeling as if her last chance to escape
was leaving with him.

"Want to come in and warm up?" Mike asked.

She shook her head. "Is there a car rental in town? No, of course not. And even if there was, there'd be no cars left. It's Christmas Eve."

But even as she felt unbearably weighed down, a car turned into the drive. It was a shiny new one, red and expensive looking, and the driver looked almost like...

Casey laughed as a man climbed out of the driver's seat. "Melvin!" She'd never been so glad to see him. "What are you doing?"

"I got my license," he said.

His voice was a trifle petulant, but she refused to let it bother her—not when he had a nice warm running car right here.

"This is wonderful," she cried. "My car doors are frozen shut and I need to get home for Christmas."

"I said you could stay here," Mike stated, with almost the same petulance as Melvin, but definitely more volume.

Melvin frowned at Mike. "And you are...?"

"This is Mike Burnette, Mrs. Jamison's nephew," Casey said. "Mike, this is my friend Melvin."

"So I gathered," Mike said, without the slightest bit of warmth in his voice. "You come all this way by yourself and in this weather? Pretty brave."

Casey gave Mike a pointed look. She knew he was mocking Melvin, but she wasn't going to allow it. "I think it is brave," she said. "Considering how terrible the roads are, I think it was very brave."

"Foolhardy even," Mike continued. "Nobody should've been out on them. Only makes more work for us cops."

"I'm a good driver," Melvin said. "And I wanted to see Casey."

"And I wanted to see you," she assured him, with a quick glance at Mike to make sure he was getting the idea. "Can you take me home?" she asked Melvin. "Do you mind?"

"Don't be silly," Mike snapped. "He's a new driver or lousy roads."

Melvin seemed to bristle. "I could do it," he said.

"And risk Casey's life?" Mike asked. "Not to mention your own."

What was Mike being so pigheaded about this morning "I could do the driving," Casey said.

"It's almost as dangerous to drive a car you aren't familiar with on these roads," Mike said.

She felt like kicking him. He was being a real jerk. If he was so in love with Darcy, he ought to be glad Casey was about to go. He should be helping her load up the car and giving Melvin directions to the expressway, not putting obstacles in her way.

"Melvin will take good care of me," Casey said, with a smile at Melvin designed to make Mike gag. Hopefully enough to also make him leave. "I'm not worried at all."

Melvin smiled back at her. There was something in his look that she found disturbing—not scary disturbing, but clingy disturbing. Maybe this wasn't the right way to make Mike go inside.

"And you shouldn't be," Melvin said, then leaned in closer. "I have a very special surprise for you."

Oh, great. She took a deep breath.

"Really," Mike said, his voice full of fake enthusiasm. "That's great. I can't wait to see it."

Casey glared in his direction, which he pretended not to notice. Why was he being such a jerk about things? She took Melvin's arm. "Let's go up to my apartment, shall we? Have you had breakfast?"

"Just some coffee," he said.

"Then you need to come in the kitchen here," Mike said. "I've got bacon and eggs and toast."

Casey's look told him to back off—but she wasn't sure he was reading it. He took hold of Melvin's other arm.

"Come on, Melvin," she said, and tugged him toward her. Mike let go with a glare, but she didn't care. "Help

ne pack up the car, then we can grab some breakfast down-
own.''

She knew Mike was watching them. She could feel his
eyes on her, but she refused to turn around. Less than an
hour and she'd be gone.

Mike watched until Casey and Melvin disappeared
through the side garage door, then kicked Melvin's tire.
What a jerk that Melvin was! How could she be thinking
of letting him drive her home?

Mike frowned at Melvin's car, then at Casey's. Maybe
he ought to sabotage both cars so they'd be stuck here. No,
she'd find a way to leave. But she would be better off in
her own car, so he had to thaw out the locks. And fast.
Maybe if he pushed it into the garage and got some space
heaters...

He glanced down at his hands, almost numb with the
cold. "Gloves," he told Gus. "I need to find my gloves.
That cat has to have hidden them somewhere in the house."

He hurried back inside, with Gus reluctantly following
him.

"She was your great buddy," Mike grumbled to his pet.
"You ought to know what she did with them."

If he did, Gus wasn't telling. He went to his corner in
the kitchen and lay down, while Mike went upstairs to the
room Casey had used. They were in here someplace, which
ought to mean they'd be easy to find, but there were boxes
piled high in one corner. A closet full of junk with a door
that wouldn't quite close. A desk, some shelves. He'd never
really realized just how much junk had been left here from
all the previous owners.

Mike shook his head and got down on his hands and
knees. He looked under the desk, behind the boxes, in back
of the shelves, and felt under the nightstand. His hand hit
something. His gloves! But when he pulled them out, something else came along. A crumpled-up piece of newspaper.
Curious, he flattened it out.

It was an article about a baby girl abandoned in Bento
Harbor twenty-seven years ago. Almost exactly twenty
seven years ago. He frowned. The baby's birth date wa
the same as Casey's. Was this her?

He read on. About the baby being left in a church base
ment. About the priest who'd found her and how bitterl
cold the night had been. About how the baby was cold bu
seemed healthy. And about the priest's view of the baby'
mother. Mike winced as he read the quote—about th
mother being "heartless, selfish, thoroughly evil" for leav
ing the child there to die, for not caring about the welfar
of her baby.

Mike sat back, feeling as if someone had knocked th
breath from him. Those were pretty strong words to hea
about your mother, birth or otherwise. The baby in the ar
ticle had to be Casey, and the article itself had to have
belonged to Casey. How else would it have gotten here
And what did it mean?

Gus came upstairs and lay on the floor next to him, rest
ing his head on Mike's knee.

"What it means is easy," Mike told him. "It means tha
she thinks her very own mother didn't care if she lived o
died. That she's been carrying a hell of a burden around
for a while now, and it also explains why she got so hype
when I said I'd find a home for you."

Gus just wagged his tail.

Mike petted his head, scratching him behind the ears the
way Gus liked. "I was only saying it because I was trying
to let Casey down easy," he told the dog. "But I made
everything ten times worse. Hell, a hundred times worse
A thousand times worse."

Gus looked up at him, big eyes all serious and question-
ing.

"I know. I know." Mike nodded. "Shows she's better
off without me, doesn't it?"

He got up and walked slowly over to the window. He
hadn't realized it, but from here he could see one of the

windows in the garage apartment. And right now, he could see Casey and Melvin talking. Casey throwing her arms around Melvin. Casey hugging Melvin and laughing. Casey leaning over to kiss Melvin.

What the hell was she doing? Aunt Myrna was right. Casey did need protection from herself, and she was going to get it!

"It's all right, Melvin, honest," Casey said, mopping the front of her sweater with a towel.

Luckily, the hot chocolate wasn't all that hot, for it had soaked through her blouse and her bra to her skin, not to mention down the front of her jeans, too. Melvin had gotten a little exuberant.

"I'm really sorry," he said, for about the millionth time.

She just shook her head and put the towel on the table, before giving him a light kiss on his cheek. "Forget it," she said. "I'm just so happy for you. I had no idea you and Jenny were seeing each other."

"We haven't been for very long," he said, grinning from ear to ear. "But sometimes these things happen fast."

"So I hear." As if she didn't know. "I'm going to get out of these wet clothes and clean up. You can tell me everything on the ride to Fort Wayne."

She took some clean clothes from her suitcase and went into the bathroom. Melvin's surprise had been quite a surprise—he was engaged, and to a wonderful young woman that Casey knew well. And to think Casey had been worried that he was seeing her in a romantic light! Oh well, it showed how silly love made one.

She stripped off her sweater, blouse, bra and jeans, then dumped them in the bathtub to rinse out the chocolate. While the water was running into the tub, she pulled on a T-shirt. It was nice to know that Melvin had found happiness. At least some people weren't like her and Mike, destined to love the unattainable.

Kneeling on the floor and leaning over the edge of the

tub, Casey turned the water on. She wished life was simpler and that there was a way to avoid getting hurt. But then, there was—never take a risk. She swished the clothes around in the water, then glanced at the door. She thought she heard Melvin talking, but she must have been wrong. Who would—

Suddenly the bathroom door crashed open, smashing up against the far wall with a crash that rivaled a sonic boom. Then a big furry dog flew in, took a gigantic leap and landed right in the bathtub!

Casey barely had time to spring back as water sprayed everywhere—over her, the wall, the whole room. "Gus!"

But even as the words came out of her mouth, she realized she wasn't alone. The door was wide open and Mike and Melvin were standing there. Casey tugged at her T-shirt, trying to make it longer, trying to make it cover more of the bare essentials.

"Haven't we done this before?" she demanded of Mike.

But Mike was busy with Melvin. "Get the hell out of here, Melvin," he snapped.

"Mike! How dare you!"

He turned back to her, his eyes dark with agitation. "How dare I? Somebody's got to be watching out for you."

"Watching out for me? What for?"

"What for?" He waved his hand around the tiny bathroom. "Just look at us all. You draw every stray for miles around. You're a stray magnet."

"What is that dog doing?" Melvin asked.

Casey looked at Gus, who had gotten her bra over his nose. She grabbed it away.

"I thought I told you to leave," Mike was saying to Melvin.

"He doesn't have to," Casey said. "He's my guest."

"It's my house."

"It's Mrs. Jamison's house." The frown on Mike's face

aid she'd gotten him there. "It's not your house because you're so damned afraid to commit to anything."

"Well, it might not be my house, but it is my job to protect you," Mike said. "That's why Myrna sent you here."

Casey crossed her arms over her chest and leaned against the sink. "She sent me here to write a family history."

"That was the story she used. The real reason was to protect you from yourself."

"What?" Casey just stared at him.

Mike turned to Melvin. "Look, Mel," he said. "I don't know what she promised, but it's a no-go. It's over. Kaput."

"Casey..." Melvin looked over at her. "What is going on?"

"Mike, this has gone far enough," she said. "I don't have any idea what you're talking about, but I think it's time you left."

"I didn't know what was going on either, Mel," Mike said, suddenly changing to a friendly tone. "I knew she collected strays, that was pretty obvious, but I didn't know why until a few minutes ago."

"And you do now?" she asked.

"I found this," he said, and held up a scrap of newspaper.

Casey's heart stopped, then she slowly let out her breath. "Where'd you find it? No, what difference does that make?" she said, more to herself than him.

"What is it?" Melvin asked.

"Just an old newspaper article," Casey said, and forced a smile. "About my being abandoned as a baby."

"Really?" He touched the article. "May I?"

Mike looked at Casey; she slowly nodded. "Why not?" she said.

Mike gave him the article, then took a step closer to Casey. "Why didn't you tell me?"

His voice was so low and caring it brought tears to her

eyes, but she really didn't want to talk about this. "Tell you what? That my mother dumped me right after birth? That she didn't care what happened to me? Mothers do it all the time. What's the big deal?"

"Casey, don't."

"Don't what? Don't admit the truth to myself? That's kind of silly, isn't it? I'm not likely to believe my lies."

Mike looked all too good, standing there in the doorway. And all too sure of himself.

"Why not?" he asked. "You believe the lies in the article."

She frowned at him. "What lies?"

"All that stuff that priest said. How do you know it's the truth?"

"How do you know it isn't?"

"If she really didn't care about you, why would she have left you in a church? Why not in a Dumpster? Or along a deserted road?"

"He's right there, Casey," Melvin said, handing the article back to Mike. "She'd pick a lousy place to dump you if she really was trying to hide your existence."

"Melvin," she snapped. "You're supposed to be on my side."

"There's nothing to take sides on. You haven't really been stewing on this long, have you?"

"Of course, she has," Mike said. "Why do you think she rescues everything in sight? Cats. Dogs. You. Me. So that's why it's not going to work between you two."

"What isn't?" Melvin asked.

What bug had gotten into Mike's head now? "Melvin just got engaged to a friend of mine," Casey interjected hotly.

"Really?" Mike smiled, and it was as if the sun had come out after a sudden storm. He stuck out his hand. "Hey, congratulations. Glad to hear it."

Melvin shook his hand, though he looked rather befuddled. "Thanks, I guess."

Casey wasn't feeling quite as friendly toward Mike as he seemed to be feeling toward Melvin, but she smiled at her friend. "Maybe it would be best if you left us," she said. "I think I need to talk to Mike alone."

Melvin looked from one to the other, then shrugged. "Okay. Want me to take the dog?"

Casey had forgotten about Gus and turned to look at him. He was sitting in the tub, looking as goofy as ever. "Yeah, you'd better take him. This isn't going to be pretty. Gus, come on out."

Gus hopped out, shook himself dry all over her, then trotted out with Melvin. Once the door was closed, Casey turned toward Mike.

"What do you—"

He'd come three steps closer and was right in front of her. Too close for her to think or speak. Putting a hand on each arm, he made her sit on the edge of the bathtub as he squatted in front of her and took her hands in his. His eyes were saying something, but she'd never been good at reading silent messages.

"I really hurt you before," he said softly. "I made up that story about Darcy, and then suddenly it was all about Gus, and I didn't know how much it would hurt you. I never would have—"

He what? She couldn't have heard him right. "Hold it." She ripped her hands from his and grabbed hold of the front of his sweater. "You made up that story about Darcy? You made it up?" Her voice had risen with each word she spat out. "You made up that you were still in love with your ex-fiancée?"

He looked a little startled at her vehemence. "Well, yeah," he said simply.

"And you made up that whole thing about giving Gus up?"

"Sort of."

"Sort of?" she cried, feeling so astonished and angry

that she was unable to do anything but echo him. "Sor
of?"

"But it was all for your own good."

"For my own good?" She was screeching now as she
rose to her feet, bringing him up, also. "You made me
completely, utterly miserable for my own good?"

"I hated to see you so worried about me and 1
thought—"

"You thought!" She shoved him back against the sink
"You didn't think at all. You ran scared! You told yourseli
it was some big, brave, save-the-little-woman, macho decision, but it was nothing more than you running scared."

"Hey!"

She realized she'd been emphasizing each word by poking him with her index finger, and she pulled her hands
back. "This wasn't at all about me being worried. It was
about you. And how afraid you were that I'd react like
Darcy. That I'd leave and you'd be hurt again."

"I was thinking of you," he retorted sharply.

"If you were thinking of me, you would have been honest," she said. "You would have treated me like an adult
and given me the choice." She took a step toward him, and
he slid along the sink until he could turn slightly. "You
wouldn't have made sure things would go as you thought
they should."

"It wasn't just up to you," he said. "You think I like
knowing someone's worrying about me? That you jump
every time the phone rings?"

"What makes you think I'd stop worrying once I left
here?" she snapped. "You think love is something you turn
on and off at will?"

"Of course, it isn't," he snapped back. "But you don't
have to let it grow, either."

"No, right. Let's chop it off at the knees. Might hurt a
little, but what's a little pain? Much better than a little
worry and a lot of happiness."

"You're taking this all wrong," he said. "I only came

ver because of that article, not to change anything between
s.''

"How did you get that paper, anyway?" she demanded.
Another reason to be furious with him.

"Hey, I wasn't poking in anything," he said, holding his
hands up in a protestation of innocence as he backed away
again. "If you've got to blame anybody, blame your cat. I
was looking for my gloves and found that. Though why I
needed your cat to explain this mystery to me when you
should have, I don't know."

"I should..." She stopped. "What did you say? My cat
explained a mystery of life to you?"

"Yeah." He looked uneasy, as if he wasn't sure what
he was getting at, and took another step back. He was up
against the tub.

Casey just grinned. Things looked mighty different all of
a sudden. "I seem to remember someone saying I was safe
from him until my cats explained the mysteries of life to
him."

He just froze. "But I didn't mean..."

"Hey, they kept up their side of the bargain," she said,
and took a step closer, then another. "Shouldn't you?"

When she reached out to put her hands on his chest, he
backed up again—and tumbled into the bathtub! Water
sprayed all around, he looked stunned and Casey laughed,
falling in on top of him.

"So what's your argument now, Mr. Macho?" she said,
wrapping her arms around his neck.

"Casey," he said with a moan.

"I love you," she whispered, and kissed his lips softly.
It had been so long, too long, since she'd tasted him. A
shudder ran through her. Or had it run through Mike and
just echoed in her heart?

"And you love me," she said. "You can't deny it. You
listened to my cats' advice. You couldn't have heard it if
you didn't care."

His arms had found their way around her, but he was still frowning. "It's not that simple."

"It's very, simple," she said. "We have a chance to be happy together or to be miserable alone. Which—"

The door crashed open again, but this time Casey knew what to expect. She braced herself, burying her face against Mike's chest as Gus leaped into the bathtub with them. Water splashed and wet fur stuck to her arm, but all she could do was laugh.

"Give your daddy a kiss, Gus," she said.

Mike sighed. "I'm not his daddy."

She laughed. "And Gus hates cats, I know."

Mike kissed her. His lips were hard and wild and devastatingly thorough. When he lifted his head, they both could barely breathe. "Do I have to be your cats' daddy too?" he asked.

"Absolutely."

"Can I assume you don't need that ride to Fort Wayne after all?"

Casey turned. Melvin was in the doorway. She just smiled at him. "Nope. Thanks, anyway."

"Then maybe I'll be on my way."

Mike raised himself up somewhat. "No," he said.

Casey just stared at him. Were they going to have to fight this all out again?

"I really meant it about the weather," Mike told Melvin. "Stay for lunch at least. The weather's supposed to clear by then."

Melvin nodded slowly, then with a sly smile took a step back into the other room. "I do think I'll take a little walk, though. At least over to the house. Come on, Gus, we know when we're not needed." Gus trotted along after him.

"Thanks, man," Mike said, and folded Casey in his arms again as the door closed.

Casey snuggled back down. "That was very very nice of you," she said, and kissed his cheek. "Aren't you uncomfortable?"

"I can think of several places where we could be a lot more comfortable," he said, and found her lips. The water should have been sizzling by the time he pulled away. "Want to go look for some?"

"I'd love to."

Epilogue

"You're sure your parents didn't mind you staying u here for Christmas?" Mike asked.

"They probably figured it was about time."

They were snuggled up on the sofa, in each other's arm Gus was sleeping on the floor at their feet, the cats wer in the easy chair and all the lights were off except for thos on the Christmas tree. It had been a wonderful Christma Casey wiggled her feet in the big fuzzy cat slippers Mik had gotten her.

"So you were a hopeless cause, huh?"

"They'd even doubled the dowry, but no takers."

"You mean I could have made money off this deal?"

"Watch it, fellow," she teased. "I'm pretty tough."

But Mike didn't follow her joking lead. He was instea frowning at the tree, staring at a spot up near the top. Sh turned to look at it also, but saw nothing.

"What are you looking at?" she asked.

"That ornament," he said. "I can't figure out what it is."

She moved so that they both could get up. She could see the one he was talking about now, and they walked over to get a better look. Mike reached up and unhooked it.

"It's a pickle."

"A pickle?" she cried. "There was no pickle ornament. I looked."

"Well, that's what this is." He handed it to her.

It was indeed a pickle, but an old one. How had they ever seen it in the dim light? Carved out of wood and at one time painted green, it was now dull with age. The carving skill could still be seen, as well as two tiny hinges.

"It opens." Casey fiddled with the tiny clasp.

It opened to reveal a tarnished brass plate. Casey held it up to the Christmas tree so that the light picked up the engraved words.

To my darling Stella—may your fondest wishes always come true. With all my love, Simon. Christmas, 1907.

Casey just stared at the words, feeling tears welling up in her eyes.

"What's it mean?" Mike asked.

She shook her head for a moment, then swallowed the sadness. "That we were all wrong. It was Stella he loved, not Priscilla. And from all I've read about his reticence, I bet he never told her."

"But he did right here," Mike said.

Casey just sighed. "She never got this. She died a few weeks before Christmas."

"Oh."

They looked at the ornament and then at the tree. An incredible sadness seemed to be in the room, but ever so slowly it lifted, until there was a rapture in the air that felt almost like the coming of spring.

"We got our most favorite wish," Mike said, pulling her into his arms. "Didn't we?"

She nodded, tears of joy filling her eyes. "And Simon made sure we didn't repeat his mistake."

"Wonder if he's going to keep springing doors on us for the rest of our lives."

Casey looked up into his face. "We're staying here?"

Mike just shook his head. "Wouldn't we be abandoning the house if we left?"

"Not to mention Simon and the rest of your family."

"Both our families."

*   *   *   *   *

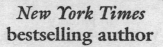

Welcome to the Towers!

In January
New York Times bestselling author

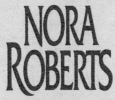

takes us to the fabulous Maine coast mansion
haunted by a generations-old secret and introduces
us to the fascinating family that lives there.

Mechanic Catherine "C.C." Calhoun and hotel magnate
Trenton St. James mix like axle grease and mineral
water—until they kiss. Efficient Amanda Calhoun finds
easygoing Sloan O'Riley insufferable—and irresistible.
And they all must race to solve the mystery
surrounding a priceless hidden emerald necklace.

Catherine and Amanda
THE Calhoun Women

A special 2-in-1 edition containing
COURTING CATHERINE and A MAN FOR AMANDA.

Look for the next installment of
THE CALHOUN WOMEN with Lilah and Suzanna's
stories, coming in March 1998.

Available at your favorite retail outlet.

SILHOUETTE WOMEN KNOW ROMANCE WHEN THEY SEE IT.

And they'll see it on **ROMANCE CLASSICS**, the new 24-hour TV channel devoted to romantic movies and original programs like the special **Romantically Speaking—Harlequin™ Goes Prime Time.**

Romantically Speaking—Harlequin™ Goes Prime Time introduces you to many of your favorite romance authors in a program developed exclusively for Harlequin® and Silhouette® readers.

Watch for **Romantically Speaking—Harlequin™ Goes Prime Time** beginning in the summer of 1997.

If you're not receiving ROMANCE CLASSICS, call your local cable operator or satellite provider and ask for it today!

ROMANCE CLASSICS

Escape to the network of your dreams.

See Ingrid Bergman and Gregory Peck in *Spellbound* on Romance Classics.